I ESCAPED SERIES COLLECTION #1

3 Survival Adventures For Kids

I ESCAPED COLLECTION
BOOK 1

SD BROWN

SCOTT PETERS

CONTENTS

I ESCAPED

THE
CALIFORNIA
CAMP FIRE

THE BESTSELLING SURVIVAL ADVENTURE SERIES

SD BROWN + SCOTT PETERS

I ESCAPED THE CALIFORNIA CAMP FIRE

MAP OF CALIFORNIA
HIGHLIGHTING BUTTE
COUNTY AND PARADISE

Eureka

Paradise ★ ◄————— Butte County

Nevada

●Sacramento

San Francisco●
●San Jose

Pacific Ocean

Santa
Barbara ●

Los Angeles ●

● San Diego

CHAPTER ONE

THURSDAY NOVEMBER 8, 2018
PARADISE CALIFORNIA
AROUND 11:05 A.M.

Fourteen-year-old Troy's hands gripped the steering wheel so hard his knuckles hurt.

The fire had jumped the road. Explosions and flames burst on both sides, chasing the Bronco from behind—a fire-breathing monster herding them toward the forest. A forest full of nature's fuel to feed the raging blaze.

He turned to his younger sister. Her face was half-covered by a wet rag to block the smoke from entering her lungs. Above the rag, her eyes bulged in terror.

She started to scream, waving her arms and pointing. "The fire's everywhere. Look! By the road. At that house. The roof just collapsed. And look at the bakery. Flames are coming out of the windows. Turn around. Go back."

"We can't," Troy said, looking into the rearview mirror.

It seemed as if the entire town behind them was lit with flames.

"We have to keep going. It's our only chance."

"We're not going to make it," she said.

"Yes, we are."

He hoped the lie would morph into truth.

```
The fire accelerated, consuming the equiv-
alent of a football field every second.
    — Cal Fire Official Statement
```

CHAPTER TWO

ONE DAY EARLIER
WEDNESDAY, NOVEMBER 7, 2018
PARADISE, CALIFORNIA
AROUND 4:00 P.M.

Fourteen-year-old Troy Benson snagged the keys to the family's blue Ford Taurus from the kitchen counter. His dad had just finished drinking a glass of water and had set it in the sink. His mom scurried around like she'd be going away for a month instead of a day.

Were they ever going to leave?

Troy said, "Hey, I can load your stuff in the car and back it out of the garage for you. Okay?"

His dad grinned. "If I didn't know better, I'd think you're trying to get rid of us. Sooner than later."

Exactly, Troy thought. Once his parents left town, he'd walk to the HOLIDAY MARKET for some serious junk-food-contraband. Since his parents had opened PARADISE HEALTH MART, he'd been drowning in organic-this and hummus-that.

He finger-shot his dad. "Wish I had a get-out-of Paradise card like you and Mom. Admit it. Living in Paradise is kind of boring."

Welcome to Paradise, California

"I'd be careful what you wish for, son," his dad said and winked. He looked at the clock on the wall. "Honey. If you still want to attend the no-host dinner, we need to get on the road."

"Almost there," Mom said. "Just one last thing."

Troy grabbed the two suitcases, lugged them into the garage and hit the remote. The garage door rumbled open like the thunder before a lightning storm. The car was parked next to his dad's SUV Bronco. The suitcases went into the car's trunk and he went into the driver's seat. Ever since he'd learned to drive the tractor on his grandparents' farm, his dad had let him pseudo-drive around the yard—mostly on the lawnmower.

At least he'd be king for twenty-four hours. His little sister would have to do what he said. Go to bed when he told her. Eat what he served. Watch what he wanted to watch on Netflix.

Using the rearview mirrors, he backed the car into the front yard and onto the yellow front lawn to make a perfect three-point turn. He grinned. At least he hadn't had to cut the grass since June because it hadn't rained in seven months. Plus, the town had water-use restrictions, which meant no outside watering.

All the yards looked the same—dried stubble, bare dirt flowerbeds, and dead bushes. Even the weeds had given up their will to live.

Everyone said the hot, dry summers were normal, but usually they'd had plenty of rain by November. This year was different. Governor Brown had declared an official end to the five-year California drought the previous April, but Paradise hadn't gotten the memo.

The only good thing about the local water-famine was that his last yard-chore had been to pull the dead plants and toss them into the compost pile in the backyard.

Troy got out of the car. It was windy and cool. After all, it was November and almost winter. Rascal, the family's large German shepherd, ran over and nudged Troy's hand. The boy rubbed her between the ears. The dog's tail slapped his leg like a drummer in a rock band.

"You're the best thing about living here," he told the dog. "Who named this place Paradise? Must have been someone's idea of a joke. Look at it. Except for the tall evergreens on the hill and around town, everything is dried up and dead. My idea of Paradise is everything green with flowers and palm trees like Hawaii. Not like this H-E-double-hockey-sticks kind of place. Minus the inferno."

There was no point in complaining. He was stuck in Paradise—a small town in Northern California along the foothills of the Sierra Nevada Mountain Range. Only 27,000 people lived in the whole town, and twenty-five percent were old—as in senior citizen old and retired.

It was an over six-hour drive to get to San Francisco and civilization.

Instead of people, Paradise had trees. Instead of streets, there was one road in and one road out. Instead of high-rise buildings, there were trailer courts tucked between small planned and unplanned neighborhoods.

If his parents had to move to the country, why hadn't they moved to the Central Valley near his grandparents? Where there was a horse to ride and a tractor to drive?

Rascal barked. The dog bounded across the yard.

She grabbed a red ball from under the skeleton of an oak tree. A black tire hung from one of the lower branches.

A gust of wind knocked the swing, making it spin. The breeze sent a few dead leaves scattering across the lawn.

Rascal ran back to Troy, dropped the ball at her master's feet, and sat.

Troy picked up the ball and tossed it high into the air. It dropped and somehow miraculously landed inside the tire. Was it the wind?

"Wow!" Troy couldn't do it again, even if he tried a million times. "Go get it, girl."

Rascal raced after the ball. She jumped on the tire, sending the black rubber Goodyear into a twirl. Rascal barked and jumped again. The branch cracked. Held for two more twists of the tire before snapping and crashing to the dry earth.

Rascal yelped.

"Come on, girl," Troy said. "It's time to go inside and hope Mom doesn't notice."

CHAPTER THREE

WEDNESDAY, NOVEMBER 7, 2018
PARADISE, CALIFORNIA
AROUND 4:15 P.M.

Troy smiled at his mom like he was listening. He wasn't. His mind was focused on his plans for the next twenty-four hours and the food he was going to eat. It was going to be stellar. Pizza. Hot dogs. Mac-N-Cheese. Chili fries. Fish sticks. Pepsi. Mountain Dew. Henry Weinhard's Root Beer. Double-stuffed Oreos. Cookie-dough ice cream. Doritos Nacho Cheese chips. And whatever else he wanted to eat. And not at the table.

"Troy, are you listening?" his mom said.

"Yeah, Mom."

"Then what did I just say?"

He held up his thumb to begin the countdown. "No friends over." Up went the index finger. "No junk food." His other fingers followed as he rattled off the rules. "Go to bed at the regular time. Get up a half hour early. Don't miss the bus." Next hand. "No fighting. No messes. Walk the dog. Feed the cat. If we have any problems, consult Mrs. Jones next door. She's a retired nurse and knows what to do in an emergency." He grinned and punched the air. "Nailed it."

"You did," his dad said. "But in case of a real emergency, call 911. Honey, we really need to get on the road."

"One last thing," Mom said.

"You said that twenty minutes ago," Dad said.

"Troy and Emma," his mom said, doing her version of Vanna White and sweeping her hand across the spotless kitchen, "this should look exactly as it does when we return." She pulled out her phone. "And so there's no argument, I'll document how things look."

She snapped shots of the big open kitchen and living area. *Click.* The sink. *Click. Click. Click.* Stove-top. Refrigerator. Microwave. *Click.* Floor. *Click. Click. Click. Click.* "Emma, use the microwave and not the stove. Remember the cookies you forgot in the oven last week? I don't want to come home to find you burned the house down. Troy, don't forget to lock up before you go to bed."

"Enough, honey," Dad said, giving Troy a wink. "If we didn't trust Troy and Emma to be responsible, we wouldn't be leaving them home alone for the night. What kind of trouble can they get into? They'll be in school all day tomorrow, and you know Mrs. Jones has an eagle-eye view from her front room window. Everything'll be fine. We'll be home tomorrow night."

"I know," Mom said. "It's just that my babies are growing up too fast."

"We're not babies," Emma chimed in. She shot Troy a look. "At least I'm not."

"That's because you're a mutant," Troy said, laughing. "A science experiment gone wrong." At his mother's frown, he added, "Just kidding. I love my little sister."

Dad pointed at the wall clock hanging over the stove, with its butter-knife hour hand and spoon minute hand.

"One last hug." Mom scooped both kids into the same tight embrace. To Troy, she said, "Be nice to your sister." To Emma, "Your brother is in charge. Do what he says."

"Do I have to?" Emma pouted.

"Come on," Dad said. "We want to get there before nightfall."

Troy grinned. His dad liked to exaggerate. It was only an hour's drive to Redding and at least three hours until sunset.

Troy and Emma waved as their parents drove around the corner and disappeared from view. Rascal barked and Midnight appeared from under a bush. Emma scooped up the kitten and cradled it like a baby.

Troy slugged his sister in the arm and yelled, "Party time!"

"Shut up, Troy." Emma pointed to Mrs. Jones' living room window with a wave and a big smile. "She's watching."

The older woman waved back from her recliner.

"Looks like her window is open. Bet she heard you."

"Don't be such a brat," Troy said and went inside with Rascal at his heels.

CHAPTER FOUR

THURSDAY, NOVEMBER 8, 2018
PARADISE, CALIFORNIA
AROUND 2:00 A.M.

The clock on the kitchen wall read 2:00 a.m.

Troy grinned. If his parents asked, he could truthfully say they were up extra, extra early for the school day. He'd just leave out the part that they hadn't gone to bed, yet. No foul. No penalty.

Emma would be stupid to rat him out unless she wanted to be on restriction, too.

Empty soda cans, candy wrappers, and half-eaten junk food littered the coffee table in the living room. Rascal had just wolfed down pizza crusts and was starting in on licking the empty paper plates. Midnight sniffed the carpet where Emma had spilled chili.

On TV, Kung Fu Panda had just rolled down a set of steep temple steps.

"I don't feel so good," Emma said, her hand clutching her stomach. "Maybe we should have eaten the tofu and chicken Mom left for us to reheat for dinner. Instead of this junk food."

"Not even," Troy said. "It's because we're watching this stupid movie."

He'd wanted to watch *Transformers*. At least the panda was better than Emma's favorite movie—*Mary Poppins* from the last century. "You didn't have to eat my food. You could have had the casserole."

"I'm going to tell Mom. You spent our emergency money on junk food."

"And I'll tell her you were in her makeup," Troy said, eyeing her clown lips. "Maybe you should go to bed. We can clean up in the morning before school." He grinned. "By then, Rascal and Midnight should take care of most of it."

"Okay," Emma said and picked up Midnight. "Aren't you going to bed?"

"In a little while," he said. As soon as she left the room, he shut off the lights, put on *Transformers* and turned it down low. He settled on the couch under one of his mom's crocheted blankets. Before long, sleep punched him into unconsciousness.

CHAPTER FIVE

Troy awoke to dog breath, a canine tongue and a cold nose nudging his face. He patted Rascal's head. "Too much pizza, girl? Can't you wait till morning?"

Rascal wined, let out a few yips and pawed his arm.

"Okay." Troy sat up on the couch and rubbed his eyes, still half asleep. "You need to go do your business. Just a minute." He reached down and felt for his shoes.

Wait. Something was off. Suddenly he was wide-awake; his eyes darted left and right. He couldn't see anything. It was black. The usual electronic lights were dead and the steady hum of the fridge silent. The electricity must be out—which was seriously *weird*. There hadn't been a storm in months.

What time was it?

Rascal began to bark, jumping on Troy. Then the dog nipped at the sleeve of his hoody and pulled.

"Okay. Okay. I'm moving." Troy stood, fumbled for his cell on the coffee table, and turned on the flashlight feature. The beam lit the room. Their food-feast remains lay strewn across the carpet like garbage art. "Wow. Look at the mess you made. Good thing Mom's not here."

The landline rang. Rascal started barking and frantically ran back and forth to the door. Whoever was calling could wait. It was the middle of the night and probably a wrong number. Plus, Troy didn't want to clean up after Rascal if she had an accident in the house. Which hadn't happened since she was a puppy.

He stumbled after Rascal and opened the door. Outside, it was pitch black. There wasn't even starlight. The wind ripped at his clothes like it was being chased by fire-breathing dragons. And smelled that way, too—smoky and warm.

Someone must have built a bonfire.

"Hurry up, girl," he said. He wanted to get back inside and back to sleep.

Rascal didn't head to her usual spot. Instead, she kept barking and barking.

"What's wrong?" he asked. She usually only got this excited when a raccoon grocery shopped in their trashcan.

"Troy?" Emma's voice shouted. Her shadow darkened the front door.

"What?"

"That was a call from my school."

Emma must be dreaming. "That's ridiculous. Your school wouldn't call in the middle of the night."

"It's not night," she said, her voice all excited and squeaky. "It's nine fifteen. In the morning."

"What?" He looked at his phone. She was right. But then why was it still dark? Were they in the middle of a solar eclipse? Mrs. Grady, his science teacher, was slipping. He looked back at his phone.

Wow. He'd missed at least fifteen text messages from his friend Jeremy. He scrolled through and read them in order. By the time he reached the last one, he knew why Rascal was acting crazy. He felt a little crazy himself.

The first one read—*where r u?*

Second one—*cutting class?*

The third to twelfth were similar jabs. Number thirteen said —*fire drill*

Fourteen—*fire for real!*

Fifteen—*yeah school's out*

The last one said—*i see flames*

CHAPTER SIX

THURSDAY, NOVEMBER 8, 2018
AROUND 9:20 A.M.

As Troy stared at his phone, the smoke hit him like a baseball bat. Troy's throat grew tight. His eyes burned.

Rascal barked and ran in circles.

"Shhh, girl," Troy said and patted her back. Rascal expected him to do something. His sister did, too. His parents had left him in charge—of Emma, Rascal, Midnight and the house.

"Hold on. What am I supposed to do? Sit, girl."

The dog obeyed and leaned up against Troy's leg. Her barks morphed into soft intermittent yips between low-pitched whines.

He looked up at the black sky and back to his phone.

Squinting, he reread the text messages from Jeremy. His friend liked to joke, but the dark sky, the intense wind, and the smoke weren't a game. The fire was real. Still, Jeremy could be trying to be funny. Trying to scare Troy. Or making a jealous jab, that Troy had cut class without him.

How worried should he be? He'd never been in a fire before.

His first instinct was to check the news—but no electricity

meant no cable. He punched in a Google search, but it was taking forever to connect.

He finally gave up and sent a quick return text to Jeremy—*slept in R you home?*

Almost immediately, Jeremy answered—*no. on the road. u?*

Troy—*home*

Jeremy—*get out of town*

Jeremy—*NOW!!!!!!*

"Troy. I'm scared," Emma called, her dark shadow moving toward him.

"Wait there. I'm coming," he said, walking back to the house with Rascal bumping his leg at every step. "We're going to be fine. Who called?"

"My Principal. The school is sending kids home because of a fire."

"Did you ask him where it is? How close to town?"

She shook her head. "It was just his voice. A recording. I called back, but no one answered. What are we going to do?"

"First, you need to get dressed." Troy pushed her inside the house. She went.

He stood in the open doorway and stared at the dark, his mind racing. What next? Think. He was a Boy Scout, but he wasn't prepared for this situation. Still, he had to run through the options.

Okay. The best weapon against fire was water. Maybe he should hose down the house and the yard. He started to cough. The smoke seemed to be getting thicker and he put his hand to his face. How close was the fire? Was there time to soak the yard and the house enough to stop a fire? Was there even enough water?

Option two—the basement. It was made of concrete. It wouldn't burn if the fire reached their neighborhood. Maybe he, Emma, Rascal, and Midnight should wait it out there—at least until the firemen came.

He squinted in the direction of the neighbor's homes but saw only blackness. It was way too gloomy to see more than a few feet. He couldn't even make out Mrs. Jones' house, which was just next door. She had lived in Paradise forever. She should know what was going on and if they should even be worried.

But first, he'd give his dad a call.

CHAPTER SEVEN

THURSDAY, NOVEMBER 8, 2018
AROUND 9:30 A.M.

Troy pulled out his cell. Dad would tell him what to do.

Troy tapped the autodial on the screen and waited.

"Come on, come on. Answer."

When it finally answered, it went straight to voice mail. He groaned and tried his mom's phone. Hers did the same thing. He left a quick message.

"There's a fire up here. They canceled school. Call me back."

Now what?

"Hey!" he yelled at Emma's bedroom door. "I'm going next door to see Mrs. Jones."

"Wait until I'm dressed. Don't leave me here alone."

He couldn't decide if she sounded scared or was just doing her usual whine. Either way, the fire could be racing toward their house. He needed answers now. She'd have to deal with her fear. He wasn't waiting the twenty minutes it'd take for her to get ready.

"I'll be right back. Rascal's here." To the dog he ordered. "Stay, girl."

Troy hurried to the neighbor's house and knocked on the front door before opening it. "Mrs. Jones? It's Troy. Are you okay?"

"I'm in the living room. Come on in." Mrs. Jones sounded cheerful.

Troy obeyed and was greeted with the scent of cinnamon mixed with something antiseptic. It always smelled like a cross between a doctor's office and a bakery in the house. What wasn't normal was the odor of smoke in the mix.

Mrs. Jones was eighty-two and had been a nurse. She always said, *kill the germs, kill the crud.*

It must be true, Troy thought. She was never sick. "Do you

know what's happening?" he asked. "Should I be worried? I tried to call my parents, but they didn't answer."

Emma burst into the room, breathless, Rascal at her side. "I told you to wait for me." She'd only gotten half dressed—flip flops, Minnie Mouse pajama top, and jeans. "You left me alone and I was scared."

"I told you I'd be right back." Troy tried to sound like his dad. Emma could be such a pain. "Stop acting like you're three. Sorry, Mrs. Jones."

"It's her first fire," Mrs. Jones said. "I understand."

"Aren't you worried?" Emma asked, the panic in her voice slowing. "It's daytime and it's dark like night. It smells like the whole town is on fire."

"Pish posh. I've lived here all my life. I've seen so many fires up here you wouldn't believe it."

"Like this?" Troy said.

"Don't worry," Mrs. Jones said. "They'll put it out. They always do."

Boom. Boom. Boom.

The three thunderous explosions blasted outside.

Rascal yipped.

"What was that?" Emma asked, her voice cracking.

CHAPTER EIGHT

THURSDAY, NOVEMBER 8, 2018
AROUND 9:40 A.M.

Bursts of fire glowed through Mrs. Jones' front room window. Trees looked like they were shooting into the dark sky.

"The hill's on fire," Troy said.

Another series of explosions boomed, sounding like a giant's machine gun mowing down the enemy.

Emma screamed.

Rascal flinched and quivered against Troy's leg.

More patches of fire spots erupted in the distance. Troy gulped, a sick feeling settling in his stomach.

Emma grabbed his hand.

"Don't worry, dears," Mrs. Jones said. "The firefighters will be here soon. Would you like a cinnamon roll? I baked them last night. With the electricity being on the fritz, you'll have to eat them cold but they're fresh."

"It sounds like a war is going on out there," Troy said, thinking Mrs. Jones was not taking the danger seriously. "My friend Jeremy's family left town. I think . . ." He frowned. "We should go, too."

"You young people overreact to everything." She sniffed. "It's not your fault. It's the excessive live media coverage you're exposed to. I predict this false-induced stress will cause your generation to have the highest rates of heart attacks and strokes in modern history."

"Look out the window," Troy said. Up the hill, the individual fire patches had joined into a huge bonfire. It looked like it was coming closer every second. "We have to leave. Now."

"Well, I'm not going anywhere," Mrs. Jones said. "And it would be prudent to check with your father before you make any rash decisions." She picked up her knitting needles and they began to click. "It's a long walk out of town. You'll be heading straight into the forest. That's more dangerous than staying put."

Troy didn't know what to think. She'd lived in Paradise most of her life. What she said made sense—but Jeremy's parents had decided to get their family out of town.

"I believe it's safer to stay right where we are," she said. "You wouldn't want to get in the way of the firefighters."

His dad's words came back to him. *You're in charge. Take care of your sister.*

"I told you. I've already tried to call my Dad," Troy said, "and my Mom."

"And I texted them," Emma said, talking at the same time.

"They didn't answer," Troy said.

Emma hit his arm. "That's because they're at the workshop, stupid. Remember they said we could only reach them on the hour." She rolled her eyes. "You never listen."

Troy let the snarky comment pass. At least she wasn't crying.

He checked the time. His parents wouldn't get his message or Emma's text for another twenty minutes. Did they have enough time to wait for Mom and Dad's advice?

Outside, the flames looked higher, wider, and closer. Red embers floated in the air, drifting like the tail-ends of a FOURTH OF JULY firework rocket. Only this was November eighth, two weeks before Thanksgiving.

Mrs. Jones might be right. Maybe the firefighters would put out the blaze, but where were they? Why was the fire spreading?

CHAPTER NINE

THURSDAY, NOVEMBER 8, 2018
AROUND 9:50 A.M.

Troy wished his dad would call. But he hadn't. It was up to Troy. He had to decide.

Stay and wait for firefighters?

Or start walking and try to get as far from the fire as possible? He pictured the one road out of town.

Through the front window, four doors down and on the opposite side of the street, a propane tank exploded into a massive firebomb. The bright fireball lit the neighborhood. Glowing debris flew as if tossed by a fire god casting destruction into the wind. Basketball-sized sparks soared into the air and then rained down onto the Merrills' and Johnsons' roofs. In seconds, their shingles began to glow.

Emma bit her lower lip, her wide eyes ping-ponging between him and the fire. Now, only the length of a football field stood between them and the advancing flames. Rascal bit Troy's sleeve and tugged.

"We're leaving," Troy said. "I think it's what Dad would tell us to do."

"Don't worry about the fire," Mrs. Jones said for like the third or fourth time. "The fire department may be taking its sweet time. But they'll come. I tell you, it's safer here than out there."

Mrs. Jones was an adult, and his parents had told him to check with her if there was a problem. Like she was semi-in-charge. So it felt wrong ignoring her advice. But it felt more wrong taking it.

They had to get out of Paradise. ASAP.

"Emma, move," Troy said and pushed his sister toward the door. "Mrs. Jones, I think you should come with us. The fire is too big and too close to stay."

"Suit yourself. See you when you get back."

Emma ran to the woman. "Don't stay, you'll die. Please, come with us. We need you to drive. Troy doesn't have a license."

"I said, I'm not leaving. This is my home. I was born here and if it's God's will, I'll die here."

"Come on, Emma," Troy shouted and grabbed her arm. "I'm sorry. We can't stay. Can't you see? The Greens' place is on fire, too. Please, Mrs. Jones. Come with us."

Mrs. Jones kept knitting.

Troy half dragged his sister from the house and ran to theirs. He led her to the front door. The hot wind pulled at their hair and clothes.

"Wait out here," he said. "I have to go through the house to get into the garage."

"Don't leave me," Emma said. "Please?"

"It's safer out here. Yell and bang on the garage door if the fire gets closer. I'll hurry. Rascal, stay."

"Where's Midnight?" Emma cried. "We can't leave Midnight behind."

"Call him, he'll come to your voice," Troy said, thinking of Jeremy's last two text messages—*get out of town NOW!!!!!!*

Why had he wasted so much time? They should have left when he read Jeremy's warning. He'd been so stupid.

"What if Midnight doesn't come?" Emma said.

"I don't have time to argue." Troy sounded as annoyed as he felt. "He will."

She started to cry. "What if he doesn't?"

Troy didn't answer. He reached for the doorknob and turned it.

CHAPTER TEN

THURSDAY, NOVEMBER 8, 2018
AROUND 9:59 A.M.

Troy twisted the doorknob and pulled open the front door.

Something black and furry shot from the house and he jumped.

"Midnight," Emma squeaked and bent to scoop up her baby. "Ouch. Ouch. Ouch," she said as the terrified cat climbed up her legs and tried to bury itself in her armpit. "Shhh, you're okay now. I've got you."

Troy felt relieved as he raced inside. Emma had Midnight to keep her occupied while he got the Bronco out of the garage.

The living room seemed darker and the garage pitch black. He couldn't see a thing and frantically felt for the Bronco's keys that should have been hanging on the wall. They weren't there.

Blindly he slapped the wall again, felt the row of hooks—no Bronco keys.

"No," he moaned. They had to be there.

He ran his hand down the wall and across the concrete floor— no keys. Stepping sideways, he bumped hard into a stack of plastic milk crates. They clattered onto the concrete. He slipped and stumbled over one. The hard plastic dug into his shin as he staggered to keep balance.

"Banana boogers," he muttered, like they were magic words to banish the throbbing pain in his leg. *You're not Emma. So stop panicking. And stop wasting time knocking around in the dark.*

Think.

He reached for his phone but it wasn't in his pocket. It must have fallen out when he fell.

Then he remembered. His mom kept an emergency flashlight on the kitchen counter next to the fridge. He ran back inside to get it. He flipped it on and flashed the kitchen. The beam spotlighted his backpack on the counter and the remains of what was left of last night's pig-out.

It only took a minute to grab his backpack, dump the schoolbooks, and shove crackers and a jar of Skippy peanut butter into the bag. His mom kept extra cash in the cookie jar. He snagged it just in case and shoved the money into his pocket. At the last second, Troy snatched a steak knife. They might need it. For exactly what, he didn't know.

Back in the garage, he spotted his phone. Grabbed it and flashed the light to where the keys should have been. The crazy thing is that they were hanging exactly where they always hung. Was his mind playing tricks? They weren't there three minutes ago. But they must have been.

He felt heat race to his ears. How could he be so brainless? Maybe the smoke had clouded his judgment—attacking him like some video game fire-breathing monster. He needed to up his game.

He ripped the keys from the hook and hit the garage-door opener button. When nothing happened, he felt even more stupid. Duh! Of course, the door-opener didn't work with the electricity dead.

He darted to the garage door, grabbed its metal handles and yanked. The door inched open painfully slowly, as if afraid to let the fire inside.

When he got it as high as his waist, he squatted and put the heels of both hands under it and bench-pressed the door open. It's a good thing they'd been weight lifting in PE.

Rascal and Emma stood waiting on the driveway.

"What took you so long?" Emma complained. "Did you lock up? Mom said to remember to do that when we left for school."

Great. Emma's attitude had rebounded.

"We're not going to school," he said.

Emma's PJ top was strangely lumpy. The Minnie Mouse design moved, making it look like a mutant body snatcher had invaded Emma's stomach.

"What's under your shirt?" He tried to sound patient like his dad but it wasn't easy.

"Midnight," she said. "He doesn't follow orders like Rascal. I stuffed him in my top. That way, he won't get lost."

Troy shook his head. "Not a good idea. What happens when

your kitty decides to scratch his way out? Get in the Bronco. Here, take the backpack. Empty it and put Midnight in it."

He opened both doors on the passenger side of the SUV. Emma scrambled into the front seat and Rascal leaped into the back.

"I'm letting you boss me for now," Emma said and unzipped the backpack. "But don't get used to it."

"Yes, your highness," he muttered and slammed both car doors. He spotted the case of emergency water his Mom kept in the garage. They might need it. Quickly, he threw it in the back and then hopped into the driver's seat.

"Ready?" he asked.

"Ready," she said.

He slid the key into the ignition, pumped the gas pedal, and turned the key. The engine caught briefly but then sputtered and died. Heart pounding, he tried it again. Same result.

"You said you knew how to drive," Emma said, clutching the backpack. Midnight yowled from inside. Rascal panted in the back seat.

"Shut up," he snapped.

Emma began to sniff as though trying not to cry.

"Sorry," he said. "I have to concentrate."

Hopefully, he hadn't flooded the engine. Then he'd have to wait at least ten minutes to try again. He didn't think they had time to spare. *Please? Let it start this time.* He held his breath and turned the key. The Bronco roared to life. Troy shoved the car into reverse and slammed his foot on the gas.

The SUV rocketed out of the garage and into the yard, bumping into the birdbath in the center of the lawn. He slammed on the brake and they jerked to a stop. Rascal slid off the backseat.

Emma shrieked.

"We're fine," Troy said to his sister. To the dog, he said, "Sorry, girl. Lay down."

"I think we should put our seatbelts on," Emma said. "Are you sure you know how to drive?"

"Of course I do," Troy said, clicking his seat belt. He shifted the clutch into drive and hoped his words were true. It stalled. He looked back. In the rearview mirror, all he could see was fire. Everywhere. And then it began snowing ash and embers. Flames licked the roof of their house.

He slammed to a stop and started to back up.

"What are you doing?" Emma cried.

"We can't leave Mrs. Jones. We have to make her come with us."

CHAPTER ELEVEN

THURSDAY, NOVEMBER 8, 2018
AROUND 10:15 A.M.

Stay here," Troy ordered Emma and Rascal. "I'll be right back."

Head down, he jumped out onto the road. The only light came from their headlights and the sparks and flames. Suddenly the air became a blizzard, but instead of snowflakes, embers and ash pelted him and the ground.

He couldn't believe this was happening. Yesterday had been normal. Now it was crazy insane. All the houses on the block were burning.

Brushing his arms and hair, he ran to Mrs. Jones's house.

He entered without knocking. "Come on," he shouted. "You have to come with us."

"I told you. I'm not leaving," Mrs. Jones said. She sat in her chair, still knitting the baby blanket.

"Come on." He grabbed her arms, lifting her from her chair. Her knitting fell to the floor. "Look. Our house is on fire. Yours is next."

She fought him and tried to pull away. "Let go of me. I'm staying here."

"But you'll die." Troy felt sick as he released her.

She bent and picked up her knitting. "My husband died in this house. If it's my time, I'll die here, too. Then we'll be together."

The Bronco's horn made three short blasts, followed by three long blasts, followed by three more short blasts. SOS. He had to leave.

"But—"

"Just go. Your sister needs you. And remember, it was my decision to stay. Not yours."

The horn started honking again, sounding frantic.

"I'm sorry. Goodbye, Mrs. Jones." He raced back to the Bronco, jumped in, and started the car moving again.

"Where's Mrs. Jones?" Emma asked.

"She wouldn't come." His jaw felt tight.

"You should have made her," Emma said. "You would have made me."

"Yeah, I would've. You're my little sister. I'd have dragged you to the car. Or carried you. Adults are different. Kids can't tell them what to do. She wouldn't leave. Said it was her decision. Not mine."

He turned a hard right and clipped the curb with the tire. The SUV bounced down hard and Emma grabbed the dash.

"Maybe she thought it was more dangerous to ride with you than face the fire," she said.

Was Emma trying to make him feel better with her teasing? It didn't work.

He felt awful.

And frightened.

He looked back. The whole street was on fire now.

"Goodbye house," Emma whispered. "Goodbye, Mrs. Jones."

CHAPTER TWELVE

THURSDAY, NOVEMBER 8, 2018
AROUND 10:25 A.M.

One last turn and they'd be on the main road heading out of town —everyone called it the Skyway to Paradise.

He rounded the corner. Got ready to punch the gas and blast out of there. Instead, he was forced to stomp on the brake and skid to a full stop.

To his horror, he realized the Skyway was jammed solid with a giant trail of bumper-to-bumper cars and trucks.

Their escape was blocked. Him and his sister, Rascal and Midnight were going nowhere. They were trapped.

And the fire was closing in.

"Put on the blinker," Emma said. "Then someone will let us in."

"Lot of good that would do," Troy snapped. "And I don't need a back seat driver telling me what to do."

He flipped the blinker on. A pickup truck gave him just enough room to join the exodus. He crept into the flow of traffic.

"See, it worked," she said. "I told you so."

Troy wished she'd shut up, but telling her that would only make her give more stupid orders. He needed to concentrate on driving. "Why don't you try to call Mom and Dad again? You said they had a break every hour on the hour. Why didn't they call?"

"Maybe they didn't get our messages," Emma said. "We have to wait until eleven to call them again. They won't pick up now." She sat silent for a whole two seconds.

"Try anyway." At least it'd give her something to do instead of arguing.

She punched the redial button. Waited. "It's Emma. I'm with Troy. Our house is on fire." She shoved the phone in her pocket and sat silent for a moment. She sniffled and wiped her cheeks. When she finally spoke, she sounded like a little girl. "Sorry I bossed you. I'm just scared."

"It's fine," he said, not bothering to make it sound like he meant it. And then added, "It looks like everyone is leaving town at the same time."

"Yeah," Emma said. "All 27,000 people."

"Minus one," Troy mumbled.

"What?"

"Minus Mrs. Jones," he said.

"It's not your fault she stayed." Emma started bouncing in her seat and pointing out the window. "Hey look! There, on the side of the road. It's Grandma Hill and her grandkids. She's waving at us."

Troy stopped in the line of traffic for the older lady. She wasn't his grandma, but everyone in town called her that. Even people older than her. Car horns behind him blared in protest. Emma rolled down her window. "Need a ride?"

Smoke rushed in like an oxygen thief. Emma began to cough.

"Bless you. Bless you," Grandma Hill said, coming up to the Bronco and gasping for breath. "My car stopped and won't start."

"Get in. Roll up the window, Emma."

Grandma Hill opened the back door. More horns started honking.

"Move over, Rascal," Troy said.

"Oh," she said, the door still wide open. "Get in, boys." Her three-year-old twin grandsons, Danny and Sammy, piled into the back seat. "I almost forgot. I left something in our car. Wait here."

Was she serious? Really? If Emma said that, he'd yell at her, but Grandma Hill was a grown up. "Hurry. Please."

The driver in the car behind them lay on the horn and didn't let up. Troy looked back and the man behind the wheel batted the air with his open palm like he could push them off the road.

"We can't stop any longer," Troy said and waved to the other driver. He shifted the Bronco into drive and they began to inch forward.

Lucky for Grandma Hill, they'd only managed to travel about ten yards before she returned lugging a cardboard box. She shoved it onto the seat. It tipped and four golden retriever puppies spilled out, yipping.

Rascal let out a few happy barks and wagged her tail. Midnight yowled from his bag.

"There's no room for the box. Get rid of it and get in," Troy said, stopping for a moment.

"Just one last trip," Grandma Hill said. "Then that's it."

The cars horns began to blare again.

"We don't have time," he said and let the car inch forward. "Please, Grandma Hill. Get in the car."

Grandma Hill ignored him. Her hand clutched the open door and she walked to keep pace. "It will only take me a minute."

"Whatever it is, you don't need it," Troy said. "Get in."

"You don't understand," she said, beginning to sound like a retired schoolteacher. "The boys need their car seats. It's against California law for them to ride in a vehicle without them. Dangerous even."

"Car seats?" Emma said. "Can't you see the flames?"

"Danger," Troy said, trying not to yell at Grandma Hill, "is the fire on the hill. It's getting closer and we need to get out of here." *What was with these old people—first Mrs. Jones and now Grandma Hill? Couldn't they see the fire eating its way toward them?*

The traffic started to move a little faster. The speedometer inched up to ten miles an hour.

"If a cop spots them just sitting in the seat—" Grandma Hill was huffing to keep up, "he'll give you a ticket."

"Do you see any cops?" Troy asked. "Or any firefighters? We're on our own here." He slowed to five miles an hour. "Get in. Now."

"Move over, boys," Grandma Hill shouted and managed to get into the back seat and shut the door. She was gasping for breath and her words sounded almost garbled—almost, but not quite. "And you were always such a nice boy. Polite. Law-abiding."

"Law-abiding," Emma said like she was trying out a new phrase. She looked at Troy and grinned. "Troy doesn't have a license."

"Oh no," Grandma Hill said.

Troy shot Emma a look and whispered. "Don't you know when to keep your big mouth shut?"

"Pull over. I'll drive," the old lady insisted.

"It's our car," he said, thinking that if she drove like she walked, who knows where they'd end up? Probably back at her house because she left some casserole in the oven. "I'm driving."

"We'll see about that," Grandma Hill said. She pulled out her cell. "I'm reporting this to my son. He's friends with the police chief."

CHAPTER THIRTEEN

THURSDAY, NOVEMBER 8, 2018
AROUND 10:38 A.M.

Every car on the road moved southwest in a slow, steady stream—all leaving town. All in the right-hand lanes. The oncoming lanes looked strangely deserted. Troy focused on driving, his hands clenched on the steering wheel. His foot hovered between the gas pedal and the brake.

Emma hadn't said a word since he'd told her she had a big mouth. She was biting her lip and her eyes brimmed with tears.

Grandma Hill and her grandsons were in the backseat. Rascal had commandeered the rear storage space. She leaned over the backseat, tongue out, ears perked, watching the boys whisper and cuddle the puppies. Grandma Hill's lips formed a tight line.

To Troy, the almost-silence felt as oppressive as the fire. He hadn't meant to be rude. He was scared. Maybe he should have let Grandma Hill drive—she was an adult. But he was the one responsible for his sister, Midnight and Rascal.

"Where's Mr. Hill?" he asked to break the silence.

"He went into Chico to renew his driver's license." Her lips relaxed into a sad smile. "Thank the Lord I don't have to worry about him out in this inferno."

"Do you know how it started?" Troy asked.

"Or where the firefighters are?" Emma added, giving up the silent treatment.

"I'm sure they're out fighting the fire. I bet they'll have it under control in no time. Right, boys?"

"Yeah, Grammie," they chimed in unison. One of them added, "And we're having a venture."

"An adventure, Sammy," Grandma Hill said. "We've had a lot of fires over the years and hardly anyone has ever died. You just have to stay out of the fire's way."

Troy hoped she was right.

At least he wasn't being blinded by oncoming traffic. And they were traveling a steady fifteen miles an hour.

He glanced at the fuel gauge. They had half a tank. Should be plenty to get them out of there. At least, he hoped it was.

Even though he'd traveled down Skyway a thousand times, it looked totally different this morning. On either side of the road, familiar businesses crouched like hulking, dark blobs. Ready to pounce. Or explode. The Wells Fargo Bank to the left. Dutch Brother's Coffee on the right. The CVS pharmacy.

He caught the Bronco's reflection in a window and glanced away. It all looked so unreal.

"The wipers on the car go swish, swish, swish," Sammy, Danny, and Grandma Hill began to sing. *"Swish, swish, swish."*

Emma joined in for the third, *"Swish, swish, swish. All around the town."*

A headache began to slam dance behind Troy's eyes. It was growing hotter and smokier with every foot they traveled. Flakes of burning ash drifted across the Bronco's hood.

The sight of a packed parking lot, highlighted by the stream of headlights headed out of town, caught Troy by surprise. The lot was alive with flashlights and camping lanterns, which bobbed amongst the moving shadows of people milling around.

"Pull into the Chin Dynasty's parking lot," said Grandma Hill, coughing. "I think I see my son's truck."

The hot, dry air made it hard to see. Trying to drum up a few moist tears, he managed to squeeze off a couple blinks and squinted at where she was pointing. The lot was full. Parked cars, headlights still blazing, spilled along the dark street.

"Where? There's got to be over seventy cars. Are you sure it's your son's?" Troy asked.

"It's the only cherry red Dodge Pickup with chrome pipes. See it? Right there."

The pickup was parked next to the main road. Troy steered to the right and parked, leaving the engine running.

"There's my son," Grandma Hill said.

"Daddy, Daddy, Daddy," the twins started chanting.

"Wait here," Grandma Hill said, jumping out of the SUV. "I'll be right back."

Not again. Troy rolled down his window and called after her. "We can't stop. We have to keep going." Quickly, he rolled it up again to keep out the smoke. Emma began to cough. The twins coughed, too.

"Dad keeps rags under the seat. Grab a bunch. Wet them down with the water bottles." He began to cough. "First tie one over your face," he said. "Then wet a couple for the boys and me."

Emma unclipped her seatbelt and set to work. When she was done, they looked like they were about to rob a bank.

To Troy's frustration, more cars streamed steadily onto the road. His fingers drummed the steering wheel. No one would ever let them back in. The traffic seemed to be moving slower while the flames spread faster down the hill.

Outside, Grandma Hill yelled, "Tom. Yoohoo. Tom."

A man in blue jeans, a plaid shirt, and a baseball cap ran to meet her. Together they returned to the Bronco.

"Are these bandits my boys?" he said, lifting Sammy and handing him to Grandma Hill. He put Danny on his shoulders and started to close the door. "Thanks for giving the family a ride."

"Don't forget the puppies," Emma said.

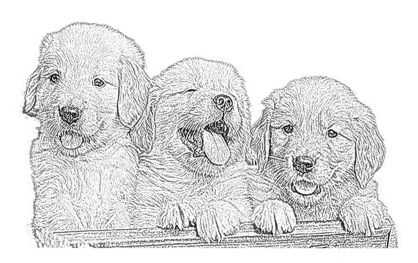

"Right," the man said. He set down his boy, scooped the wriggling puppies into his hands. "Come on, Danny. You're a big boy. You can walk."

"Aren't you going to leave town?" Troy asked.

"No. There's lots of pavement in this lot. It won't burn. We plan to wait it out here. Maybe you should, too. Might be safer." The man pushed the door shut with his hip.

Emma looked at Troy. "Do you think he's right? Should we stay?"

At that moment, another volley of explosions erupted. The Family Health Clinic's wall punched out from inside, sending sparks and debris onto the sidewalk. The pharmacy looked like a crematorium—all in flames. Down the block, he saw his parents' health food store. It looked okay—for the moment.

Then the front window shattered as fire danced in its aisles.

CHAPTER FOURTEEN

THURSDAY, NOVEMBER 8, 2018
AROUND 10:52 A.M.

What if he's right?" Emma asked a second time and stared at the packed parking lot. "Maybe we better stay here and wait it out? He's a grown-up."

"No. We need to keep going," Troy said. "Just like all these other drivers leaving town."

"But what if he's right?" she said.

"What if he's wrong?" Troy shot back. "Mrs. Jones didn't want to leave either."

He shifted into drive and tried not to picture her house in flames.

Rascal moved up between the front bucket seats, leaned over and licked Troy's neck. She barked once as if to say, *get moving*. He put on the blinker and forcefully nosed the Bronco in between a Toyota sedan and a Subaru Outback.

They drove in silence until both cell phones rang at the same time.

"Mom," Emma cried. "There's fire everywhere. And the smoke stinks."

"Dad, we're fine," Troy said, pushing up his face rag to talk. "We're in the Bronco and headed out of town."

"Who's driving?" his dad asked.

"Me."

"Why isn't Mrs. Jones driving, son?"

"She wouldn't leave." Troy felt a hitch in his voice. The car in front of him suddenly stopped. Troy slammed his foot on the brake pedal. "I . . . maybe I should hang up and save the battery. Emma can put her phone on speaker. Okay?"

"Good thinking, son."

"I'm scared, but we have Midnight and Rascal with us," Emma said and listened. "Okay. I'll put it on speaker."

"Troy," came his mom's worried voice. "Are you kids okay?"

He sucked in a deep breath. This might be the last time he ever talked to his parents. And he wanted to be strong. "Yeah. We have plenty of gas, food, and water. I hope you're not mad I'm driving without a license, but we had to leave."

"Good thinking," Dad's voice said. "You did the right thing. Where are you now?"

"We just passed Elliott Drive," Troy said. "I think. It's hard to tell. Everything's so dark. It's like midnight. All the electricity is out. There's no street lights or anything."

"Don't drive too fast," Mom said. "Take it slow and easy. Be safe."

Emma laughed. "That's funny. Troy couldn't speed if he wanted to. There's too many cars and they're all going slow."

The cars began to move again and the Bronco inched forward.

"We love you both, so much," Mom said. Her voice sounded like she was crying. "We shouldn't have left you home alone."

"We love you, too," Emma said.

"Troy?" Dad interrupted. "Take care of your sister."

"Yes, sir."

"Emma, do what your brother tells you to do. No arguing."

"Yes, Daddy."

"Let's pray," Mom said in a quiet voice. "Dear Lord in heaven, like Shadrach, Meshach, and Abednego, give my babies safe passage through the flames, amen."

"Amen," echoed his dad and sister.

Troy wished he believed in praying and God, like the rest of his family, but he knew the Bible stuff was just a bunch of fairy tales. Because if God existed, Mrs. Jones would still be alive.

"I'm proud of you both," Dad said. "Head for Chico. We'll meet you on the road."

CHAPTER FIFTEEN

THURSDAY, NOVEMBER 8, 2018
AROUND 11:05 A.M.

Troy's sweaty hands gripped the steering wheel so hard his knuckles hurt. The fire had jumped the road. Explosions and flames burst on both sides, chasing the Bronco from behind—a fire-breathing monster herding them toward the forest.

Mrs. Jones's warning came back to him . . . *You'll be heading straight into the forest. That's more dangerous than staying put*. He prayed she was wrong because there was no turning back.

The trees loomed ahead: more fuel to feed the raging blaze. Thick stands of it. He turned to look at his younger sister. Her eyes bulged in terror.

A wet rag still covered half of Emma's face to keep the smoke at bay, but it didn't stop her from screaming. Or flapping her arms and pointing everywhere at once. "The fire's all over the place. Look! There's another house in flames next to the road. And the bakery. It's in flames, too. You have to turn around. Go back the other way."

"We can't," he said, looking into the rearview mirror. It seemed as if the entire town behind them was lit with flames. "We have to keep going. It's our only chance."

"We're not going to make it," she said.

"Yes we are," he said, hoping the lie would morph into truth.

Rascal edged between the bucket seats again and tried to climb into the front.

"Back, girl," he ordered the dog. "Emma, please stop. You're wasting your breath. You'll only choke on more smoke. We'll be fine if we don't panic. Wet your face-rag again. And pour water on Rascal's head and on Midnight in the backpack. But don't let him out."

Emma's shrieks turned into sniffles as she did what she'd been told.

The cat yowled.

"Midnight doesn't like getting wet. He's not too happy. He scratched my hand."

"Don't worry. He'll forgive and forget."

"I'm sorry," Emma said. "I didn't mean to act like a baby." She rubbed the scratch on her hand. "Do you really think we're going to be okay?"

"Yeah," Troy said, even though he wasn't sure. Fire spots had sprouted on both sides of the highway. "We just have to get out of town. Which is what we're doing."

The car in front of them ground to a sudden halt and Troy almost rammed into its back bumper. What was the driver thinking? Why was he stopping when it was obvious the traffic in front of the guy was still moving? Why was he blocking up the whole lane? This was the only way out of town—unless you made a U-turn, and headed back into the fire.

Troy hit the horn—tapped a message urging the car to move. The pickup truck on Troy's bumper did the same.

It was like the stopped driver hadn't heard. The fire from behind bore down on them in an avalanche of molten ash. "Move," Troy ordered the parked car. "Can't you see? We're sitting ducks."

Heat from the fire pressed into the car through the rolled-up windows. Troy knew he couldn't wait a second longer. He wrenched the steering wheel right, pressed the gas, bumped up over the curb, and drove around the car. He tried to look inside, wondering why they'd stopped.

He couldn't see anything. Part of him felt like he should check on the driver. Part of him was afraid to waste precious time. If they'd wanted a ride, he reasoned, they would have jumped out and flagged him down.

A siren wailed. Flashing lights appeared in his rearview mirror and raced toward him. He let out a breath in relief. Finally, the firefighters had shown up. Or the police.

Emma twisted in her seat. "Boo. I thought it was a fire truck. It's an ambulance. And it's leaving town, too." It passed them on the left in the empty lane for oncoming traffic. "Hey, that's not fair."

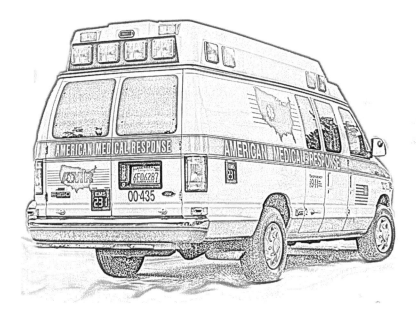

"What's not fair?" Troy asked.

"They get to drive in that lane and no one else does."

"That's because the fire trucks will need to use it when they come racing into town to fight the fire."

"When are they coming?" Emma asked. "Shouldn't they have been here by now?"

He stared at her, his mind turning. "You know what? You're not so dumb after all. At least, not all the time."

He steered into the open lane and hit the gas. Freedom at last! Who cared if he was driving the wrong way down the oncoming lane? He sped along the open road, past the slug-train of law-abiding drivers. Other cars pulled out to chase after him as he zoomed to catch up with the ambulance's flashing lights.

The opening lyrics to *Ain't No Stoppin' Us Now* burst out of his mouth. A little muffled by the face-rag. Usually, he only sang in the shower, but he couldn't help himself. The town limits were just ahead. It felt like they were going to make it.

Emma let out a whoop and joined in. "We're on the move!"

CHAPTER SIXTEEN

THURSDAY, NOVEMBER 8, 2018
AROUND 11:15 A.M.

They were flying down the road now, but inside the car, it felt like an oven cranked up to broil. Troy kept two car lengths between the Bronco and the ambulance in case it had to stop suddenly.

Both vehicles were doing forty miles per hour, and it was the fastest he'd ever driven.

"You should go on *America's Got Talent*," Emma said through the rag that covered her mouth. She bounced on the seat like a hot potato. "You could win. And get rich. And we could go somewhere cool. Like Africa. We could take Rascal and Midnight. They could meet their cousins. You could ride an elephant. I'd pet a lion."

"Africa's hot," he said. He swiped sweat from his forehead with the back of his hand. "The equator runs right through it. I'd rather be somewhere cold."

"Oh." Emma stopped bouncing. And although he couldn't see her mouth, he knew she'd lost the smile he'd heard in her voice. Instead, she stared out the windshield at a giant piece of ash gusting and swirling in the headlights. "Me, too."

Troy could have slapped his head except he was afraid to take his hands off the steering wheel. Why did he have to ruin Emma's daydream? She'd forgotten the danger they were in for a moment and he'd brought her back to reality.

"Let's pretend," he said. "It's snowing real snow out there. Like in, what's that movie?"

She shrugged.

"You know," he said, playing dumb. "The cartoon. The one with that weird-looking snowman with the funny name. Otis? Oopsie?"

"Olaf," Emma said, sitting straighter. "And he's not weird look- ing. He's cute. And he's funny. The movie's called—"

"Wait. Don't tell me. I got it," Troy said. His eyes were trained on the gap between the Bronco and the ambulance. "*Chilled*."

Emma rolled her eyes. "*Frozen*. It's called *Frozen*."

"Chilled. Frozen. Same thing." He forced a laugh. An annoyed Emma was preferable to a terrified Emma. "That's what I'd like right now. A gallon of frozen cookie-dough ice cream."

Emma said nothing.

"What would you like?" he asked her. "If you could have anything right now? This second."

A shower of flaming embers dropped from the sky, igniting trees and vegetation.

"For this to stop."

"Emma," Troy said. "Wet down Rascal and Midnight again. And splash more water on your face-rag. Save enough for mine."

She went to work, focusing on her task instead of what was going on outside. Flames engulfed the east side of the road, devouring trees like a starving dragon.

A shower ball of embers landed on the ambulance. It slowed and seemed to weave in the lane. Had the driver taken in too much smoke?

Troy tried to stay calm as he steered his vehicle through the smoke and flames. Everywhere, the patchy flares merged to become walls of fire moving closer to the road. He slowed and left more space between him and the ambulance.

A Honda Accord from the slower lane took advantage of the gap; it darted in front of the Bronco. Another car tried to do the same, but Troy sped up. The car clipped their rear bumper. The whole frame shuddered and the Bronco swerved. Troy fought the wheel for control. Maybe he should have let them in but he'd promised to keep Emma safe.

"No. No. No. No. No. No. No. No," Emma chanted in rhythm to a new sound of scraping, bumping metal that was now coming from the back of the vehicle.

"Emma?"

She kept up her mantra. The car behind began to blare its horn.

"Emma! Stop. Roll down the window. Use the flashlight and tell me what's making that noise."

Coughing, she craned her head out. "I can't see anything."

"Nothing's on the tire?"

"No."

"It must be the bumper dragging on the ground," Troy said. "Roll up the window. Ignore it."

In front of the Honda Accord, the ambulance slid to a stop and parked sideways in the lane. The Honda Accord swerved to miss it and landed in the left ditch. Troy stopped dead center in the lane. It was obvious no one was going anywhere for at least a minute or two.

He jumped out and raced to the back of the Bronco. The pavement was as hot as the surface of Mars at noon. As he'd suspected, the bumper was dragging. Another driver got out and joined Troy.

"Let me help you pull that off," the man said.

"It's fine," Troy said.

"No, it's not fine. It's creating sparks. We got to get it off."

"Should have thought of that."

Troy grabbed the loose end, and the man pulled the attached section. Together they wrenched the bumper free and tossed it to the side.

"Thanks," Troy managed, his skin feeling so tight and hot it felt like he'd been sunburned.

"Look out," the man shouted and raced back to his car.

Burning tree limbs were crashing to the ground. One smashed onto the road just five feet from where Troy stood. It shattered into a volley of sparks. The noise and blazing light rooted Troy to the spot.

A flying spark zapped his arm, stinging him into motion. He wrenched opened the Bronco's door just as a huge burning limb dropped onto the roof of the ambulance.

He stared opened-mouthed as the vehicle caught fire.

CHAPTER SEVENTEEN

THURSDAY, NOVEMBER 8, 2018
AROUND 11:25 A.M.

Emma started to shriek. "It's on fire. It's on fire."

Troy dry-swallowed. If the flames reached the ambulance's gas tank, it would explode like a bomb. He slammed the gearshift into reverse and tried to back up. Except he couldn't—only a few feet separated the Bronco and the car behind them.

The car was hot. "Emma, grab three waters. Pass me one."

She handed it over.

"Thanks. Splash more water on your head and face. Take a drink and see to Midnight."

Troy used half the water to wet his hair, face-rag, and shoulders. It was warm but felt soothing. He poured the other half on Rascal's head and back. Tossing the empty, he opened the second bottle and took a long swig.

"Drink," he told Emma as he made a cup with his hand and poured water for Rascal. "Try to get Midnight to drink some, too."

Overhead, a roaring whoop-whoop-whoop beat the air.

"What's that noise?" Emma asked.

"I don't know."

From above, a bright beam spot-lit the gridlock of cars, tracing over them.

Emma leaned into the windshield, twisted and looked skyward. "It's a helicopter. I've never seen one so close."

The whoop-whoop-whoops grew louder.

"It's got a bucket hanging down. It's tipping, like a teapot. Oh!" She jerked back.

A gush of water doused the ambulance. Seconds later, water splashed onto the Bronco's roof and trickled down the windows.

The windshield made a cracking noise and a tiny one-inch line appeared on the driver's side at eye level.

Noooo . . . Don't let it grow any bigger.

Troy kept the thought inside. Maybe Emma wouldn't notice the crack. And if she did, she probably wouldn't realize what would happen if it ran the length of the window.

The windshield was more than just a windshield.

It was a fire-shield.

CHAPTER EIGHTEEN

THURSDAY, NOVEMBER 8, 2018
AROUND 11:34 A.M.

The ambulance backed out of its skid, straightened and shot down the road. In less than twenty seconds it was headed down the highway once again. Lights flashing. Siren wailing.

Another wall of fire flared on the west flank. Trees glowed neon-orange about fifty yards to the right, half the length of a football field. It was moving fast, like ten yards every couple of minutes—an infernal quarterback going for the touchdown.

"Go! Go! Go!" Emma shouted like she was his personal cheerleader.

Troy gunned the engine and tried to close the gap between him and the flashing lights. Half of the other cars had the same idea at the same time. His only advantage was that he was already in the lane.

They flew down the highway toward safety. The ambulance led the charge like a beacon of life. Troy hardly noticed the side roads they passed as he drove. Concentrating on the road, he tried to ignore the spot fires igniting along on both sides of the pavement.

It looked like it was clearing up ahead.

Troy whooped. They were going to make it. They were out-running the fire.

Emma started to sing again. *"Ain't No Stoppin' Us Now!"*

He tapped the song's rhythm on the steering wheel and slowed for a sharp curve in the road. The ambulance had shot ahead, followed by the other lead cars except for one. A Corvette. Troy accelerated to close the gap between them when it happened.

A giant fir tree toppled, smashing onto the pavement. The song died on Emma' lips. The Corvette skidded and shot across the road in front of them and landed in the ditch. The downed tree had blocked their only escape.

Troy swerved and just missed clipping the Corvette before coming to a stop. He gulped in air. Unless miracles were real, they weren't going anywhere.

Emma squealed.

Rascal nosed his ear and licked.

"Don't panic, Emma," Troy said. "You okay?"

"Yes." Emma's voice was barely a whisper.

"Good."

He checked the rearview mirror. The fire behind had morphed into a unified giant wall of flames headed toward them—licking and consuming everything in its path.

A Dodge Ram Truck passed him on the right and rammed the downed tree. The truck high-centered on the tree trunk, but the tree didn't move. The driver jumped out, ran through the flames and disappeared from view.

Troy watched the truck's tires catch fire and burn. He wanted to cry but for Emma's sake, he kept up his brave front.

"What do we do now?" she asked.

"Let me think," he said, knowing they were going nowhere. He stared at the burning pickup and tree. Looked left at the Corvette in the ditch. Looked right and saw a dirt side-road winding into the trees. Checked the review mirror. Behind them, the two-lane road had turned into an eerie car lot. Cars were parked at odd angles. Headlights aimed uselessly at their doom.

What were the people in them thinking?

Up until that moment, even though Troy had been afraid, he'd believed they'd make it out. For the first time since he'd received Jeremy's text, real fear crept into Troy's gut. He felt numb. His mouth had gone dry. His heart ached.

He'd failed.

Failed to convince Mrs. Jones to leave.

Failed his parents.

Failed to protect his sister.

Failed to protect their pets.

They were going to die.

He swallowed hard, turned off the ignition and shut off the headlights.

CHAPTER NINETEEN

Troy!" Emma said. "What's that?"

She pointed to a pair of bright lights to her right. They were high in the air, like the headlights on a big semi-truck. But what would a semi-truck be doing on a small dirt road in the middle of the forest? And why were trees being knocked down in its wake?

He squinted, flipped on the headlights, and started the Bronco. Whatever it was, he wanted to be seen.

The big vehicle half-straddled the ditch and the shoulder as it drove. It was huge—a yellow Bulldozer with a wide blade raised in front like a shield.

"It's an earthmover. To cut roads," he said, grinning. "Like Scrapper."

"Who?"

"Scrapper," Troy repeated. He shifted into reverse and looked back. "He's a *Constructicon.*"

"A what?" she asked.

"A kind of Transformer." He backed the SUV and stopped two

feet from the Volkswagen Beetle parked behind them in the road. "He's one of the good guys."

"Oh," Emma said. "Is it going to save us?"

"I hope so."

The Bulldozer crept onto the road. Its running tracks tore into the pavement as it inched toward the pickup and the downed tree. At the same time, the giant blade lowered itself to the ground. In one big move, it shovel-scooped the pickup and burning tree off to the side of the road.

The driver looked back and waved for the cars to move.

Troy beeped a thank you and put the Bronco in drive. He rolled down his window and yelled to the man. "Do you need a ride? We have room."

The man shook his head. "I've got my ride. And work to do."

"You sure?"

"Yeah, a lot of people live off the grid. I'm clearing their side roads so they can get out. My partner is working the east fork. You go on now."

"Thanks!" Troy repeated.

"Thank you, Mr. Scrapper," Emma yelled in Troy's ear.

"Get going," the man said. "You're not out of the woods yet."

Troy gave him a salute and pressed the gas pedal.

"We're on the road again," Emma sang out and then laughed. "You hate that song, don't you?"

"Not at the moment," he said, thankful Emma couldn't read his mind. Or feel his fear.

God, if you're real. Let us outrun this fire.

CHAPTER TWENTY

BUTTE COUNTY, CALIFORNIA
THURSDAY, NOVEMBER 8, 2018
AROUND 11:56 A.M.

They were moving again. Troy drove at a steady clip. Not too fast. Not too slow. He was getting pretty good at this driving business. A few cars passed him when they hit the first straightaway but he didn't care. It looked like they were all going to outrun the fire.

"See, I told you we were going to make it," he said.

"Then why are those cars stopped?" Emma asked, pointing up ahead. "What's wrong now?"

"I don't know. Not again."

He took his foot off the gas and let the Bronco coast until they reached the cluster of cars before coming to a stop.

Troy saw a man climb out of his car and jog over to a parked Jeep.

"Stay here with Rascal and Midnight," Troy ordered.

"Where are you going?"

"To see what's up. I'll be fast." He got out of the Bronco. It was hot and super windy, like someone had turned on a blast furnace.

"I'm timing you," she said, her eyes bloodshot and scared above the bandana. She twisted in her seat and looked back. "And so is the fire."

Troy glanced back at the route they'd driven to get this far. The fire was advancing—moving fast. Ahead, the cars weren't moving at all. In the gloom, he could see a few people getting out of their cars and running down the road.

God, if you're real, this is the time to show yourself. Tell me what to do.

He didn't hear an answer.

Troy looked back at the approaching wall of flames. Watched it licking trees and tasting the sky. Knew it wasn't stopping its rampage. Where were the firefighters? Why weren't they coming? Didn't anyone care? A lot of people were going to die. And why didn't they send more than one helicopter? Didn't they know what was happening?

He made a split-second decision and ran to the passenger side of the car.

He yanked open the door. "Get out. We're going to run for it."

"What about Midnight and Rascal?"

"Rascal can run. Give me the backpack."

She handed it to him.

Troy held the backpack to his chest and slipped the straps over his shoulders. He remembered the flashlight and grabbed it. They wouldn't use it until they had to.

"You've got it on backward," Emma said.

"I know." He crouched with his back to her. "Climb on. I can run faster with you riding piggyback than I can dragging you."

She giggled nervously and climbed on.

"Hold tight," Troy said and set off at a fast jog. His face-rag slapped his mouth. "Come on Rascal. Good girl."

He knew all-out sprinting would be a mistake, unless absolutely necessary. It'd tire him too soon and he'd inhale too much smoke deep into his lungs. Rascal kept pace at an easy dog-trot. Midnight bounced on his chest and yowled a complaint.

Troy and Emma both began to hack and cough. He wouldn't stop until they were safe. Or . . . the fire caught them.

He ran past parked cars—some with people still sitting in them. Others abandoned like the Bronco. He and Emma weren't the only ones running for their lives.

He stumbled but managed to stay on his feet. His chest and legs hurt, but that wouldn't stop him.

Behind them, pops of shattering glass went off like firecrackers. He chanced a backward glance and saw cars burning. It was time to sprint.

"Don't look back," he told Emma, hoping she hadn't seen anything. He didn't want to think about the people still in their cars. And he didn't want Emma to, either.

Rascal raced ahead.

"Wait, girl!" he yelled. "Stay with us."

Rascal ignored his command and ran toward the side of the road about twenty feet away.

Then Troy spotted the fox.

Rascal chased it over the bank and into the woods.

"Rascal! Come back."

Troy ran toward where the dog had disappeared, calling her name.

"Why did Rascal run away?" Emma asked.

They'd reached the spot and Troy stopped. He gasped for breath. "You're going to have to run for a bit. Okay?"

She nodded.

"Rascal," he yelled again. Emma joined him.

He looked back at the fire. They had to keep going.

CHAPTER TWENTY-ONE

BUTTE COUNTY, CALIFORNIA
THURSDAY, NOVEMBER 8, 2018
AROUND 12:14 P.M.

Tears streaked from Emma's eyes into her face-rag. She voiced the words he'd been thinking. "Why did Rascal run away from us?"

"I don't know," Troy said, panting. Each breath felt like it was wrenched from his lungs. He'd had Rascal longer than he'd had a little sister. "But we have to keep going. Come on, climb back on."

"But you said—"

"Forget what I said. Get on my back." He turned and bent his knees. "Up you go."

Barking came from the woods. Rascal burst through the smoke. Emma flung her hands around the dog. "She didn't leave us. Did you, girl?"

Rascal barked again, nipped Troy's hand and grabbed the cuff of his hoodie—pulled hard, tried to drag him down the steep embankment and away from the road.

"NO!" Troy said, pulling his hand free. "We've got to go this way."

The dog let go and ran down the hill a few paces, stopped, turned back, barked again. She waited. Tail wagging. When Troy didn't follow, she raced back up the bank. She grabbed him again and pulled hard enough to make him lose his footing.

Suddenly he was sliding down the steep bank of loose rocky soil. He felt his jeans rip and the flashlight jab into his ribs. Midnight yowled and thrashed in the backpack as he slid to a stop at the bottom. Rascal yelped and licked his face.

Emma scrambled down after them. Rascal barked once more and pushed through a wall of brush.

"Rascal," Emma cried as she helped Troy to his feet. "She wants us to follow her."

He looked up. They'd never be able to climb back to the road and outrun the fire now. It was better to keep going down.

Maybe Emma was right. Rascal wanted them to follow her into the wilderness. And then he remembered a Boy Scout camping trip he'd gone on two years earlier. They'd spent a weekend roughing it somewhere near here. It wasn't a real campground, but it had a stream running through it.

He jumped up, grabbed Emma's hand and pulled her into the brush, going as fast as they could manage. He had a stupid thought. *Don't let it be poison oak. That's all they'd need if they survived.*

Rascal kept up her frantic barking, leading them down into a narrow ravine.

Troy's legs were cramping. He didn't think he could walk much further, let alone run. And he knew Emma couldn't either.

"Where is Rascal taking us?" Emma asked.

They stepped from the thicket and found themselves at the edge of a shallow stream. Rascal was gulping water.

"Good girl. You led us to water," Troy said.

Emma waded in, but the water only came to her ankles. "It feels good. Hurry. Get in."

Troy stepped into the creek. The water was icy cold. It did feel good, but it wasn't deep enough to save them from a raging fire. They needed to find a hole at least three feet deep and big enough for all of them.

"We have to keep moving," Troy said. "Look at the hill." Flames were spilling down it. Trees and brush flared as the fire claimed them. "Stay in the center of the stream. Hold onto the back of my shirt to keep your balance. Okay?"

"Okay."

He pulled out the flashlight and switched it on, pointing it into the water to keep an eye out for boulders. They couldn't afford to trip now. The four of them sloshed down the center of the shallow creek. It widened for about forty feet before it narrowed again.

Troy smiled. *Maybe there was a God* because the water was growing deeper with each step. When it reached his knees, he raised the light.

He knew where they were, recognized the big rock at the edge of the swimming hole that his Boy Scout troop had splashed in for a whole week. Another thirty feet and they'd be there.

On the hill, the fire was picking up speed. Hot wind whipped the air. Embers swirled like fireflies, lighting mini-flares in their wake.

"Hurry," he said. "Almost there."

He started to run, slipped on submerged rocks—windmilled his arms and fought to keep balance. Emma slid but held on, dragging his shirt down until it almost choked him.

He managed to dig his feet in and grabbed her arm. They stood panting for a moment.

He pointed at the flames. "We don't have much time."

Troy picked Emma up, squishing the backpack in the process. Midnight cried.

"You're hurting him," Emma sobbed and struggled to get free.

"He'll be fine," Troy said and slogged ahead with Emma in his arms.

She stopped fighting and Troy struggled to make the last few feet without dropping her.

Rascal splashed on ahead.

Five feet. Four Feet. Three. Two. One. They made it to the rock. Hopefully, the little swimming hole was as big as Troy remembered.

CHAPTER TWENTY-TWO

BUTTE COUNTY, CALIFORNIA
THURSDAY, NOVEMBER 8, 2018
AROUND 12:32 P.M.

Troy set Emma next to the rock.

The fire was raging down the hill. They didn't have much time.

The creek water was barely above his knees. He swept the flashlight's beam left and right. The hole was much smaller than he remembered. He'd have to make it work. He prayed it was big enough for the four of them.

"Hold on to the rock," he told her. "And make your way around to the other side. I'm going to check it out. I think it's deeper."

The water came up to his waist, but the hole was small—only half the size of a hot tub. It would do. It would have to. He slipped off the backpack with Midnight growling inside and carefully set it on the rock. The bag wobbled and rolled as Midnight fought to get free.

Troy had more important things to worry about. Like getting his sister into the pool before the fire attacked the trees and brush alongside the stream.

"What's taking you so long?" he said, and he slipped back around the rock.

"My foot's stuck," Emma said. "Between two rocks."

He heard a splash. Hoped it wasn't Midnight. He rushed to Emma and pulled on her leg.

"That hurts."

"I'm sorry. But the fire will be here any second."

A large flaming leaf floated down and hit the water with a hiss.

Troy reached into the cool water and felt for her foot. Her shoe was wedged between the large rock and a smaller boulder. He wished he could see what he was doing. Wished he didn't have to hurt her but knew he had to get her foot free.

Using both hands he felt the shoe again. It was her favorite hot pink high-top Converse. He fumbled with the laces. Why did his sister always have to tie a double knot?

The fire had reached the bottom of the ravine. A thicket of brush, like the one they'd pushed through, burst into flames.

Frantically he pulled at the laces, loosening them. Putting both hands around her ankle, he jerked.

She yelped but her foot slipped free. "What about my shoe?" she wailed.

"You can get it later."

He lifted her, took two steps and plopped her into the deeper pool. Rascal was there, with the backpack in her mouth and Midnight crying from inside.

The flames lit the ravine. It looked like a movie filmed in Hades.

Emma screamed. "It's cold."

"Good girl, Rascal," he said and took the backpack. He unzipped it a quarter of an inch and let about two inches of water inside. Midnight howled in protest. There was a rock ledge. Troy set the backpack where Midnight wouldn't drown, half in and half out of the pool.

"Stay as low as you can," he said. "Do what I do."

He dunked his head. The cool closed around his steaming scalp.

It felt awesome. After a long second, he raised his nose and mouth just high enough to breathe. Next, he pulled the rag from his face, soaked it and put it on his head like a hat. Rascal huddled, propped on Troy's lap. Emma clung to them both.

They stared at each other as the fire overtook the little canyon. Other than dunking Midnight's bag and re-soaking their rag hats, they waited in silence, hoping the fire would burn itself out.

It took ten minutes for the water to go from ice-cold to cool. After ten more minutes, the water barely felt lukewarm. It took another ten minutes for the stream to turn hot. Really hot. Then, the shallow river became the hottest hot tub Troy had ever soaked in.

For what seemed like an hour, it felt like they were boiling and being cooked alive. His heart was slamming. His hands and feet began to swell. He wanted to get out, but knew they couldn't.

The fire raged so loud, it sounded like an endless freight train headed for the underworld. The crackling roar seemed to go on forever and ever.

CHAPTER TWENTY-THREE

BUTTE COUNTY, CALIFORNIA
THURSDAY, NOVEMBER 8, 2018
AROUND 12:37 P.M.

Troy eased his ears out of the water. The silence felt deafening. Not a single bird chirped. No sounds of movement came from the forest. At first, it seemed darker without the flames.

A sweet wind whipped over him, bringing smoke and then taking it away.

"Come on." Troy straightened, rising until his shoulders were clear of the water. The air was still smoky but not as bad as before. He motioned for Emma to rise, pulled the rag from his head, dipped it, and washed his face. "It's cooler now out of the water."

Emma bobbed up next to him. Her face looked puffy. She was crying.

"We're going to be okay," Troy said and helped her stand. "The fire is gone and I think the sky is starting to turn gray. Out you go, Rascal."

With more room in the pool, he stood. Hot water streamed off him. He breathed in. It still smelled like he was in the wrong seat at a campfire. But after being submerged for at least forty-five minutes in near-scalding water, the air felt amazingly cool.

The hungry monster fire had run away in search of more fuel to devour. Smoke hung in the air. Here and there, it rose from the scorched earth in wisps.

He squinted in the dim light, but it was still too dark to really see well. The few trees he could just make out looked like scorched skeletons. The bushes had been reduced to heaps of ashes.

"I'm hot," Emma said. She peeked into the backpack. "And so is Midnight. Shhh. You're okay. As soon as we get somewhere safe you can get out."

"Don't worry, we'll cool down now," he said.

He thought of their last mad dash down the hillside, of the fox and of Rascal pulling at his sleeve. How lucky they'd been to find this pool of water! As he stared at his sister, he started to grin.

"What are you smiling for?" she demanded.

"We made it. We did it! We made it out."

She started to smile, too. "You're right. We did, didn't we? We made it!"

"Yep. Maybe there is a God."

She wiped her eyes, water dripping from her hair. "Of course, you silly," Emma said, "I learned all about him in Sunday school."

He rolled his eyes.

Rascal barked and scrambled onto the creek bank.

"Now that the fire's over," Emma said. "I need my shoe."

Troy laughed and gave his sister a knuckle rub to the head.

"Hey," she said and punched his shoulder. "I'm telling Mom."

CHAPTER TWENTY-FOUR

BUTTE COUNTY, CALIFORNIA
THURSDAY, NOVEMBER 8, 2018
AROUND 1:12 P.M.

They followed the creek back to where Troy thought they'd come down the embankment. He couldn't be sure. The world was colored in shades of gray. It felt like they'd stepped into a black-and-white movie. The only color came from orange embers still glowing here and there, clinging to life.

Nothing in the forest was left untouched.

In the eerie silence, they crept along, careful to keep their feet away from the burning coals. Emma carried Midnight, but kept the cat in the bag. If he ran away, she'd never find him.

Rascal kept pace at Troy's side.

"You're a good girl," he said, patting her head. "You saved us."

Up ahead, he spotted the fire-scarred hillside. He felt pretty sure it led up to the road. They stopped at the bottom for a short rest.

"Can I call Mom and Dad?" Emma said.

"Why not?" Troy said, tearing the rag he'd used as a facemask into strips.

She frowned. "Can I use your cell? Mine got wet."

He grinned and pulled his cell from his back pocket. "Mine, too." He laughed. "Not sure we have service here, anyway."

Emma eyed the rag strips. "What are you going to do with those?"

Troy pointed to the smoking ground. "Rascal doesn't have shoes. The ground's hot."

"Oh," Emma said. "I see. You're going to make her shoes." She frowned. "Do you think it'll work?"

"If it doesn't, I'll carry her. Rascal. Come here, girl." Troy sat on the ground and carefully wrapped the rag strips around all four of his dog's feet and tied them. When he was done, Rascal sniffed them and then bounded up the hill, barking as she raced to the top.

Troy and Emma followed.

He wondered what they'd find at the top. When he came over the lip of the hill, he glanced left and right.

The strip of asphalt snaked away into the gloom. Not a single car was in sight.

Rascal lay on the road panting and trying to chew the makeshift shoes from her feet. Troy squatted next to the dog and unwound the rags. He wrapped them into a ball and shoved them into the front belly pocket of his hoodie.

"Why are you keeping those?"

Troy stood. "Just in case Rascal needs them again."

Emma's eyes went wide. "You don't think the fire's coming back?"

He shook his head. "There's nothing left to burn. Okay, ready for a hike?" he asked, stretching his back. He was still wary but was pretty sure they were safe.

He felt sore all over like someone had stuffed him in a sack and beat him with a baseball bat. But still, it felt good to be alive. Hiking was the last thing his feet wanted to do but they couldn't just sit there. "Let's hit the road."

"Why are we going this way instead of back home?" she asked. "Wouldn't Paradise be closer?"

"Probably, but Mom and Dad are this way. Remember? We said we'd head for Chico?" What he didn't tell her was that first of all, home was gone. Second of all, he didn't want to walk back past the cars that had burned. Third, the fire could still be burning back there and he'd had enough fire for a lifetime.

"You're limping," Emma said. "And you tore your jeans. And your face is dirty."

He grinned. "You think I look bad? Just be glad you don't have a mirror."

She slugged him in the shoulder.

"Hey! Take it easy."

She laughed.

Fifteen minutes later they heard engines coming up the road from the Sacramento Valley. Three minutes later, a caravan crawled around the corner—a caterpillar of red trucks and blinking lights. A horn blasted.

"Yeah!" Emma shouted and waved both arms. "Firefighters!"

"And a ride," Troy said, feeling the weight of responsibility being lifted from his shoulders.

The truth was, he was exhausted. Although they'd escaped the fire, he'd been afraid he didn't have the energy to get his sister back to civilization before he dropped.

The first truck didn't stop. The driver waved and shouted words that were lost in the engine's roar.

Three more vehicles drove past. Then another. And another.

Were they still on their own?

Wasn't anyone going to help them?

CHAPTER TWENTY-FIVE

BUTTE COUNTY, CALIFORNIA
THURSDAY, NOVEMBER 8, 2018
AROUND 1:59 P.M.

A big red pickup truck peeled away from the train of fire fighting vehicles and parked. A guy in fire protection gear hopped out.

"Hey, kids. Need a lift?"

"You could say that," Troy said.

"Even though we're not supposed to take rides from strangers," Emma said.

The man held out his hand. "Hi. I'm Tom Williams, Transportation. And from the looks of you, you must have had quite a morning. I can see you're a resilient pair of kids."

"Yes, we are," Emma said. "We were never going to give up. Right, Troy?"

"No, we didn't." Even though it had seemed hopeless at least a dozen times.

"What are your names?" Mr. Williams asked.

"Emma. Emma Benson." She took his hand and shook it. "This is my big brother Troy. Who's pretty cool sometimes when he's not being a boring pain. And that's Rascal." She lowered her voice. "Midnight's in the bag. So. Now we're not strangers, my feet would love a ride."

Mr. Williams laughed. "Climb in. You kids are incredible. Great job for making it through."

They piled into the front seat. Emma turned into *Chatty Cathy* and by the time they left the forest and reached the rolling fields of yellowed grass in the valley, she'd told the fireman their entire life history. Including both their mom's and dad's cell numbers.

"I had to memorize their numbers because I kept losing my phone," she said.

"You're a bright one," Mr. Williams said and handed her his phone. She passed it to Troy.

Emma rattled off a number and Troy punched it in. It didn't even make it through half a ring.

"Hello?" his dad said, sounding panicked.

"Dad. It's me. We're okay."

"Troy! Thank God? Where are you? You still driving? Emma's fine?"

"I want to talk," Emma said and grabbed the phone. "Me and Rascal, Midnight and Troy are just fine. A fireman is giving us a ride to—where are you taking us?"

"To an evacuation center in Chico." He gave her the address.

She repeated the information into the phone.

Troy took the phone back. "See you soon, Dad."

"Troy," his dad said. "I'm sorry we weren't there. I'm proud of you. We'll be waiting when you arrive.

The evacuation center was like a giant ant-farm of activity. People were everywhere. Coming. Going. Waiting. Arriving. Talking. Reporting.

An ambulance with flashing lights pulled out of the lot as they drove in.

Troy couldn't spot his parents in the chaos. Had they been held up on the road?

His eyes scanned everything at once. A stream of people carried cases of bottled water into the building. The Salvation Army had brought boxes and trays of food. The Red Cross had set up a medical triage station.

Mr. Williams parked the truck in a space reserved for CAL FIRE. A news-crew spotted them and pointed a camera their way. The reporter started toward them.

Emma pulled down the visor and looked in the mirror at her soot-streaked face, red eyes and crazy hair. "I don't want my picture taken," Emma said. "I just want to see Mom and Dad. Where are they? They said they'd be here."

"I'm looking," Troy said and spotted them. "There they are! See, Mom's waving."

"And running," Emma squealed. "Hurry up. Open the door, Troy."

Troy already had the door open. He turned to Mr. Williams. "Thanks for the ride."

"Good luck, kids," he said.

"Hurry, Troy." Emma pushed her brother's shoulder. He hopped out, followed by Rascal and Emma with Midnight.

"You did well," Mr. Williams said through the open window of the truck. "Tell your dad he should be proud of you both." He shifted into reverse, waved and drove away.

"He didn't wait to meet Mom and Dad," Emma said.

"He doesn't have time," Troy said. "The fire isn't out."

Before Emma could say anything else, his parents reached them.

His mom was crying and scooped them all up, including Rascal, into a group hug.

"I've been so afraid," Mom said, squeezing them tight. She whispered in Troy's ear, "I love you. Thanks for keeping your sister safe."

Midnight yowled, not liking the squishing hug.

Mom released them and wiped tears from her cheeks. "You two need a bath. And clean clothes. We're going to Grandma's house."

"Can we stop for ice cream on the way?" Emma said. "We missed breakfast. I'm starving."

"Of course," Mom said.

"Dad?" Troy said. "Can I borrow your phone to send a text to Jeremy? I want to let him know I'm okay."

"Sure, son," Dad said and ruffled Troy's hair. "So proud of you."

"Really?"

"More than really. You kept your head. Saved your sister. Did the Benson name fine."

CHAPTER TWENTY-SIX

TWO WEEKS LATER...
CHICO, CALIFORNIA

It's funny, now that they couldn't go back to Paradise, he realized how much he missed the place. He missed being able to walk over to Jeremy's. He missed his old bedroom. He even missed the tire swing that had been busted on the front lawn. It would be a long time before life got back to normal. He was glad he had his family, though, and he knew that having survived the fire, they could get through anything together.

What was crazy, his dad had gotten a call that the Bronco had been located. It had been towed to a junkyard in Chico. If they couldn't go home, maybe some small memento had survived the fire.

"Do you think we'll find anything?" Troy asked as they pulled into the yard and parked.

"Maybe," Dad said. "Maybe not. We'll see."

Rows and rows of junked cars waited to be stripped of usable parts before being crushed. One whole row was made up of burnt vehicles from the fire.

They got out and Troy's dad went into the office. Troy started down the row of car skeletons.

The vehicles looked like they'd all been tricked-out by the same fire-breathing mechanic. Lights, bumpers, tires, chrome trims and any other pieces on the outside had melted. The paint jobs were scorched into angry patterns.

Troy found their Bronco near the end of the row. Its windows were gone and it looked like the others but seemed worse. Before the fire, it had been the coolest car ever. He put his hand on the rough metal and patted the hood like it was an old friend. "You got us through the worst of it," he said to the car.

Even though it had rained, the SUV still smelled of smoke and soot.

His dad and the yard-attendant joined him. "You're welcome to take what you find, but I doubt it'll be much," the man said.

Troy leaned in through the missing window. Everything from the seats to the ceiling had been charred. The only thing that appeared to have survived were the keys dangling from the ignition.

The man said, "You're lucky you kids didn't stay with the car."

Troy winced as he nodded, remembering his and Emma's final run.

The man returned to his office. Troy and his dad spent ten more minutes searching and came up empty-handed.

"Guess this was a wasted trip," Troy said.

"Don't know about that." Dad reached in through the driver's door and pulled the key from the ignition. "I still have the keys to my first ride. You should have yours." He tossed them to Troy, who caught them easily.

Troy stared down at them and closed his fingers around them. He nodded. "Thanks."

"You know son, you're amazing. Your quick thinking saved you and your sister."

Troy smiled. Those keys were proof that the four of them had beaten the fire. He'd keep them forever as a trophy. They'd won. He'd driven the Bronco through flames. Kept his sister safe. Saved the family pets. Out-ran the fire on foot. Huddled in a stream while the fire raged through the ravine. But the Camp Fire didn't get them.

Troy felt like shouting, *I made it.*
I escaped California's deadliest fire!

———

THE END

Turn the page for facts about
Wildfires and fire safety

The California Camp Fire raged on for 18 days.

Three people are still listed as missing.

Eighty-six people are listed as deceased.

More than 50,000 people were evacuated. Many are still struggling to find new homes.

Our thoughts are with the brave people and their pets whose lives were turned upside-down on that fateful day.

TEN FACTS ABOUT THE CALIFORNIA CAMP FIRE

- The Camp Fire is California's deadliest and most destructive wildfire.
- 6th deadliest wildfire in the US
- Many evacuees spent over 3 hours driving through the raging fire
- The blaze was so hot it melted cars and wheels, and reduced bodies to bone.
- It spread at 80 football fields a minute.
- 240 square miles burned. That's larger than the city of Chicago.
- The fire burned for 18 days: from November 8, 2018 at 6:29 a.m. until November 25, 2018
- The Camp Fire is named after where it began: near the Camp Creek and Pulga Roads, close to the Jarbo Gap in Butte County, CA. Fires are often named according to their starting location.
- Number of buildings destroyed: 13,972 homes, 528 restaurants, stores, offices, schools, churches, rest homes, and a hospital, plus 4,293 other structures.
- 50,000 people were evacuated and 86 people lost their lives.

———

CAMP FIRE TIMELINE
Thursday, Nov 8, 2018

- **6:30 a.m.** (approx.) Fire sparks to life near the Feather River.
- **6:51 a.m.** The fire now covers 10 acres.
- **7:23 a.m.** (one hour has passed) The first evacuation order for Pulga, CA is tweeted by the Butte County sheriff. Unfortunately, most residents do not receive the tweet.
- Wind speeds are approaching 50 miles per hour. The fire is growing rapidly. It's consuming the equivalent of a football field *every second*. (Cal Fire)
- The fire's speed makes it impossible for most Paradise residents to evacuate before it arrives.
- **Around 8 a.m.** The fire reaches the town of Paradise, CA.
- **10:30 a.m. It looks like night.**
- **10:45 a.m.** The fire has grown to nearly 20,000 acres. (satellite image records)
- **6 p.m.** Less than twelve hours have passed. The Camp Fire has traveled 17 miles and burned almost everything in its path.

Did you know?

WHERE IS PARADISE, CALIFORNIA?

Longitude: 121.434700 Latitude: 39.813400

Paradise is located around one hundred and forty miles northeast of San Francisco and eighty miles north of California's state capital, Sacramento. The closest big town is Chico, around a forty-minute drive away. Until the fire, the small town was nestled in evergreen forests with beautiful views of the Sierra foothills.

WHO LIVED IN PARADISE?

Around 27,000 people lived in Paradise itself. According to the latest census, over twenty-five percent of its residents were 65-years or older. It has been described as a tight close-knit community.

WHAT WAS LOST?

Ninety percent of homes and buildings in Paradise were destroyed in the first twenty-four hours.

By November 11th, three days after the fire began, 52,000 people had been evacuated from Paradise and the surrounding area.

The *Honey Run Covered Bridge* nearby Butte Creek was the last three-span Pratt-style truss bridge in the United States. The fire incinerated it on November 10.

FAST FACTS
Start Date: 11/8/2018
Start Time: 6:29 a.m.
Incident Type: Vegetation Fire
Location: Camp Creek and Pulga Roads, Butte County
CAL Fire Unit: Butte County

WHAT CAUSED THE FIRE?

Power lines belonging to Pacific Gas and Electric caused the deadly fire.

The California Department of Forestry and Fire Protection said, *"After a very meticulous and thorough investigation, Cal Fire has determined that the Camp Fire was caused by electrical transmission lines owned and operated by Pacific Gas and Electricity located in the Pulga area."*

"The tinder dry vegetation and Red Flag conditions consisting of strong winds, low humidity and warm temperatures promoted this fire and caused extreme rates of spread."

Cal Fire said that a second ignition site was caused by *"vegetation into electrical distribution lines owned and operated by PG&E."* The second fire merged into the original fire, officials said.

A number of factors contributed to the spread of the blaze.

NO RAIN = LOW HUMIDITY

Although the five-year California drought had officially ended the previous April, Butte County had had no rain for seven months. While summers are normally hot and dry, autumn rains usually arrive long before November. This year they did not.

The state's water restrictions were still in effect. Yards were dry and kindle-ready.

HIGH WINDS + FIRE = DEVASTATION

Through the morning of November 9, the National Weather Service issued a *Red Flag high-wind warning* for most of Northern California's interior.

The high-wind warnings proved true.

Once the PG&E downed power lines touched the dry plants and sparked the fire, the wind took hold. A high-powered, fifty-mile-an-hour gale tore though the area, fanning the blaze and driving it forward.

The fire moved at a rate of eighty football fields per minute. No runner, no matter how fast, could cross eighty football fields in a minute. It took less than twenty-four hours for the flames to devour Paradise and its surrounding communities.

"Pretty much the community of Paradise is destroyed, it's that kind of devastation. The wind that was predicted came and just wiped it out," Captain Scott McLean (Cal Fire) said.

WHY WEREN'T PEOPLE WARNED IN TIME TO ESCAPE?

There are many reasons why people didn't receive the information to evacuate in time.

Living in the Sierra Foothills above the Sacramento Valley has a strong pull for those in search of small communities, a lower cost of living, less urban bustle or planning, beautiful views and less bureaucracy. With the warm summers, it's a great place to retire. It's a peaceful life, but it comes with a price.

Many homes don't have cell phone service, access to WiFi, or cable television. While this might seem strange to some, many retirees lived in Paradise, people who aren't tied to their devices. Unfortunately, this meant they did not have easy access to information, such as Tweets and emergency cell phone alerts.

Those with service in town were also at a disadvantage. One cell tower was down. Many homes had replaced their landlines for cell phones. Electricity was out, so TV was unavailable.

Butte County had actually beefed up its emergency warning notification system because of the 2017 California wildfires. However, their efforts were in vain. They sent evacuation warnings over landlines, cell phones, and Twitter. Unfortunately, only twelve percent of county residents had opted in to receive the reverse 911 notifications. The rest either failed to sign up or chose to opt out.

The fire moved too fast for officials to use other means of notifying residents, such as door-to-door warnings.

Most people found out about the evacuation by word-of-mouth from friends, neighbors, and/or family.

Some people chose to ignore the evacuation order until it was too late to escape.

BE INFORMED ABOUT WILDFIRES

- Sign up for emergency alerts.
- Know your community's evacuation plans and find several ways to leave the area. Drive the evacuation routes and find shelter locations. Have a plan for pets and livestock.
- Leave if told to do so.
- If trapped, call 9-1-1. Turn on lights to help rescuers find you.
- Listen for emergency information and alerts.
- Use N95 masks to keep particles out of the air you breathe.
- If you are not ordered to evacuate but smoky conditions exist, stay inside in a safe location or go to a community building where smoke levels are lower.

For more information, visit:
https://www.ready.gov/wildfires

I ESCAPED

THE
GOLD RUSH FEVER

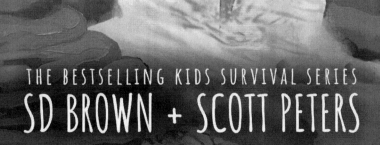

THE BESTSELLING KIDS SURVIVAL SERIES
SD BROWN + SCOTT PETERS

I ESCAPED THE GOLD RUSH FEVER

CHAPTER ONE

The Klamath River, California
August 1852

Pale moonlight filtered through the madrone tree's gnarled branches. Crouched in the shadows, fourteen-year-old Amelia Hudson Taylor had just enough light to recognize the figure at her feet. It was Ned Pepper, the Indian boy from a downriver nation. He lay on his side, gagged and hogtied.

How had this happened?

Amelia, or *Hudson* as everyone called her, knelt and whispered, "Do you have a knife?"

Unable to answer, Ned wriggled onto his side and glanced down at his pants.

"Front pocket?" Hudson whispered.

He nodded.

The knife was an obsidian blade—no handle—and razor-sharp. Hudson sawed through the heavy hemp rope. She nicked her fingers, winced, and kept sawing.

Finally free, Ned ripped off the gag. "How many?" he whispered into her ear. "White men?"

"At least three."

"More will come. Follow me."

Hudson grabbed his arm. "I heard them talking. They're going to burn the village at first light."

"Before long, sun rays will come," he said. "We must move like the raccoon. Low and silent."

The two teens reached the big rock at the river's edge where Ned had beached his dugout-canoe. To the east, an ominous hint of gray crept into the sky. Time was running out for the village.

"Wait here," Ned said. "I will warn them."

"I tried," Hudson said. "They're still chanting over my father. They wouldn't listen."

"They will listen to me." He got to his feet.

Hudson rose, too.

"No," he said, "you wait here."

"You're not my father. You can't tell me what to do. Father is trapped in the sweathouse. He's hurt and needs my help. I'm going with you, whether you like it or not."

The boy frowned, and she followed him up the rocky bank.

Crouched low, Hudson slipped, releasing a clatter of pebbles. Startled birds squawked. Wings beat the air, and a murder of crows burst into flight.

Ned turned and glared, shaking his head and tapping his finger to his lips.

She mouthed, "Sorry."

Ned pointed to her, walked his fingers up his arm, and then pointed to the big rock.

What? Was he ordering her to go back and wait?

Hudson shook her head. No way. Her father needed her. She wasn't some helpless girl.

Ned grabbed her arm and whispered, "Go. Wait."

"No," she hissed, jerking free. She hardly knew this boy. They'd met only a few days ago. There was no way she'd trust him with her father's life. "I'm coming with you."

He gave her a long hard look.

"And stop acting like I'm a girl. I may not be Indian, and I may be smaller, but who just rescued who? Besides we're almost the same age."

A gunshot broke the deadly calm.

Hudson flinched and dropped to the ground.

A woman screamed.

Eerie silence followed. The only noise was the hammering of Hudson's heart, pounding like a drum warning of impending doom.

CHAPTER TWO

Five Days Earlier

Amelia Hudson Taylor, frequently called young lady by her strict domineering aunt, had run away from San Francisco three weeks earlier. To cover her tracks, she'd disguised herself as a boy and used her middle name. Hudson. She liked the sound of it; the name suited her just fine.

Hudson had traveled for long, weary days, getting through by hiding, trickery, and the skin of her teeth. She had finally arrived at the remote Klamath River Gold Strike in Northern California.

Now came the tricky part: Hudson had to find her estranged father, convince him she was his daughter, and persuade him to let her live with him.

She looked down from the trail she'd followed from Union on the coast. Trails framed the river, running parallel on each side. Both were up high, well above the winter flood-line.

Her eyes scanned the river bar. This section of the river was long and wide. She could see a quarter of a mile in each direction. The miner's settlement was a hodgepodge of makeshift tents and campsites scattered throughout the trees and brush that overlooked the river's north side.

As for the shining Klamath River, its shores were crammed with at least a hundred or more men. They crouched along both edges. Dark trails of muddy water ran from their gold pans and bled downstream.

The miners all wore the same sturdy dungarees with shirtsleeves rolled up to their elbows. Most wore crumpled, wide-brimmed hats. It was hard to tell one from the other.

Which man was her father?

Hoisting her travel pack, she started down the path toward the river. A three-minute scramble, and she reached the rocky bar edging the water. Just ahead, a big, red-haired man squatted over a gold pan. A scrawny black mule stood next to him, hobbled so it couldn't wander away. White scars, and a few fresh red ones, traced patterns over its face and back.

Seeing the poor creature with its soft brown eyes made Hudson wince.

"Excuse me?" Hudson said, taking a tentative step toward the man. "Do you know Miles Taylor?"

The red-haired miner didn't look up. He grabbed a huge handful of dirt from a bucket and dumped it into his gold pan.

"Excuse me? Sir? Can you help me? I'm looking for my father."

No answer. Not even a grunt.

He dipped the edge of his gold pan into the river. Swirling the pan to mix the water with the dirt, the contents turned brown. He poured off the excess and dipped three more times until the dirt washed away, leaving just the gravel and rocks.

"Sir?"

Why was he ignoring her? Maybe he was deaf.

She leaned closer and raised her voice. "Miles Taylor. He's my father. I need to find him."

The man swore and dumped the contents of his gold pan into the river.

He stood, hoisting his pick, and shot her a feverish glare. "Don't know. Don't care."

He spit a stream of tobacco juice onto the gray gravel. The heat dried it almost on contact, and, for a second, it looked like blood splatters. "Get lost. Quit bothering me, boy. Or you'll get a beating like old Blackie here."

Hearing its name, the poor mule brayed and lowered its head as if in fear.

The miner picked up a fist-sized rock and flung it at her. She side-jumped, and it clipped her shoulder—sharp and painful.

Hudson backed away, thankful when his glare returned to his gold pan. She beat a hasty retreat, tripping over uneven gravel the size of baseballs.

Panting, she bent double to catch her breath. Finding her father would be tougher than she thought. She bit her lip. Hopefully, he wasn't like the red-headed miner.

She rubbed her shoulder; it felt bruised and hot. Maybe even a little swollen.

"You should avoid Red Duncan," said a voice behind her. "He is a bad man."

Hudson spun around and gulped.

She stood face-to-face with an Indian boy. Even though he was taller, he looked about her age—fifteen or sixteen. His hair was tied back like a girl's in a ponytail. Like Hudson, he wore canvas dungarees, but that was all he wore. No shirt. No shoes. She'd never seen anyone half-dressed walking around in public.

She couldn't help it; she grinned. Aunt Gertrude would have been scandalized.

"You are asking about Mr. Miles Taylor?" the boy said. "I know Mr. Taylor. Come, I will take you to him."

This boy was a stranger. He might be just as dangerous as the miner.

"That's okay. Just tell me where to find him," she said.

"It is easier to take you."

Forcing a smile, she said, "But I don't know you."

"I'm Ned. Ned Pepper."

CHAPTER THREE

Ned did as he promised. He delivered her to her father.

"Mr. Taylor, here is your child," Ned said and left.

Hudson locked eyes with the father she'd never met. It was almost like looking into a mirror, except he was older and a man. He had the same shaped mouth, the same hazel eyes, and the same unruly curly hair.

Oh, please be glad I've come. Be the father I've imagined. Let me stay.

Her father stared at her with a look that could only be described as shock. And then, confusion. He shook his head as if to refocus his vision. A shadow passed over him, and his face grew grim.

"Father?" she said.

"You don't belong here." He sounded angry. "This is no place for a girl. Why are you here?"

"I came to find you."

"Go home."

"I can't go back to San Francisco. I won't," she said.

A frown creased the corners of his mouth.

"Please?" she said. "You don't know what it was like living with Aunt Gertrude."

"I'm sure it was fine."

"Let me show you."

Hudson slipped the suspenders from her shoulders and let them dangle at her waist. She held up her oversized baggy boy-pants with her left hand. Turning, she pulled up the back of her rough cotton shirt for him to see the scars that zigzagged across her skin.

She heard her father's sharp intake of breath.

"Everything I did was wrong." She fingered a two-inch raised patch of scar tissue in the center of her back. She knew it looked pink and ragged. "Aunt said it would remind me to be obedient."

At this, her father's frown deepened.

Hudson pointed at two more. "These stripes are for the day I snuck food scraps to a beggar." She turned and tucked the shirttail back into the pants. "If you ever loved Mother, you'll let me stay. I won't be a bother. I promise."

He stared up into the cloudless blue sky as if it would make her disappear.

Hudson added, "I'll work hard. And I can cook a little."

They eyed each other for a long moment.

"Why did you feed the beggar?" he asked.

"Because he was hungry."

"I see," he said, without any hint of a smile. He sighed, his face softening. "You can stay under three conditions."

"I agree," Hudson blurted.

He held up his hand. "You haven't heard my conditions. Only a fool agrees to the unknown." He bent until their noses were just inches apart. "Are you a fool?"

"I . . ." Hudson shrugged and stepped back. Why had her mother married this man? He seemed so unfeeling. So stern. "I hope not."

"Good." He held up his index finger. "One. You will work as hard as a real boy."

"I will."

"How old are you?"

"Almost fifteen," she whispered, thinking he should have at least remembered her birth year.

"You're small and can pass for younger. Let's say twelve." He held up a second finger. "Two, you will do as I say. Even if I decide to send you back to live with Gertrude."

Hudson nodded, crossing her fingers behind her back. She'd rather die than return.

"And three." A third finger went up. "You are a boy. Hud. Don't forget it."

"I won't." It sounded easy. After all, pretending to be a boy had gotten her this far.

She wouldn't miss the endless layers of clothing her aunt had insisted proper young ladies wore. The mid-calf skirts and crinoline petticoats. The ankle-length pantalets and long-sleeved dresses buttoned to the neck. The obligatory pinafore apron to keep the dress looking new for as long as possible.

It didn't matter what you were doing or how hot it was. In Aunt Gertrude's house, you dressed properly. You acted like her version of a young lady. Were obedient. A slave to her every whim.

The last straw was forcing Hudson to accept a proposal of marriage from the son of the largest mercantile owner—Luther Albert Banks. He was mean, rude, and a disgusting pig.

She'd rather die than marry him.

Hudson didn't tell her father this because he might agree with her aunt.

She tucked in her shirt.

As long as she didn't mess up, she was here to stay.

CHAPTER FOUR

Hudson spent a fitful and sleepless night, worried he'd send her back. But the following day, he put her to work. She was glad; no matter how hard the job, she'd give it her best. She was never—ever —returning to Aunt Gertrude's. Or worse, forced into marriage with Luther Albert Banks.

Hudson struggled under the weight of two twenty-five-pound buckets filled with dirt and rock. Someone had replaced the bucket's original wire handles with rope; the sisal cord cut into the fresh blisters on her palms.

Adding to her discomfort, the miner's pick strapped to her back dug into the tender flesh of her shoulders, rubbing against the old scar tissue.

Gritting her teeth, her breath came hard. No matter what it took, she refused to give up.

Sweat prickled Hudson's skin and streamed down her neck. If only it wasn't so hot. It must be a hundred degrees. In San Francisco, the fog rolled in and kept things cool. But here, the relentless sun beat down, even in the shade.

Hudson set the buckets down, flexed her fingers, and breathed deep. She finger-combed her auburn hair. Even short, it preferred tangles to curls.

Humph. Complaining solved nothing. At least the forest smelled sweet. Plus, sweat and blisters trumped being beat with a hairbrush.

After stretching her back, she smiled. She'd solve two problems with one solution.

She unstrapped the miner's pick and slipped the bucket handles onto either end. Then she hefted the pick to her shoulder. One bucket dangled in front and the other behind. They were still heavy, but at least it gave her blisters a rest.

Hud continued down the trail. Tall fir and pine trees reached for the sky. Bent double under the weight, she wound in and out of their shadows, following the narrow path.

This was her twelfth trip from her father's secret dig-site to the river. She'd bring him the dirt and he'd process it, sifting and cleaning it and hoping for a nugget of gold. As far as Hudson could tell, her father's secret dig-site was not going to be a lucky strike. So far, nothing had panned out.

The Klamath River's rushing water hummed on the breeze. Almost there—just one last twist in the path, and she could rest.

Her stomach growled. Hopefully, Father was ready for a lunch break.

A loud rustle sounded in the brush. She gulped, remembering her father's warning about bears.

She thought he'd been kidding. Picking up her pace, she shouted, "Go away, bear. I'm too tough to be a tasty morsel."

Grrrrrrrrrrr.

It *was* a bear! Hudson ran, forgetting her father's instructions to freeze, face the animal, and raise her hands.

The growls grew louder. She put on a burst of speed, the buckets swinging wildly as she slipped and slid over the rough trail.

Grrrrrrrrrrr.

She glanced back. A stand of huckleberry bushes shook violently.

Panic pushed her into overdrive. The buckets slammed her chest and back, the pick handle pressing deeper into one shoulder. Ragged gasps tore from her lungs.

A loud whistle split the air followed by a loud, "Ha, ha, ha!"

She stumbled, sending the buckets flying, and went down hard. A rock stabbed her left shoulder. Panting, she rolled onto her side and grabbed a half-rotten tree limb from the ground.

Armed, she scrabbled to her knees and used the branch to pry herself upward. Halfway to her feet, the stick cracked and broke.

She teetered but managed to remain upright, still clutching the short half. Stabbing the air, she yelled, "Whoever you are, you're not funny."

Her eyes darted to where the buckets landed. Miraculously, they both stood upright.

"Grrrrrrrrrr!" Jason Brancet, the only boy in the miner's camp, lumbered toward Hud.

Her father had pointed him out the night before. He'd warned that both Jason and his stepfather—the grouchy red-headed miner —were trouble.

"Jerk!" Hudson said, rubbing her shin.

Jason looked more like an orangutan than a bear with his long arms and orange-colored hair.

Jason loomed over her and growled again.

"Give it up," Hudson said, taking a step back. "You're pathetic. You sound nothing like a bear. More like a mouse with constipation."

Jason's cheeks turned an angry shade of red. "Oh yeah? Then why'd you run? Scaredy cat. Didn't anyone ever tell you—only stupid people run from a bear!" He reached to poke her in the center of her chest.

Before he could strike, she batted away his hand. "Don't touch me. Ever."

"Oooo. I'm so scared. *Grrrr!*" He fake-smiled, baring his dirty snaggleteeth. "How's your dad like having a feeble-minded son?"

"Maybe you should ask your stepfather," Hudson said, inching toward her fallen buckets.

"What?" he said, scratching his head like it housed a nest of fleas. "Why would I ask my stepfather? He doesn't even know your father."

She held back a giggle. Clearly, that one went right over his head.

Jason narrowed his eyes. "What's funny?"

She mentally kicked herself. There was no point in making enemies. Not when half the miners were already at odds. Even if he was a bully. She was here to work with her dad, and she wouldn't get far like this.

Swallowing her pride, she said, "Nothing. Just that your growls did almost sound real."

"Huh. Well. Yeah. There you go." He crossed his arms. "I was right."

Talk about self-centered. Jason was big, but maybe he was younger than he looked. That would explain why he acted so immature. And lacked basic hygiene.

Too bad she couldn't send him to live with Aunt Gertrude to learn proper manners. Coughing to cover a laugh, she nodded. "Yep. Well. Got to go. My father is waiting."

"For what? You got something in here?" Jason poked into one of her buckets then raised his finger to his nose. He sniffed, smudging a grimy mustache onto his lip. "There ain't no gold in these here pails. It's just plain old stinking dirt."

She shrugged, retrieved her miner's pick, and re-strapped it to her back.

He wiped his finger on his pants. "Want to play kick the can?"

"Sorry. Can't," Hudson said.

"Well, I do." He grinned and kicked the nearest bucket. It tipped over and rolled, spilling rocks and dirt.

Hudson gritted her teeth and clenched her fists. How dare he? If she were a real boy, six inches taller and twenty pounds heavier with muscles and a big fist, then she'd show him.

But she wasn't. Hitting him would be like a gnat attacking a buffalo.

"What's a matter? Bear got your tongue? *Grrrrrrr!*" He slapped his thighs and let out a huge, gut-busting laugh.

"Quit it."

"Why? This is fun." He kicked the second bucket.

It slammed into her shin, exploding into a blast of pain. Afraid he'd see the tears blurring her vision, she stared at the ground and swiped her hand across her eyes.

She blinked and stifled a gasp.

Cradled in the black dirt, just peeking out from beneath the bucket's rim, lay a gleaming flash of gold. She snatched up the nugget.

Eureka! she thought, her mind reeling. The nugget was the size of a large chicken egg! It had to be worth a fortune.

"Hey!" growled Jason. "That's mine. Give it to me. Now."

His big hand swung at her.

116

CHAPTER FIVE

Jason's fist zoomed straight at her face. Hud dodged, and his hand plunged past her.

Panting, Hudson snatched up the empty bucket and took a shot, swinging it at him. The bucket totally missed, but at least he jumped back. Both crouched in a fighting stance, frozen and eyeing one another.

Jason's dark gaze darted to the nugget in her free hand. "Just give it to me," he said, licking his lips. "And I won't hurt you."

She dry-swallowed, shoved the nugget into her pocket. "No."

The boy might be bigger, stronger, and meaner.

But she doubted he was faster. All she needed was a head start.

Unfortunately, that looked impossible. Jason straddled the narrow path to the river like a giant, raging grizzly. It was easy to imagine his teeth sprouting into sharp fangs, ready to tear her apart. She'd never squeeze past him.

Which left only one option. Retreat into the unfamiliar woods. Run fast enough to lose him and then double back to the river bar.

He inched closer.

She swung the bucket in a wider arc—stepping back and forcing herself to breathe through her nose. Then she took another step. And a third.

Jason kept coming, his face sinister. "Give me the nugget."

"You're crazy. It's mine," Hudson said. "I found it. Not you."

"Give. Me. The. Nugget." He stretched out his hand, his eyes berserk with gold fever.

If only she could swing her pick instead of the old bucket. Talk about a pathetic weapon. But her miner's pick was strapped to her back.

Jason feinted left, then kicked high, aiming for her stomach. As his leg shot forward, he skidded on a stone and lost his balance. His arm flailed. Hudson grasped the bucket with both hands and slammed it into his gut.

Perfect shot.

"Oomph." He groaned and bent double.

Hudson took off, running for her life. Once around the bend, she found a spot where the wall of brush thinned into random clumps and slipped into the forest. Moving quickly and silently, she crept uphill.

Below, footsteps pounded along the trail.

Hud's heart slammed. He was coming—he'd see her. *Hide*, her mind screamed. But where?

To the right, a huckleberry bush sprouted from a fallen fir log. The log was small, but the brush was thick. She put on a last desperate burst of speed, dropped behind it, and hugged the ground.

The running footsteps stopped.

Had he seen her?

Fear raced along Hudson's spine. Please, God, don't let him find me.

"Hud!" called Jason. He sounded close.

She held her breath. Why had he stopped? Was he winded? Or had he spotted her footprints leaving the trail?

"Hey," he said in a loud voice. "I was kidding. Come out. We can be friends. You don't have to hide."

Hudson stayed put. He wasn't a very convincing liar.

A heavy-sounding object clunked to the ground.

"I won't hurt you. Promise." He sounded like a little boy who'd been caught with his fingers in a cookie jar. "I didn't mean to scare you."

Silence.

"I brought your other bucket. It's still full of dirt."

Hudson pushed aside a twig to make a tiny peek-hole in the thick huckleberry bush.

Jason stood with his back to her, facing toward the river. Her father's best bucket sat on the trail. The fingers of his right hand clenched and opened like a tarantula on the hunt—over and over again.

Why couldn't he just leave?

Instead, he paced, waiting. Did he think she'd forget that he'd tried to steal the nugget? Did he think she was stupid?

By the time he sauntered off, her legs had grown stiff.

Just to be safe, Hudson counted to five hundred before making her next move.

CHAPTER SIX

Early afternoon sunlight slanted through the trees. Hudson couldn't sit there forever; her dad would be worried. He might even be mad at her for taking so long. He'd definitely be angry when he learned she'd already made an enemy.

Still, what if Jason was waiting by the river to ambush her? He wouldn't give up that gold nugget easily.

Hud sighed, realizing it'd be foolish to take the path straight to her father. That left her forging a roundabout path through the woods, even if she risked getting lost. If she brought her father the nugget, he'd be so happy he'd forget about her scuffle with Jason. He'd definitely let her stay.

Hudson glanced into the tangle of trees. It wasn't San Francisco, and the forest might not have street signs pointing the way, but if she stuck close to the river, it would eventually lead back to her father.

Hudson stood, shoved the nugget deeper in her pocket, and unstrapped the miner's pick from her back. She gripped it like a weapon. The bucket would be her shield.

Quickly, she tramped through the woods, putting more distance between her and Jason. She clambered over downed logs, climbed up and down steep hills, and shoved through thickets of brush. Hopefully, none was the poison oak that Dad had warned her about. The last thing she needed was an itchy rash.

She eyed the nearest bush. What had he said? Leaves of three, leave it be.

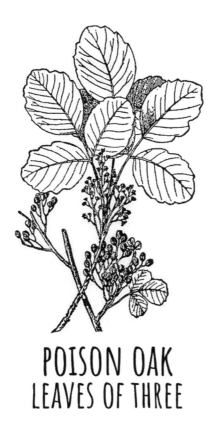

POISON OAK
LEAVES OF THREE

Fortunately, this bush looked safe. She kept going.

Finally, the river flashed brightly through the trees. It was time to circle back downstream. She breathed deep, and immediately wished she hadn't. Something smelled bad. She struggled to keep from gagging.

What the heck was it?

Hudson held her breath and bolted from the trees into a grassy meadow fronting the river. It should have been a peaceful view; wildflowers danced in the breeze beneath a bright blue sky. But what met her eyes was horrible.

The stench was even worse, and her hand flew to cover her nose.

Three cows lay on their sides. Angry horseflies buzzed in massive clouds around the poor beasts. The animals were clearly dead. Five red-headed vultures tore at one of the bloated carcasses. Hudson's stomach clenched.

What had happened to these poor cattle?

Voices startled her. The vultures took flight and Hudson ducked into the forest.

Two armed miners appeared, dragging an Indian boy by his long black hair. The brave looked about her age. Maybe a little older, but not much. He struggled to stay on his feet.

A third miner followed, shoving his gun into the brave's back. "Murdering savage! Killing our cows. They're worth more than three of you injuns."

Hudson stared, open-mouthed, breathing through a cupped hand. The armed men looked familiar. Maybe because they were miners.

This didn't feel right. These miners must have it wrong.

Why would the boy kill their cows unless he was starving? And that didn't make sense. He wouldn't leave the dead cows for the buzzards to eat. Or let the meat rot in the hot sun. For that matter, why kill three cows? One cow would probably feed a whole village.

An awful feeling tightened her stomach. Alarm bells rang in her head. An innocent Indian boy was about to be punished for something he didn't do.

The men shoved the boy to his knees next to one of the rotting carcasses. They pushed the boy's bruised cheek against the cow's bloated face. His dark eyes flicked to the woods, his gaze locking onto hers.

She gasped and drew back.

How had he spotted her when the others hadn't?

To her surprise, his eyes seemed to warn her. *Don't let them see you.*

She shrank lower.

"Look at our cows. Take a good, close look, boy," one miner said. "See what you gone and done, you mealy-mouthed—"

"You gonna pay," the taller man said, cutting in. "You gonna pay big time."

The boy struggled and spoke in ragged gulps. "We do not kill what belongs to another. We do not let meat rot in the sun."

"Liar!" the miner said.

"The cows, they have eaten the Klamath weed. It poisoned them," the boy said. "This is not our doing."

A pair of Indian men dressed in deerskin loincloths melted out of the trees and into view. Only Hudson saw them. Both carried rifles like the miners; they crept forward and took aim.

One Indian had long black hair, tied back and hanging almost to his waist. Three tattooed lines marked his inner forearm. He said, "Release my son."

The miners practically jumped out of their skins. They spun around. The man holding the gun jerked and fired.

The miner's shot went wide, and a branch exploded near Hudson. Bark flew in all directions. A piece hit Hudson's cheek, and she gasped.

"The next one goes in your son's head," the miner shouted.

He aimed at the boy thrashing to free himself. Two men held the youth down. They ground their feet into the boy's back and neck.

The boy's father said, "Shoot him, and we will shoot you dead."

Hudson watched the standoff in horror. There was nothing she could do. And then it happened. Guns exploded on both sides.

Time seemed to slow. Muzzles flashed, boomed, spewing the acrid scent of gunpowder. Men screamed. Bodies fell, crumpling to the ground.

Hudson felt dizzy and grabbed onto a tree to keep balance. She waited for someone to stand, to groan in agony, but no one moved.

A flush of crows rose, flapping and cawing into the air. Then the world fell silent, laced with the odor of gun smoke and the gurgle of the rushing Klamath River.

Hudson began to shiver. It was hot, but she was freezing cold. She stood on trembling legs and vomited.

Was anyone still alive? Cautiously Hudson forced her feet into the grass. She checked the boy first. It was too late.

"This was senseless. You died for nothing."

Her head clutched in her hands, she rocked back and forth on her knees and sobbed. How naïve she'd been to think Aunt Gertrude was the epitome of evil.

Tears streamed down her cheeks as she checked each man in turn. Not one had survived.

Nine bodies lay crumpled in the grass—three Indians, three miners, and three cows.

Straightening and spinning on wobbly feet, Hudson plunged across the field and ran.

CHAPTER SEVEN

Hudson leaned against a fir tree to catch her breath. The bark felt rough, but the tree's support was comforting. She'd been running forever, scrabbling through brush and climbing over fallen logs. Following the river. Using the brush as cover. Avoiding anyone who might make trouble for her. Like Jason. Or his stepfather, Red Duncan, the angry miner with the fiery hair.

The pick weighed painfully on her shoulders, but it was too valuable to abandon. That's when she realized her mistake: she'd left Father's bucket next to the poor Indian boy. Now both buckets were lost. He'd be furious.

A new worry struck. Would the miners think her father had been there? That he'd abandoned the fight and left the other miners to die? What else *could* they think?

She had to find him. He'd know what to do. She started to run.

Up ahead, a huge hill towered too steep and rocky to climb. It was time to chance exposure on the river bar. It'd be flatter, easier to walk on, and a direct route. She prayed Jason was still watching for her on the trail.

Hudson stepped onto the deserted gravel bar. A pair of mallard ducks floated in the current. There were no miners in sight.

The air was sweet, but the odor of blood and decay clung to her. She dropped to her knees and splashed water on her face and into her nostrils. The wetness felt good even though the water was murky.

She scooped up sand, scrubbed her face, rinsed, and could almost hear Aunt Gertrude's voice. "Amelia! Remember, cleanliness is next to Godliness. Therefore, dirt is next to evil."

Hudson's whispered, "No, Aunt Gertrude. Dirt has nothing to do with evil. Evil is the work of cruel, mean, and selfish people. People even worse than you."

Suddenly she felt hot, exhausted, and fearful. Her blisters had blisters.

She wanted to just sit and wait for her father to find her. To pretend that nothing bad had happened, that she could erase what she'd seen. That everything would be okay.

A horsefly landed on her hand, and she shooed it away. Fairytale daydreams didn't solve anything.

Hudson stood and brushed off her knees. It was time to get going.

The mallards quacked, beat the water with their wings, and rose into the air. They circled once and glided off, flying low over the water.

"Wait for me," Hudson called after the birds. She hurried along, ignoring the pain in her feet.

Around the next bend, miners hunched over gold pans. They were spaced at intervals along both sides of the sixty-foot-wide river. Some worked in groups. Some worked solo. All guarded their areas on the riverbank.

She finger-combed twigs, leaves, and cobwebs from her curls.

Odd. Why wasn't Father at his usual spot?

Instead, a stranger squatted there, dipping his gold pan into the river.

She thought about the abandoned bucket, recalling how his name was scratched into its side. Could someone have discovered the awful scene already?

Fear crept into her stomach.

"Father?" she whispered. "Where are you?"

CHAPTER EIGHT

Panic raced from Hudson's toenails to the tips of her curly hair. Where was her father? Miners were everywhere, but it was impossible to tell which were decent and which were evil—like Red Duncan.

This section of the Klamath River ran straight, long, and wide. Rock, sand, gravel, and boulders framed both sides. One huge white rock on her side towered high enough to hide a team of horses.

Hudson jogged past the white rock. Her stomach rumbled painfully. It was long past the mid-day meal. Wait. That's probably what happened. Tired of waiting for her to return, Father had gone back to camp for food.

She had to find him fast to explain what she'd seen and why they needed to go back for the bucket. At least if they ran onto Jason, the bully wouldn't dare try anything with her father present.

She felt for the lump of gold, glad to find it still in her pocket. Father would be furious with her, but the gold nugget would make him happy. Wouldn't it?

Not if he's implicated in murder, her mind shouted.

Red Duncan's voice startled her; she froze. He stood with his back to her, less than a dozen paces away.

"You stupid imbecile," he shouted. "Do you even know what a gold nugget looks like?"

Red Duncan was the last person she wanted to run into. The miner had to be at least six-and-half-feet tall, with over three-hundred pounds of mean muscle. His massive body blocked the identity of his latest victim. Still, Hud had a good idea who lay on the ground.

"I'm not lying. I saw it."

Hudson tiptoed backward.

"Sure you did," sneered Red. "I'm supposed to believe Miles Taylor and his boy hit the motherlode? You're nothing but a worthless lout. Lazy. Dumb. I have a half a mind to put you out of your misery."

"Look, Mr. Red," Jason's voice whined. "I got the kid's other bucket. See?"

Hudson recognized the first bucket she'd lost, sitting on the bank.

"I found another nugget in there, in the dirt," Jason said. "Not as big, but it's gold. See?"

Another gold nugget. That was hers!

Hudson had a mad impulse to run over and demand her bucket and gold.

"Keep your voice down," Red growled. "Haven't you learned nothing? Stupid boy. You don't advertise your pickings."

As if sensing her presence, the brute began to turn.

Hudson threw herself behind a redwood log and prayed. Her father had been right. He'd warned her. *Avoid that man. He's cruel. He'll kill for gold if he thinks he can get away with it.*

Sweat snaked down her neck as understanding washed over her.

Her father had downplayed the horrible truth. The Klamath Gold Rush was a place where honor and justice didn't exist.

"You find that boy," Red Duncan snarled. "Got that? Find him!"

"Yes sir," came the mumbled reply.

"Do what you have to, boy. Get me that nugget. Hear me?"

"I will."

"Find the kid. Bring me that gold. I'd hate to have to arrange three accidents." Red laughed.

"Three?" Jason's voice cracked.

"That's what I said."

"But there's only the boy and his father. That's two."

"You'll be number three if you don't deliver." Red spat a wad of chewing tobacco on the ground. "I don't leave witnesses. Got it?"

"Yeah." Jason sounded as scared as Hudson felt. "I got it."

Suddenly the gold nugget in her pocket felt like a huge weight. Red Duncan would stop at nothing to get it. And when he did, he'd kill them and keep it for himself. If he found Father's bucket, that would be the perfect excuse to string Father up as a traitor.

It was all Hudson's fault. If she'd never come, none of this would be happening.

"Now get out of here," Red barked. "Don't come back empty-handed."

CHAPTER NINE

Hudson waited for Red Duncan to wander away. Then, she ran. Her feet felt like they'd been filled with lead buckshot—every step sapped her hope and energy.

Red Duncan had as good as pasted targets on Hud and her father's backs.

Ahead, five men huddled by the water. They seemed excited—arms waving, fingers pointing, everyone talking at once.

Bile slithered up her throat. Were they talking about the dead men? Had they discovered father's bucket?

Giving the miners a wide berth, she rushed toward the camp.

Moments later, she reached the edge of the sprawling tent city. It wasn't a proper city like San Francisco with streets and signs. It was a haphazard maze of canvas tarps, wooden crates, and stone-circled fire pits.

Thank goodness it looked deserted.

Skirting the empty canvas huts, Hudson used the trees and bushes to navigate—left at the burnt oak tree, right at a clump of huckleberry brush, left again at the red-bark madrone tree.

Just past a thicket, their campsite squatted amongst a stand of young pine trees.

A huge sigh burst from her lungs. Father stood next to their tent.

Thank you, Lord.

"Father!"

"Hud, where have you been?" His eyes blazed.

"I—"

"It's been over two hours since you disappeared."

"I can explain," Hudson blurted. "Something's happened—"

He cut her off. "I thought we had an agreement." He untied a rope stretched between two trees. Their white tarp tent fluttered to the ground like an empty ghost. "No more excuses."

"You're taking down the tent. Are we leaving?" she said, feeling hopeful for the first time since her run-in with Jason. Leaving would solve everything. "How soon?"

"Now." He yanked the rope free, looped it on his arm, and tied it into a neat coil.

"Father." She swallowed. "I saw something—bad." The words

stuck in her throat. She dry-swallowed again. "And I lost your bucket. And . . ."

"We'll deal with that later," he huffed. "Just pack the supplies. I'll get the bedding."

"But I have to tell you. It's urgent. Your name is on the bucket."

"Quit your jabbering and dilly-dallying. Get packing."

"It's important—"

He raised his hand. "Enough! Do as I say. Now." He lowered their food sack from its perch high in a tree and handed it to her.

"But—"

"Pack up, Hudson."

Hud gritted her teeth. She shoved the cast iron pan into a burlap gunnysack, and dumped everything else on top—flour, hard-tack, venison jerky, tin plates, knives, forks, and cups.

"Why won't you listen?" She blinked back tears. "You're as stubborn as Aunt Gertrude."

"It's a trait you've inherited as well," he said sharply. But seeing her face, his eyes softened. "Trust me. You're not safe here."

"And neither are you. That's what I'm telling you. I saw—"

"There's no time. Tell me later." He tied the top of the gunny sack. "We have to leave before trouble starts. Indians shot three miners this morning. Killed two."

"But that's not what—"

Father talked over her. "One miner lived to tell the tale."

Wait, *one lived?* But she'd checked. Everyone was dead.

"One survived?" she asked, breathless.

"Yes. Apparently, a fourth miner was there and left him to die. The fourth man sided with the Indians."

"That's a lie," Hudson shouted.

He frowned.

Finally, she had her father's attention. "I was there. I'm the fourth miner."

A flicker of shock crossed his brow. "You?" His eyes lit with anger. "You were there? Why didn't you tell me?"

"I've been trying to. But I didn't leave the miner to die. I thought he was dead!"

Her father stared at the sky, rubbing the worry lines on his forehead. "What happened?"

The whole story came out in a rush. When it was over, their eyes locked.

"I panicked." Her voice choked. "And I left your bucket. With your name on it. Red Duncan's going to kill us. He'll say you were there, that you sided with the Indians."

He reached out and rubbed her curls. She shivered. It was the first time he'd shown any affection since she'd arrived. Then he pulled her into a tight hug and patted her back like she was a baby in need of an emotional burp.

"It's going to be okay," he said. "I'll get you to safety."

She clung to him, smelling the woodsy odor of fire on his clothes. A loud rustle sounded in the brush behind them.

Father stiffened and pushed her to the side. He pulled a pistol from his pocket and held it high.

She sucked in a breath. Had Jason given up waiting at the trailhead? Had he grown a brain and come looking for her?

"Who's there?" Father called out. "Show yourself."

CHAPTER TEN

A raucous donkey's bray split the silence.

The brush quivered, and Ned Pepper appeared. The unsmiling young Indian nodded to Hudson's father. Today the boy's dark hair hung loose. Other than that, Ned looked the same as when she'd met him. He was still barefoot and bare-chested.

A long-eared mule followed on his heels. One of its ears drooped forward and the other back. It was cute. It brayed again and rushed to sniff Hudson's hair.

"That tickles." She rubbed its neck. The fur felt smooth and coarse at the same time.

Father shook the boy's hand. "New plan. Red Duncan is on the warpath. It's serious, we have to leave. Now."

Ned's frown tightened. "What fire ant ran up his pants?"

"You haven't heard?" Hudson blurted. "Miners and Indians were both killed over the death of some cows. I . . . ."

Father shot her a look that silenced her. She stopped petting the mule.

"Duncan's gathering a hunting party," Father said. "He plans to attack the Indian villages tonight." He frowned. "He's looking for the miner who helped the Indians."

Ned's eyes flicked to Hudson. He couldn't know she was there, could he?

The mule chose that moment to give Hudson an unexpected nudge. She stumbled.

"Chewed Ear!" Ned's hand sliced the air.

The mule hung its head like it had been slapped. Hudson took pity on the poor creature and scratched its mane. The mule snuffled.

"I'm going to Happy Camp to see Redick McKee," Father said. "He has the governor's ear."

Hudson frowned. "What good will that do? It won't stop tonight's attack."

"No. But it might stop the next one. The men are on the warpath, they won't stop at one attack." He reached into his pocket and handed Ned a handwritten note. "You head to Parker Ranch, drop my things with Gray Morgan, and give him this letter. Tell him I hope to see him within the week."

Ned nodded.

"See that my son, Hud, gets to the coast safely. Stay with him until he boards a ship bound for San Francisco."

The words were like a scatter shotgun blast to her heart.

"No," she cried, grabbing her father's arm. "Let me stay."

"That's not possible."

"Then why can't you take me to the coast? Why Ned? He's just a boy."

"Ned's a trail guide. I trust him," he said.

And not me, she thought.

"Less talk. More hustle. Grab the supplies and load up the donkey."

"Don't send me away," Hudson said. "The Klamath River is a hundred-and-eighty miles long. Can't we find another spot to pan for gold? Away from Red Duncan and his men?"

Father made no reply.

Frowning, she swallowed the urge to cry. Her dream that they'd be a family slipped away. Her clenched jaws ached.

Her father was a stubborn old mule.

Well, she could be mulish, too. She'd go. But not back to Aunt Gertrude's. She'd find a job—maybe on the docks.

The three worked in silence. Soon the supplies were tied onto the mule. Ned whistled and started off. Chewed Ear followed.

Father squeezed her shoulder and leaned closer. She waited for him to say something nice, like that he'd miss her.

"One last thing," he whispered. "Ned doesn't know you're a girl. Keep it that way."

She scowled. "I thought you trusted him?"

"Trust only goes so far. Now hurry. Red will be looking for us."

They hurried single file toward the river and Ned's canoe. She jogged to keep up.

At the gravel bar, they slowed. Here and there, angry men stood in clusters. She heard snatches of talk about the dead cows, the dead Indians, and the dead miners.

"Eyes down, Hud," Father warned. "Don't look at anyone."

"Yes, sir," she said.

It was only a matter of time before someone read the name scratched into the abandoned bucket and raised the alarm.

"Whatever happens, don't talk," he said. "Ned? Where's the canoe?"

Ned pointed past the largest mob.

Father gave a quick nod. "Flank Hud on the right. Keep the mule on your left. Be ready to run. If something happens to me, keep my boy safe."

All around, the voices grew louder, swelling like the wild river—dark, turbulent, and frothing.

CHAPTER ELEVEN

Hudson kept her eyes downcast but snuck quick, frightened glances. The miners gathered at the river bar seemed to have doubled. They grew rowdier, angrier. It was clear some were liquored up.

"Should we retreat?" Ned said. "Until the wolves leave the lair."

"No," Father said. "The sooner we go, the better. Follow my lead."

The mob ignored them—until one miner spotted Ned.

"Hey," the man shouted, pointing. "Ain't that thieving White Feather's brother?"

The mob swarmed like angry hornets. Every eye fastened on Ned as they closed in.

"Your brother poisoned our cows," one snarled.

"We could arrange a family reunion," shouted another, waving a bottle of whiskey. He took a swig of the firewater, licked his lips, and pulled out a pistol. "Would you like that?"

Hudson's father cleared his throat. "What's got everyone all riled up?"

"Why don't you ask your Indian friend where he was this morning?"

"I already know. I hired him to strike my camp," Father said. "Took us most of the morning."

"You sure?"

Father pointed to the loaded mule. "That's my gear. I'm heading downriver."

"What's the big hurry?" shouted another miner.

"You'll miss the hunting party," said another.

Hudson felt her father's hand on her shoulder. "Get in the canoe," he whispered.

"What about Ned? And our things?"

"Do as I say. If you can, shove the boat into the water." He pushed her toward the beached canoe and turned back to the mob.

Hud took two steps and got no further. The men attacked. She was caught in a man-stampede—jostled left and right. A fist slammed into her ribs. She crashed to her knees, and a heavy boot crushed her little finger.

Gasping, Hudson scrunched into a ball and tucked both arms over her head. Chewed Ear bolted, clanking into the trees. Father and Ned were lost to sight, trapped in the surging horde.

Dread gripped her. Dread that her father and Ned would die like the men in the field.

Please. Please, God. Make this madness stop. Please, keep Father and Ned safe.

A shotgun blasted upriver.

Hudson rolled sideways as the men scattered left and right. Rising, she blinked to clear her eyes, desperate to try and spot her father.

Men were everywhere, clamoring and shouting.

Chewed Ear stood atop the bank eating dry grass—their supplies still tied onto the donkey's back. Ned's canoe lay abandoned on a sandy patch of shore just ahead.

As for Father and Ned, they'd disappeared.

He'd come back. He just had to!

Red Duncan's voice rose above the chaos. He'd climbed atop a massive boulder and was punching a smoking shotgun into the air.

The men roared, drowning out the sound of the rushing Klamath.

Duncan fired off another blast and motioned for the men to quiet.

Silence fell. Red Duncan spoke but was too far away to understand.

Swiftly, she headed for the canoe. When Father returned, she'd be ready for him. Because he *would* return, she had to believe that! She'd get the canoe in the water first and then fetch the donkey.

Up close, the boat was huge—at least twelve feet long. It looked like a hollowed-out redwood tree that had been burned and scraped smooth.

Hudson went to the canoe's far side, using it as a block between herself and the mob. She shoved, and nothing happened. Wow. It was twice as heavy as it looked.

She planted her feet on the shore and shoved hard. Again.

It didn't budge.

Maybe if she pulled from the floating end, the buoyancy would make it lighter and easier to maneuver.

Hudson slipped off her boots, tossed them into the canoe, and rolled up her pants. The rushing water felt cool as she waded to her knees.

Red Duncan shot off another gun blast.

She held onto the canoe for balance and waded deeper. Soon, the water reached her thighs. She grabbed the stern, jumped up, and shoved it down, using all of her weight to pull the canoe into the water.

At first, nothing happened. She jumped again. Tugged harder. Leaned back farther. The next jerk made her arms feel like they were being pulled from their sockets. But it moved.

Another hard jerk and the boat floated free.

"Yes!" Finally, she'd done something right.

Hudson stood waist-high in the river, panting.

Uh oh, how was she supposed to get the donkey? The current tugged at the boat, threatening to drag it downstream.

Upriver, Red Duncan was climbing down from his rock. The mob splintered into groups. Thirty men followed Duncan toward the main camp.

She had a bad feeling about this.

A second, smaller group headed toward Hudson. To her surprise, every few yards, two or three men peeled away to return to their gold panning. Only about fifteen men remained by the time the rag-tag group reached her. They were still arguing.

Hudson spotted her father and Ned bringing up the rear. She gasped in relief. Both looked unscathed. Then she saw Ned's wrists.

They were tied with twine.

Ned kept his eyes to the ground, his feet shuffling. Hudson gulped.

Father led the boy with a rope leash—like Ned was an animal. Why would her father do such a thing? It was horrible.

"Hud," Father called out. "Push the boat back onto shore."

"But, I just—"

"Do it. Now." He shot her a dark look.

CHAPTER TWELVE

Hudson's jaw clenched. There was no pleasing her father. Do this. Do that. Put the canoe into the river. Take it out. All her efforts had been for nothing. And now he was leading Ned like a bad dog on a leash. It was humiliating and cruel.

Father and Aunt Gertrude were cut from the same cloth after all.

She gave the boat one hard shove. It sailed forward and lodged in the sand. Her soaked pants chafed as she waded after it.

Father handed her Ned's leash and whispered, "Untie Ned."

Her eyes met his. "What's going on?"

"Do it. Now." Father hissed and then spoke loudly to the men. "This boy will be punished for what he did. After I get some work out of him."

Hudson grabbed his arm. "Why? Ned didn't do anything."

Father shrugged off her hand, whispering, "Be quick. The men might change their minds and take him."

"Oh." She shouldn't have jumped to conclusions.

To her surprise, Father bent and washed his hands in the river. Was he trying to act casual, like they weren't in a hurry to get away?

Ned held his bound hands to her, and she fumbled with the knots. Danger sparked on the breeze.

"Hurry," Father urged. "We need to skedaddle."

Hands free, Ned tied his hair back and reached into the boat for his long paddle.

"Sure you don't need help with that injun?" a miner called out. "Be glad to oblige."

"We got it," Father yelled back and waved. "My boy and I can handle one Indian youth."

The man shrugged and walked on.

"Ned's mule is over there." Hudson pointed to where Chewed Ear was munching grass. "It's still loaded with your stuff."

Ned put two fingers into his mouth and whistled three sharp blasts.

Chewed Ear raised its head.

Ned whistled again.

The mule raced down the steep bank, hit the flat ground, and trotted straight toward them. It veered to avoid two men without losing pace. The jolt sent the muslin bag that held their venison jerky flying. Hudson ran to catch the sack, but it bounced off her fingers and landed in the gravel at a stranger's feet. The stranger quickly swept it up.

"That's ours," she said.

"Was." The black-bearded man opened the sack, snagged a piece of jerky, and chewed. His white ceramic Burley pipe bounced with each bite. "Mine now and mighty fine."

"Hud," Father shouted. "Get on back."

She scowled, wishing she could call the man what he was—a no-good thief.

"What's the hurry, boy?" The man drew a flask from his pocket and took a swig. Then he held it out. "Want some? It'll put fire in your belly."

"No, thanks," she said.

The man's chin went up, and he squinted at her. It was a creepy stare. Hot shivers raced up her arms.

"How about a pull on the pipe? Got my own special blend of tobacco. Cinnamon and nutmeg."

She shook her head.

"What's your pa want with that injun boy?" he asked.

"Don't know. Didn't tell me." She shrugged. "All I know is I got to get back."

"Stop him!" someone called out. "He's the traitor. I saw him."

Hud froze.

The voice belonged to Jason Brancet. He stood on the overlook. Their eyes locked, and she gave him a quick shake of her head. This only made him smile. An awful, nasty smile. He raised one arm and pointed straight at her.

In a loud voice, Jason shouted, "That boy was the fourth miner. And here's proof. He left this bucket behind." Jason raised the bucket high.

The bottom dropped out of Hudson's stomach.

The bearded man grabbed her arm. "You killed the miners?"

"He's lying!" Hudson tried to wriggle free. "Let me go."

"That's not all," Jason yelled.

A dozen men had gathered around Jason.

"He held a gun to my head and stole my gold."

"That's a lie!" Hudson screamed, outraged.

Jason and the men streamed onto the beach like wild dogs. The bearded man's grip tightened.

"He's lying," she yelled. "Jason's the thief. Let go."

A gun blast sounded. At the canoe, her father held his pistol in the air.

"Let go of my son," he roared.

The miner's hand squeezed harder. "Shoot me and you're dead."

Hudson bit the man's wrist. He howled and let go, and she bolted.

The mob thundered after her, their shouts narrowing the gap. She reached the canoe and jumped in. Her father took aim at the crowd.

Ned shoved the canoe into the current and clambered in over

the side. The boat rocked as Ned used the long paddle to push them into the current.

The horde reached the river's edge, too late to stop them. Jason arrived last, panting and glaring at Hud.

She waved. "Bye."

The bully reached down, grabbed a baseball-sized rock, and flung it. The projectile whizzed by, landing in the water.

Jason grabbed another and sent it flying with a volley of insults.

Hudson laughed as the current carried them out of reach.

But then, to her horror, her father let out a fearsome cry and crumpled sideways. A bloodstained rock lay next to him in the canoe. He'd been hit.

"Father?" she cried.

Blood streamed down his temple, across his jaw, and soaked into his shirt.

"No," she cried. "No!"

CHAPTER THIRTEEN

Ned steered the canoe into the current.

The miner's shouts faded in the distance. Still, they had to keep moving because trails ran both sides of the river. A man in the saddle could catch up. The miners would be on the warpath.

Hudson cradled her father's head in her lap. He was unconscious, his face pale. She dipped her handkerchief into the river and wiped blood from his forehead. She rinsed the cloth and pressed it against her father's wound, trying to stop the bleeding.

Please, Lord. Don't let him die. Let him wake with nothing more than a headache.

She was afraid to the voice the words—afraid Ned would hear the sobs that threatened to tumble from her lips and realize she was a girl.

Stop this nonsense. Father needed her to be strong and focused.

Trails tracked the river. They needed to find a safe hiding place. Ned knelt at the back of the canoe, clearly worried. Suddenly he looked almost younger than her.

He gripped the paddle, using twists of his wrists to steer the canoe around boulders in the turbulent water. Hudson noticed a black line tattooed on his inner forearm. She turned away, her chest tightening at the reminder of the dead Indian in the field.

The afternoon stretched on, and still Father did not wake.

Now and then, Ned called out to shore in another language. Each time, Hudson saw no one.

"What are you saying?" she asked.

"I try to warn the Indian villages."

"Is anyone hearing you?" she said.

"I do not know."

An afternoon breeze blew as the canoe rounded a bend. The river spread out, and the current slowed to a near standstill.

Ned stowed the paddle, grabbed the long pole, and stood, shoving the pole into the water. It dug into the riverbed. He leaned onto it to push the boat through the still water. The canoe rocked gently with each forward shove.

"How is your father?" he asked.

Worried, she lifted the wadded handkerchief from the wound. "I'm not sure. His head stopped bleeding, but he hasn't awoken."

Ned stood. "That is good."

"How is that good?"

"No more blood. His sleep will allow his spirit to heal him."

She hoped Ned was right.

"When we reach the village," Ned said, "I will take him to the sweathouse. The medicine man will banish the evil spirit that is pressing your father's soul."

Hudson drew back. "No. We can't go there. The miners plan to raid the villages tonight. We'll be caught in the middle of it all."

"Do you want your father to die?"

"Staying in a village isn't safe."

"Not safe for who?"

"For anyone," she said. "Father. You. Me. The villagers. We need to warn them and keep going. Then find a place to hide until it's over."

"We have come far. It will be hard for Duncan to reach us tonight. We will be safe there."

"I wish I could believe that, but you saw how mad they were."

On shore, a gray squirrel paused to stare at Hudson.

She stared back, watching as it scampered away. The river narrowed, and the current picked up again. Ned pulled the pole from the water and stashed it in the canoe. He dropped back to his knees, taking up the paddle.

"If your father is to live, we must take him to the medicine man." He repositioned the paddle as a rudder.

"No," she said. "I told you, Red Duncan's men are coming. They'll find my father."

"He will die unless we bring him to the medicine man."

"You don't know that. He's my father. The decision's mine. Not yours."

A knot formed in Ned's jaw.

Hudson touched her father's pale cheek and whispered, "Please wake up. It's going to be okay. Don't leave me. I love you."

But he showed no sign of waking. Hud knew Ned was right; Father needed help, desperately. She felt sick. For her father, for the dead men in the field, for the innocent villagers who stood in harm's way. She never should have come to the gold fields. This was all her fault.

Ned wedged the long pole into the riverbed, stopping the canoe, and pointed at the shore. "Look. There."

Hudson squinted. She saw only the river, the brush, the rocks, and the trees. "Where? What am I looking for?"

"See the tallest tree? Look to the brush at its feet."

Hudson stared harder. It was just a ratty-looking bush, yellow and already dead.

The bush moved, and Hud gasped.

A warrior brave crouched low, clutching a spear, aiming straight at them.

The blood in her veins turned to ice.

CHAPTER FOURTEEN

Hudson stared at the warrior in terror. Then Ned raised his arms and whistled. It sounded like a blue jay's cry.

The warrior straightened. Like Ned, he was bare-chested with long dark hair. Unlike Ned, the man's hair hung loose to below his shoulders.

Ned called out in words she didn't understand.

The man nodded and jabbered a long reply.

"Is he friend or foe?" Hudson asked.

"He watches. I have told him what has happened upriver. He will send word we are coming." Ned pushed off. "We should arrive soon."

"You said that before. How much longer?"

"The river decides. You must be patient."

She puffed out her cheeks in frustration.

Her father moaned.

"Father? Can you hear me?"

His eyes moved under his pale lids. Maybe if she talked to him, he'd wake.

"We're in the canoe. Ned is taking us downriver. He says there is a medicine man who can help you heal."

Father's face gave no sign that he heard.

Hudson looked at Ned. "Can your medicine man really cure him?"

"He is skilled."

"But what about when the attack comes? What then?"

Ned's lips tightened. "It will not come tonight. You must be calm. It is all you can do. Think of something else."

"You talk like an old man," she mumbled.

He acted like he was as old as her father or something. They were the same age or close. Then she remembered the dead Indian boy. A miner had called him Ned's brother. Maybe that was why Ned was so serious. He was grieving.

"I'm sorry about your brother," she said.

Ned frowned. "I do not have a brother. Only a sister."

"Oh," she said, confused and embarrassed. She shot him another glance. If she had to trust this boy, she needed to know more about him. It was time to apply one of Aunt Gertrude's sayings: knowledge is power.

"How old are you, Ned?"

"I believe I am fifteen of your years." He traded the pole for the paddle.

"We're the same age, then."

He nodded

"Why are you helping us? Won't it anger your tribe?"

"The Karuk are not my tribe. They are upriver people. My people are Yurok, downriver people. We share the river, but we are not the same."

"Oh." She could think of nothing more to say, and Ned clearly had no interest in talking.

Hudson rinsed the rag, wrung it out, and placed it on her father's forehead. If only she could wave a magic wand and heal him. All she had were prayers, and God seemed to be ignoring them.

Why did men like Red Duncan exist? How could they kill innocent people?

She knew the answer. Her hand went to the lump in her pocket. *Gold fever.* The nugget felt twice as big and heavy as before.

Had gold lust ruled her father like it ruled the crazed miners? Is that why he'd abandoned her?

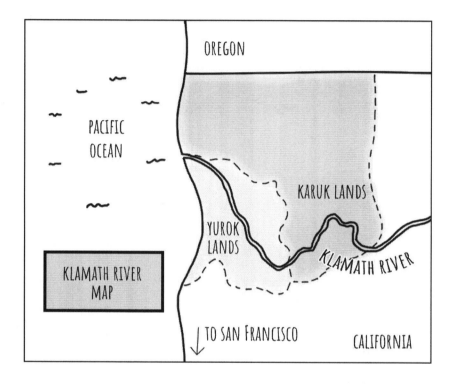

"Ned, you never answered my question. Why are you helping us?"

His gaze didn't leave the river. "Your father is not like the others."

"Did you know the Indian boy that was killed this morning?"

"You are like a blue jay. Talk. Talk. Talk. Don't you like to hear the birds sing? Or the crickets chatter?"

"I'm sorry. But don't you want revenge?"

"Revenge?" Ned's frown hardened. "You cannot change what is past. To survive, you do not stand in the way of an enemy's arrow. There are better ways."

"What does that mean? Like wh—"

Her father's breathing suddenly grew ragged, and choking sounds came from his throat. His face turned blue-gray.

Could an unconscious person swallow their tongue and choke? Frantic, Hudson flipped him onto his side. The movement seemed to ease his breathing. He sighed and muttered in his sleep.

"Shh," she said, patting his back. "Hang on. We're almost there."

She glanced at Ned, her eyes questioning.

He nodded, repeating her words, "Almost there."

Hudson prayed that this time the words were true.

CHAPTER FIFTEEN

The wind picked up, drying the sweat on Hudson's forehead. The air smelled sweet, scented with forest spice and willow blooms. For a brief moment, she pretended everything was perfect.

If only daydreams could be true.

Her father stirred. "Hud?" His voice sounded thick. "Where are we?"

"You're awake," she gasped.

"Barely. What happened?"

"Ned's taking us to a village."

Father winced. "My head hurts." He struggled to sit.

Hudson gently held him down. "Don't move. You're hurt."

He blinked. "How?"

"You don't remember?" Pause. "The miners attacked us."

"Why?" Confusion flickered in his eyes. "Why would they hurt me?"

"It's a long story," Hudson began, but before she could continue, he lapsed back into unconsciousness. "No, Father. Wake up. Please, wake up."

Treetops swayed, casting shadows. They wavered like angry

ancestor spirits dancing to purge the invaders who'd spoiled the Klamath with their gold lust.

ALLART VAN EVERDINGEN

"Let him rest," Ned said. "It will ease the pain."

"Stop telling me what to do. You're not in charge."

Ned might be right, but he had no right to boss her and act like he knew more than she did.

Ned looked away, his shoulders tense.

She sighed. Maybe she shouldn't have snapped at him. "Ned? Can I ask a question?"

He made a noise like a wild pig's snort.

"Is Ned Pepper your real name?"

"It is my white man name." His eyes sparkled with mischief, and for once, he looked his age. "If you were a Karuk, your name would be Kachakaâch."

"Catch-u-ca...atch? What does that mean?"

"It is your spirit animal."

"Which is?"

"You must figure that out for yourself."

"That's not fair," she muttered and shot him a dark look.

He pointed. "We are here."

She glanced ashore. "This is a village? There are only three houses. And they aren't very big."

"They are big enough."

She rolled her eyes.

The canoe slid up the sandy bank next to a massive rock monolith. They leaped out, beaching it higher.

"Stay with your father," he said. "It is best if I go alone. I must warn them that trouble flies like a snake in an eagle's beak."

This time, she agreed.

CHAPTER SIXTEEN

Hudson sat on the edge of the canoe kicking patterns into the sand. Her father looked almost peaceful as he slept.

Two small children peeked at her from the tall grass a dozen yards away.

What was taking Ned so long?

The village was nothing like she'd expected. Instead of a cluster of teepees, it held three houses made of split redwood planks weathered to a smoky grey. Even weirder, the houses stood only about four feet high. The doors were round holes placed at ground level, and they faced upriver.

Hudson stretched to ease her sore muscles. The two Indian boys mimicked her moves.

She waved. They waved back.

She stretched. They stretched.

She squatted. They squatted.

"Hello," she called to them.

They yelled something, laughed, and jumped up and down. Smiling, she copied their movements.

The game went on for some time. Then it suddenly stopped.

An Indian woman appeared with a basket on her back. She wore a deerskin shift, was barefoot, and had three dark-blue lines tattooed on her chin. They reminded Hudson of the tattoo on Ned's arm.

One clap of the woman's hands sent the children scooting into the nearest house.

Distraction gone, Hud's mind raced to the dangers hanging over their heads. She knelt by her father and stroked the damp hair from his forehead.

Judging by the sky, it had to be less than two hours until dark. Was it true what Ned said—that they'd traveled far enough to be safe? Her stomach churned.

Father's skin was hot.

Why was Ned wasting precious time?

The woman stood outside the nearest house. She watched Hudson, then turned and headed to the center building. That's where Ned had gone earlier. Instead of entering, the woman set her basket outside, called through the round door, and left.

A minute later, an ancient-looking man climbed out of the short house. A trail of smoke tumbled into the air, followed by Ned and two others. One carried what appeared to be a rolled-up deerskin.

The old man used a staff to stay upright, wobbling as he walked. Snow white hair fell down his back, and deep lines dug creases into his dark skin. He wore a woven basket decorated with what looked like red woodpecker feathers on his head. Around his neck dangled a pouch on a leather strip.

He was chanting. It sounded like, "Hon yee all you oh."

He must be the medicine man, she thought.

The others followed in single file. Ned brought up the rear. Unsmiling, he nodded at Hudson.

The procession stopped a few feet from the canoe. The medicine man raised his strange-looking staff. It was burned black, and an eagle feather dangled from its top.

"You must step aside," Ned said. He now wore a pouch around his neck, too.

"I'm staying with him," Hud said.

"No. You must trust the healer. We will carry your father to the sweathouse. The medicine man will banish the evil spirits that have stolen your father's health. You must wait."

She gritted her teeth, weighing her choices. It seemed she had none. Reluctantly, she stepped back. "How long will it take?"

"That is not for me to say," Ned answered.

Hud's eyes darted to the trail above. "They know the miners are on the warpath, right?"

Ned nodded.

The medicine man started to sing in a high and reedy voice. Shivers raced from her neck to her toes.

The shorter man unrolled the deerskin and laid it on the ground. The taller man had a scar on his chest. He, together with Ned, lifted her father from the canoe. They placed him on the skin.

Father groaned, and Hudson rushed forward.

"Stay out of the way," Ned ordered.

The medicine man turned and started up the trail to the

sweathouse. He sang louder. Ned and the other two carried her father in the deerskin stretcher, heads bowed.

Despite Ned's orders, Hudson trailed behind. This might be Ned's world, but they were carrying her father. She wasn't leaving his side, and that was that.

She said a silent prayer. Let Father recover. Soon. Before Red Duncan attacks.

The procession reached the sweathouse. The medicine man pulled aside the animal skin door-flap that covered the round hole. He entered feet first but facing out. The men set the stretcher on the ground. They entered the house the same way, one at a time. Ned waited outside with her father.

The tall man with the scar reached out and lifted one end of the stretcher. Ned took the other end. Together they maneuvered her father into the sweathouse. Last, Ned went inside.

The deerskin door-flap dropped and blocked Hudson's view.

She rushed to push aside the animal skin. Smoky heat blasted her face, and she coughed.

Ned appeared. "Go."

"He's my father," she said. "I'm coming in."

"You are not allowed to enter."

"Why not?"

"Only men may come inside. No women. No children."

"You and I are almost the same age. We're both boys. If you can enter, why can't I?"

"You are small. You look like a child," he said and dropped the skin curtain.

It wasn't fair. Just because she was small, it didn't mean she was a child. Doubt assaulted her. What did this medicine man really know? He was no doctor! Could she trust Ned to protect her father?

Hud leaned against the rough redwood-plank wall until her shoulder went numb. She pushed away and paced. Sat. Stood. Leaned and paced. Sat again.

What was taking so long? It had been hours. Faint stars began to sparkle overhead. Danger whispered in the air.

She turned, her eyes peeled on the trail that cut along the hillside.

A hand touched her shoulder, and she jumped.

CHAPTER SEVENTEEN

Panic shot up Hudson's spine.

She spun to find the woman she'd seen earlier, the one who'd called the children.

"Come with me," the woman said. "The air grows cold."

Hudson's heart slowed to a trot. "My father is inside. I can't leave him."

"Your presence does more hurt than good."

"I have to watch for Red Duncan's men. They're planning to burn the villages down."

"We are far from the miner's camp, and there are many villages along the river."

"That won't stop them. As long as we're here, you're in danger," Hudson said.

"How do you know this?"

"They'll be looking for revenge—on your people and on my father."

"We are one village of many. They can't attack every village. You need rest. And strength to help your father."

"No, I'm fine," Hudson said.

The woman gently took Hudson's arm and pulled her to the next house. "Come. Sleep. It is late."

I won't sleep Hudson thought. Not until Father and I are safely back in that canoe. Still, she allowed herself to be led to one of the short houses.

The woman spoke to someone inside and then motioned for Hudson to enter— feet first, facing out.

Hudson nodded. Backing into the house was clearly important, and she wondered what it meant. It seemed a little odd, but these people were trying to help her father, and she would respect their traditions.

Hud dropped to her knees and crawled backward into the door. Hands grabbed her legs. She started to panic. Then she realized the hands were guiding her feet onto a step.

Climbing down, her eyes adjusted to the darkness. A small fire in the room's center gave just enough light to see. She stared in awe.

The houses might look short from the outside, but inside they were tall. They'd been dug deep so that the bottom half was below ground. A wide shelf carved into the wall ran around the whole perimeter. Positioned along the ledge at intervals lay at least a dozen sleeping kids.

The woman led Hudson to her place to rest and then lay with the other women dozing on the floor. Many snored or wheezed.

Hudson rubbed her face. Maybe the raids were just a drunken man's ranting—full of talk and no action.

No, she'd never believe that.

But were all the miners bad? They couldn't be. Her dad was a miner, and he was a good man. There had to be more like him. So why were people like Red Duncan allowed to take control? Why didn't the others stop him?

She knew the answer.

Fear. Duncan was a bully of the worst kind, and he had the size and muscle to back it up. Out here in the Wild West, there was no law. Ruthless men could threaten, beat, steal, and murder without consequences.

Someone had to put a stop to Duncan's ruthless tyranny. Perhaps the man that her father had mentioned could do so. What was his name? Redick McKee. The man who had the governor's ear.

When her father awoke, they'd escape and go see McKee and tell him about the atrocities.

It had been a long day. Hud felt bruised all over. Was it only this morning she'd lost the buckets? She yawned. Just for a minute, she'd rest.

A noise jerked Hud awake. Confused, she bolted upright and realized she was in an Indian house and not a San Francisco Victorian home.

A woman snorted in her sleep. That must be what had awakened Hud. Still, fear shivered down her back. What had she been thinking coming in here?

Propelled by worry, she tiptoed through the sleeping bodies and climbed outside. Cautiously, she peered around.

The fresh night air felt good after the stuffiness inside the house. Bright stars twinkled overhead. She saw no sign of any watchmen, but then they were probably well hidden. No sounds came from the sweathouse. It seemed the whole village was dozing.

She needed to use the bathroom. Did the Indians have a desig-nated bathroom spot? It wouldn't be in the village. She crept away from the houses, looking for a private place.

The crescent moon gave her just enough light to navigate the shadows. Hudson headed southwest, hoping she wouldn't mistake poison oak for a huckleberry bush. She took care of business and went down to the river to wash her hands. Halfway back, she heard a noise—an animal moving on the hillside?

Uneasiness crept up her throat.

Another sound. *A thud?*

Could Ned be trying to get her attention?

"Ned?" she whisper-shouted. "Are you out here?"

No answer.

Ned didn't seem the type to play games.

A whiff of cinnamon-scented pipe tobacco wound tendrils in the air. It reminded her of the black-bearded miner who'd stolen their jerky, the one with the ceramic pipe. She remembered how he'd grabbed her in his tight clutch.

The scent came again, awful and familiar.

Every hair on Hudson's neck sprang to attention.

Be silent and move fast.

Scrunching low, Hudson reached the short house undetected. She woke the English-speaking woman and whispered in her ear.

"The miners are outside."

"How do you know this?" the woman whispered.

"There's no time to explain. Get everyone out quietly. I have to find Ned and my father."

CHAPTER EIGHTEEN

The woman scrambled to her feet as Hudson crept outside. Clouds floated across the night sky, blotting out the moonlight. In the blackness, she sniffed, tracking the scent of the cinnamon-scented tobacco smoke. It came from up the hill, near the trail.

A thought struck. It couldn't be the angry mob Red Duncan had whipped into a frenzy. The Indians would have heard them coming from a mile away. This must be a scouting party, with the black-bearded man and one or two others.

Keeping low, she hurried to the sweathouse, pushed aside the deerskin-curtain, and hooted. Hopefully, the black-bearded miner would mistake her hoot for an owl.

A hand grabbed her wrist. "You do not belong here. Go."

"My father is—"

"Is sleeping," hissed the gruff voice.

"—in danger," Hudson whispered. "And so are you. There is a white man on the hill."

The hand tightened on her wrist.

"Warn, Ned," the voice said. "He keeps guard under the madrone tree above the river."

"You need to get everyone out, now," Hudson urged.

"There are more medicine words to be said."

"There's no time. My father's life depends on it."

"Your father's spirit depends on the words."

Hudson backed away from the door, frustrated. She had to find Ned. She only hoped the miners hadn't found him first.

The air grew suddenly cold. It must be almost dawn.

The giant madrone tree stood on the hillside, halfway between the river and the high trail. Could she reach the tree without alerting the miners? If Ned was up there, what was he doing? He had to have smelled the pipe smoke.

Hud crept from bush to bush, squinting in the darkness, praying she wouldn't be spotted. The clouds parted for a second. Five paces away, the big madrone tree's lower branches draped down to create a kind of hiding place for deer.

She scooted under the tree's covering.

"Ned?" Her soft words blended with the breeze.

Ten feet up the slope, a shadow moved.

It was a man's silhouette wearing a wide-brimmed miner's hat.

Terror trickled down her neck.

The miner carried a stick slung over one shoulder. It poked skyward.

Wait. That wasn't a stick—it was a gun! A rifle or a shotgun.

Hudson inched deeper into the leafy tree cave, her heart slamming. Through the branches, she saw the man's shadow shift. Had he heard her?

The red glow of a pipe was followed by a smoky exhalation. The man said, "Quit yer pacing, Bud. The attack's not 'till first light. You're wearing me out with yer pacing. Sit down and wait for Red's signal."

"You keep your trap shut," growled a rasping voice. "I know how to follow orders."

"How's about you check on our prize?"

"Lay off. He's not going anywhere."

Hud could make out three shadows. How many more?

And where on earth was Ned? She swallowed down an awful foreboding. Is that what they meant by their prize?

Suddenly, it all seemed impossible. She pressed her hands to her face; they were shaking. She'd tried to be brave; she'd tried to keep her chin up. She'd been running and fighting and doing her best. Now, though, the truth crashed down. They'd soon be surrounded with no way to run.

She huddled against the madrone's sturdy trunk. When her foot bumped something soft, her heart skipped.

Not a log.

Logs didn't grunt and move away.

CHAPTER NINETEEN

Hudson had just enough light to recognize the bound and gagged figure at her feet.

Ned!

He lay on his side, hogtied, his mouth silenced with a rag. Hud shot a rapid glance at the miners. She'd found their prize. She had to free him before they came to check on him.

Hud bent close to his ear and murmured. "Got a knife?"

Ned nodded, wriggled onto his side, and gestured at his front pocket with his chin.

The knife was an obsidian blade—no handle—razor sharp. She withdrew it from its leather sheath and sawed through the heavy hemp rope. Hud nicked her fingers. Winced. Kept sawing.

Free, Ned ripped off the gag. Before he could speak, she slapped a hand over her mouth and shook her head. Then she pointed downhill, hoping he understood that they'd need to move silently.

The two teens crawled until it was safe to stand, then sprinted to the big rock at the river's edge where they'd beached Ned's dugout-canoe.

"What happened?" Hud said.

"I was foolish. I did not expect the miners to come so quickly. You were right."

He'd said she was right? Her eyes widened, but only for a moment. What did it matter, being right? They were still in trouble.

"How many men did you see?" he asked.

"At least three."

"We must hurry."

She grabbed his arm. "They're going to burn the village at first light."

He nodded. "I, too, heard them speak. Before long, sun rays will come."

As if in confirmation, an ominous hint of gray crept into the eastern sky. Time was running out.

"I tried to warn everyone," she said.

Ned nodded. "Good. Wait here."

"No, I'm not going to wait here."

"I must move like the raccoon. Swift and silent. You wait."

She could hardly believe it. She'd saved him, and now he was trying to suggest she was noisy?

"You're not my father," she sputtered. "You can't tell me what to do. Father is trapped in the sweathouse. He's hurt and needs my help. I'm going with you whether you like it or not."

The boy frowned, and she followed him up the rocky bank.

Hudson slipped, releasing a clatter of pebbles. Startled birds squawked.

Ned turned and glared.

She held her breath. Mouthed, "Sorry."

Ned held up an open palm. He pointed to her, walked his fingers up his arm, and then pointed to the big rock.

What? Was he ordering her to go back and wait?

Hudson shook her head. No way. Her father needed her. She wasn't some helpless girl.

Ned grabbed her arm. He whispered in her ear. "Go. Wait."

"No," she hissed, jerking free. She hardly knew this boy. They'd met only a few days ago. There was no way she'd trust him with her father's life.

He gave her a long hard look.

"And stop treating me like I'm a girl. I may be smaller than you but we're almost the same age."

A gunshot broke the deadly calm.

Hudson flinched and dropped to the ground.

A woman screamed.

Eerie silence followed, except for the pounding of Hudson's heart. She pushed up into a crawling position, ignoring the rocks digging into her knees. Stared at the village. Squinted.

Dark shadows slipped between the Indian houses. Shadows of men—men with guns.

Snick. Snick. Snick. Flint strikes ignited torches. They were everywhere. Suddenly the flaming sticks were flying through the air. They would burn everything to the ground. The wood houses were like tinder waiting to be lit.

Hudson bolted toward the sweathouse with one goal in mind. Saving her father.

Halfway there, the tall grass surrounding the village burst into flames. Everything would be burned to the ground. Hopefully, the women and children had fled.

The fire raced toward the sweathouse. Flames caught the edge. They licked upward, consuming the dry, weathered boards.

Heat blasted Hudson. Acrid smoke assaulted her nose, and the taste of fire filled her mouth.

"No," she cried, rushing forward.

Loud shouts and shotgun blasts pierced the air.

A body slammed her from behind. She went down—her attacker rolled onto her and trapped her. Angry tears streaked her face. She thrashed. Kicked. Bit the arm wrapped around her jaw.

To her horror, the sweathouse exploded into flames.

"Father," she screamed. "No." This couldn't be happening. She strained, desperate to see him come bursting out. To see his familiar form. The flames leaped higher. The roof collapsed with a *whoof*.

Her heart stopped. She knew he wasn't coming back to her. Ever.

Then like a pack of ravenous wolves, miners swarmed the village from all directions. Shouting curses. Shooting at anything that moved—men, dogs, women, and children.

Hudson felt numb. How had the beautiful dream of joining her father for the Klamath River Gold Rush turned out like this?

CHAPTER TWENTY

Ned dragged Hudson toward the river and the canoe.

"Let me go." Hudson tried to free herself from his grasp.

"Stop fighting," Ned said. "I am not the enemy."

"Father needs help." She fought back tears, refusing to accept he was dead. "I won't run away."

"Look." Ned pointed to flames high enough to singe the sky. The raging inferno had swallowed all three buildings. "Your father flies with the great spirit. We must go."

Hudson hesitated.

More gunshots rang out.

"I am going." Ned released his grip on her arm. "Stay if you want."

He pushed the canoe into the river and jumped aboard. He held it in place with the long pole. "Decide."

Ned was right. Father would want her to live. He wouldn't want her to stand there and let Red Duncan mow her down with his shotgun. She tore her eyes from the blazing sweathouse. She could almost hear his voice in her mind shouting, "Run. *Run!*"

Hudson scrambled into the water. Her foot skidded off a rock.

Her arms shot out and caught the edge of the canoe. She clambered aboard and stood, staring back at the village.

Ned used the pole to push into the current.

"Look!" shouted a man from the hillside. "In the river! Two more are trying to escape."

Three men raised their guns and aimed.

"Shoot 'em!" shouted one. "Don't let them get away."

Hudson dropped to her knees. "Ned! Get down."

He dropped next to her as three rifle blasts sounded. Two bullets hit the water. One thudded into the side of the thick redwood canoe.

The canoe was tipping in the rough current. On instinct, Hudson wrapped an arm around his shoulder and rolled into the river pulling him with her.

They sputtered, coming to the surface. Using the canoe as a shield, they aimed it into the current. The canoe dragged them downriver like rag dolls.

More gun blasts—three more bullets hit the canoe. The boat rammed into a rock and careened sideways.

Hudson went under, and came up gasping. Blinded by the surging water, everything looked blurry. Frantic, her arms flailed like a spinning waterwheel.

She surfaced, gulped for air, and was dragged under again. The current sucked her to the bottom, hurling her downriver. Hudson fought but couldn't break free of the river's relentless surge. Her lungs began to ache. Tiny air bubbles escaped her lips.

Had she survived the attack on the village only to drown?

The thought made her fighting mad. Her arms churned. Her feet kicked off the bottom, and she shot to the surface. Gulping in precious air, she scanned for Ned.

The current had swept her around a rocky outcrop, out of sight of the miners. Still, she could hear gunshots. Had Ned been hit? Where was he? Then she spotted him. He floated face down, twenty yards away.

A fresh boost of energy spun her legs into action. She swam to him and, treading water, flipped him onto his back.

"You better not have drowned," she cried and slapped his face.

His eyes popped open. "A bullet came close. I cried out. Like a possum, I died and floated downstream."

"An old Indian trick?" she said, relieved he was alive.

"To survive, you must become one with nature."

"To survive, we must swim for shore," she said.

"We must swim downstream," he said. "Put distance between us and the men."

"No. You gave me a better idea. Follow me. We don't have much time." She swam toward the village side of the river.

"You are confused," he said. "We swim toward the wrong side. The crazy men will capture and kill us."

"No, they won't. I have a plan."

He scowled but followed.

There would be time to mourn later. Right now, she needed to survive. She had to get justice for her father. She had to escape.

Huge gray boulders jutted like tombstones along the bank. Reeds and big-leafed water plants grew between them. The jutting stones reminded her of a church graveyard.

They were exactly what she needed. Hudson crawled between two of the larger rocks.

"What are you doing?" Ned asked. "We must go."

She grabbed mud and moss from the river bottom and slapped it on her head. "I am becoming one with nature."

"This is not a good idea. The miners will track us. They saw us lose the canoe."

"Sit. Now. Before they come."

He sat but didn't look happy. Hudson plopped a pile of moss on his head and grabbed two big clumps of reeds. She handed one to him. "Now we are one with the river."

She put her finger to her mouth. "We wait until they grow tired."

Sliding into the water, she disappeared into the reeds.

Waiting.

Remembering.

The vision of the sweathouse in flames was seared into her eyes. Which led to grieving. For her father and what might have been. At least she didn't have to hide her tears from Ned. He couldn't see them.

———

The sun inched skyward until it reached high noon. They'd been submerged for hours. Hud's teeth began to chatter.

Had the miners moved on? Had the plan worked?

Just as she decided it was safe, a shadow moved to her right.

She froze, but her eyes swiveled. In her side vision, she saw the creature. It was inches from her face—a hungry-looking fox leaning down to lap the water. She gasped.

Should she freeze, fight, or flee?

CHAPTER TWENTY-ONE

Terrified, Hudson sprang to her feet and shook the reeds, hissing, "Shoo! Go away."

Water droplets flew from her arms.

The mangy fox bolted off up the hill toward the trail—the trail that led back to the miner's village.

"Quiet," Ned hissed. "The fox only drinks the water. He did not come to kill." He stood, waded ashore, and started up the steep bank.

"Where are you going?" she asked, still submerged to her ankles.

"I go to look from the top."

Dragging muck, she hobbled after him. Stiff from crouching so long, her half-numb legs were slow to respond. Wet pants chafed her legs. The long soak had turned the cuts on her hands pale and puckered. Her boots squished with each step. Ned, on the other hand, sprinted upward.

When she reached the trail, Ned had disappeared.

Her mind ran wild. Had the miners captured Ned? Or had he abandoned her?

"Ned?" she called. Then, throwing caution to the wind, she shouted, "Ned!"

"Help," came a voice.

It didn't sound like Ned. But she thought she recognized that voice.

"Help," the voice cried. "I'm hurt. I can't walk."

Jason.

Warily, she stood her ground. Was this a trick? He was the one who started this nightmare. Was he pretending to sound injured so she'd come out of hiding?

"Please," Jason cried. "It hurts."

Crouching in the brush, she grimaced. Where was Ned?

"Hurry, please, oooh!" Jason said in a half-sob. "I'm under the pine tree with the dead top. Overlooking the river."

She scanned the skyline and spotted the dead treetop.

"Ned?" she called. "I wouldn't take off on a friend. Unless they deserved it."

"I'm here, Kachakaâch," Ned said in a low voice.

She jumped. "Where did you go? Why didn't you answer? And stop calling me Catch-u-ca...atch. What-ever it means."

"I look for canoe."

"Did you find it?"

Ned shook his head. "You should talk silent. It still is not safe."

Jason's voice came again. "Don't leave me." This time his whine was laced with pain, and it sounded real. "Please, Hud."

So, he knew it was her.

"It's your fault my father is dead," Hudson shouted, not caring

179

who might hear or that the village was dangerously close. "Why should I lift a finger to help you?"

"Because your father isn't dead." Pause. "Yet." Pause. "And I know where they took him."

Hope flared in Hudson's heart. But she wasn't stupid.

"Why should I believe you?" She tried to sound like she didn't care, but she was already moving in his direction.

Ned grabbed her arm; she fought him off.

"I thought you were Red Duncan's best boy," she called.

"He left me here to die. I'm scared. I think my leg's broke."

Hudson followed the sound of Jason's pleading voice with a reluctant Ned at her heels.

"Don't trust him," Ned said.

"What if he's telling the truth?" Her voice was soft, desperate.

"I never wanted to hurt you," Jason cried. "I wanted to be friends."

She hesitated, certain that was a lie. She couldn't stop herself, though.

A squirrel scurried across the trail and up a pine tree.

Ned said, "Stay back. I will go look."

"No. It's my father. My call," she said. "I'll deal with Jason."

After a moment, Ned nodded.

Jason called, "Hurry, you can still save your father. I couldn't save mine. Red murdered him." He was blubbering now. "I saw him do it. He said he'd kill me if I told anyone. That's why he kept me close and brought me up here where I knew no one. I was like his slave. And he made me do things I didn't want to do. Like ratting on you."

The pine tree with the dead top was close. Hudson made a beeline for it. Here, so near to the village, the smell of smoldering smoke lingered from the attack.

She burst into a small clearing.

Jason lay half-propped against the trunk. Leaves and burrs clung to his orange-colored hair. Tears left streaks on his dirty skin. His right leg was twisted at an unnatural angle.

Jason had told the truth. He'd been abandoned and left to die.

She almost felt sorry for him. Then she caught sight of the charred remains of the village below. Smoke shrouds hung over the remains of the ravaged settlement. Tendrils reached skyward, wafting from the charred Indian houses.

Squeezing her eyes shut for a moment, she saw the two little children waving at her. Hudson's chest tightened. Even if they'd run into the woods, she doubted the villagers had escaped the guns and rampaging miners.

Those children had had no idea they were waving goodbye forever.

She turned hard eyes on Jason.

"Where's my father?"

CHAPTER TWENTY-TWO

"I'm waiting," Hudson said, staring at Jason. "Where is my father?"

"Red Duncan took him." Jason wouldn't meet her gaze. His voice sounded weak. "They're holding a trial. Tomorrow morning, Red will hang your father."

"A trial? He's not a judge. He can't do that." Hudson's heart thudded like war drums. "It's against the law."

"No one can stop Duncan."

"I will," she said.

Jason looked at her, his eyes bloodshot. "Grown men can't stop him."

Ned knelt examined Jason's leg.

"Then why did you say I could save my father? I'm not afraid of Red Duncan. Even if you are." Her heart was quaking. "I will rescue my father." She started to walk away. "Are you coming, Ned?"

"First, I must straighten his leg. So he may walk again." Ned grabbed Jason's foot and pulled.

The boy yowled.

"Now we go."

"You can't leave me," Jason blubbered. "I said I was sorry. And I am. Very sorry."

"You're sorry?" Hudson said. "Prove it. Tell us everything you know about Red Duncan."

"He's mean. Likes his whiskey. And has killed lots of men."

Hudson snorted. "Tell us something we don't know. Something that will give us an edge."

Jason winced. "He doesn't like being called Irish."

"You're wasting our time. Come on, Ned."

"Wait," Jason pleaded. "He sleeps with his shotgun." His words came out in a rush.

Hudson breathed deep. This might be useful information.

"He has a secret signal. When he puts his finger to his nose, it means no mercy." Jason's voice grew bolder. "And I know where he keeps his stash of gold. I'll tell you where it is when you come back for me."

Hudson took off at a brisk walk and called over her shoulder, "I don't want his gold. It's gold fever that's caused all this death."

"You haven't got a chance of saving your father," Jason shouted. "Duncan will kill you. Then what will I do?"

"Pray for our success," she said. "Then we can rescue you." Under her breath, "Even if you don't deserve it."

They walked in silence. Hudson led, and Ned followed.

The hot afternoon breeze dried her shirt and then her pants.

Hudson stopped counting her steps when they reached five thousand and the blisters on her feet went numb.

They were nearing the point in the trail that she traveled only days earlier when she'd arrived in search of her father. She'd dreamed of a better life. The mountains, trees, and river had seemed magical and pure. But today, she noticed the dead treetops and vultures circling on the breeze.

Her fairytale dream of a life free of Aunt Gertrude's tyranny had given her the strength to escape San Francisco. Miles Taylor had been just a name, not a face back then. He'd been a stranger, not the father she loved. He was her family, the only true family she had, the only person she could remember who really seemed to love her.

She was terrified, but she'd face her fear head-on. If she had to, she'd grab its red beard and shake it until it toppled.

That would not happen without a solid plan. Her thoughts turned to what they needed to do when they reached the miner's camp.

The sky turned to dusk, and they were still walking.

"Ned, we need to hurry. Are we close?"

He nodded.

"Good. I have a plan of attack." She told him and ended with, "Once we spy out what we're up against, we can adjust things."

"Your plan is smart. But you and I should change jobs. You rescue Chewed Ear. I will rescue your father."

"Do we always have to argue?" Hudson said. "Chewed Ear is your mule. Father is my father."

They rounded a bend, and Hudson knew where she was. They were close, and it was time to leave the trail. They slipped into the trees and walked parallel to the path. The sky grew dark.

Ahead, the tent city was just visible. Strong winds gusted

upriver and buffeted the white tents. They flapped like ghosts beneath the darkening sky.

"A storm is coming," said Ned.

"Good. It'll help hide us."

They reached the tent city. It was deserted, but the men were nearby. Loud, drunken shouts and laughter drifted on the breeze. It was time to act.

She glanced into a tent and spotted a hat. "Forgive me for stealing this," she mumbled and shoved the hat on her head.

She and Ned slipped through the shadows. The men's voices grew louder, more raucous. A flickering glow lit the misty air ahead. Then, a big bonfire came into view, burning bright on the river bar.

Hudson and Ned inched through a stand of brush.

Beyond the flames, Red Duncan sat on an eight-foot-high rock, guzzling whisky. King-like, he held his shotgun as if it were a royal scepter. Wearing a wide grin, he surveyed his subjects below— eating, drinking, fighting, laughing, yelling. There had to be at least fifty men.

So many. Too many.

Duncan took a last pull on the bottle then tossed it high in the air. At the same time, he raised his shotgun and fired. The blast shattered the glass to a roar of cheers.

"Where's Father?" Hudson whispered.

Ned pointed to a giant oak tree. It stood on a rise at some distance from the party, away from the river bar.

Sweat broke out on her forehead. "Oh no. What have they done to him?

CHAPTER TWENTY-THREE

The towering oak tree might be far from the mob, but four burly men stood guard next to it. Their prisoner was tied to the trunk.

Hudson nearly crumpled with fear.

Father!

His arms dangled, and his head lolled to the side. She was too late.

Squeezing back tears, she whispered to Ned. "Lend me your obsidian knife."

"Why? The mob will kill you," Ned said.

"Lend me your knife."

Ned growled. "We'll do this together."

"No. You find Chewed Ear."

"I'm not letting you—"

"Don't argue," Hudson said. "I have to do this."

Sending him away would get him out of danger, and she owed him that much. She knew he'd never find Chewed Ear in time. The donkey could be anywhere in the wilderness by now. But at least Ned wouldn't be caught in the crossfire. He'd done so much to help her and Father, and this was no longer his fight.

Ned's shoulders slumped. "Kachakaâch . . ."

She met his eyes.

He said, "You have the heart of a mountain lion."

"I'm sorry for what's happened," she said.

"It's not your fault."

"Maybe, but it feels like it. I'm glad I got to know you. Tell your people that we're not all bad."

He handed her his sheathed blade, laying it gently on her open palm. He squeezed her shoulder and slipped away.

Hudson stood alone in the darkness, searching for the courage that wasn't there.

She slid the razor-sharp tool into her pants pocket. If she'd been smart, she'd have torn a strip of material to wrap a handle around one end of the blade. But what would be the point? There was no need for that now. She'd reached the end of the line.

Time to get going.

Pulling the hat low to hide her face, she moved casually and quietly toward the towering oak. Fifty yards away, she paused in the shadows to study the three guards. One was tall and lanky. A second was large and bald. The third had a black handlebar mustache. The fourth was short, with a scar running down his cheek.

The tall man said, "My turn."

To Hudson's shock, he pulled a knife from his boot, took aim flung it at her father.

Hudson sucked in her breath, helpless to stop it.

Thunk!

The knife struck the tree inches from her father's drooping head.

Yet father flinched. He flinched! Hope flickered. He was still alive.

"Missed," shouted the scarred man.

His friend leaned on a big stick and glared. "Think you can do better?"

"Watch this. I'll show you a bullseye." The man's words were slurred. He stumbled, dropped his knife. Bending to pick it up, he toppled facedown to the ground.

His companions laughed, and the man with the handlebar mustache stepped up. He carried a big stick.

"Hey! Wait your turn," Baldy said. He pulled a small knife from his pocket, kissed it, and let it fly. It somersaulted three times and stuck in the toe of her father's right boot.

Her father grunted.

"Nice throw, you win." The mustache man passed his whiskey bottle to the bald man. "I say we change games. It's my turn, and I choose Stick and Ball." He hefted a smooth, hand-sized stone, tossed it in the air, and smacked it with his stick.

It flew faster than he could have thrown it, and hit her father dead center in the stomach. Father's eyes popped open.

Hudson clenched her fists in rage.

She glanced at the river bar to see how many in the mob were still standing. At least a dozen lay slumped against rocks, heads lolling, mouths open and snoring.

Red Duncan got to his feet. He raised his gun and fired off three shotgun blasts, jerking the crowd awake. Then, he tapped the side of his nose.

"Gather round. It's time for the verdict. Miles Taylor is about to be sentenced."

CHAPTER TWENTY-FOUR

Hudson realized she'd come too late. It was over. Duncan would have Father hauled onto the bar for execution.

However, the crowd yelled, "Speech! Speech! Speech!"

Red Duncan waved them to quiet down, but they continued to yell.

Then, to her amazement, the three guards quit their evil game and left their post, heading to join them. Was Lady Luck finally on her side?

Wait.

She'd chosen a terrible hiding spot. They were walking straight toward her! She lay flat and squeezed her eyes shut as if that would keep them from seeing her.

Boots scratched the ground less than two feet away. Hud waited to be hauled up by her suspenders. The four pairs of boots kept going. They'd missed her.

Rising, she stealthily crept toward her father—one bush, rock, and tree at a time. She kept one eye on the rowdy crowd, hoping they were too riled up to notice her.

Down on the river bar, Duncan motioned the men into silence.

"Let the trial begin!" He tapped his chin and made a show of looking thoughtful. Then, he grinned. "After a long consideration of the facts, I find Miles Taylor—" Duncan pointed his shotgun into the crowd before raising and aiming it at her father.

In the shadows, Hudson went stock still and waited for the blast

The miners scattered, tripping and falling over each other.

Duncan laughed loud and long. "It's not execution time. Yet. I have to list his crimes." He drank more whiskey and wiped his mouth with the back of his hand.

The miners had settled down, all eyes on Duncan.

She started to crawl.

Duncan raised a finger. "Count number one, I find Miles Taylor guilty of colluding with the enemy."

Cheers from the men. Several shots rang out.

Duncan's second finger went up. "Count number two, I find Miles Taylor guilty of murder."

More whoops and cheers.

"Lynch him!" shouted someone in the crowd. Soon they were all chanting together. "Lynch him!"

Duncan raised the shotgun overhead in both hands, punching the sky in time with the chants. "Lynch him! Lynch him!"

For the moment, they seemed more interested in chanting and grinning at one another than attacking. But that wouldn't last long.

Hudson crept into position behind the oak tree.

"Father. I'm here."

"Hud?" His shocked voice was weak—barely loud as a whisper. "You shouldn't be here. Ned promised he'd get you to safety."

"Lynch him! Lynch him! Lynch him!"

Hudson ran her hands over the rope and felt for the knot. "I'm going to cut you free. Keep standing until I'm finished."

"Lynch him! Lynch him! Lynch him!"

"You need to leave," Father said. "I can barely stand. Let alone walk."

"Please just try." She reached in her pocket and pulled out Ned's obsidian knife. "When I cut you loose, try not to fall."

"I can't run." He gasped out his words. "I'll slow you down. Get away. While you can."

"Lynch him! Lynch him! Lynch him!"

All of a sudden, the crowd silenced.

Uh oh. Were they coming? She didn't dare look.

She hurried, fumbling with the knife. It slipped from her grasp. She heard a chink, like the sound of breaking glass. *No. Not Ned's obsidian knife. Not now.* God, *why aren't you helping me?*

Maybe it only broke in two. She dropped to her knees and felt around but only came up with shards.

Red Duncan's voice roared. "Count number three, I find Miles Taylor guilty of stealing another man's gold."

"WAHOO!" The wild shouts resumed, louder than before. It seemed to go on and on forever.

"I'm sorry, Father," Hudson said, fumbling with the knot. "I broke the knife. It'll just take a little longer."

"No. You must escape," he said. "I'm sorry I wasn't a better father. I love you. Now go."

"I love you, too. And I'm not leaving without you."

"You're more stubborn than your aunt Gertrude."

"I learned from the best. Now try to stand taller and push your back against the tree trunk. It might put a little slack in the rope. Enough to loosen it so I can untie the knot."

He groaned and began to pant. "Does that help?"

"A little."

It didn't, but she wouldn't admit it. Not to him or herself. Panic settled in. She pulled and pushed at the knot. Refusing to give up. Refusing to leave her father for target practice. Refusing to let Red Duncan commit murder in the name of fake justice.

Wait. She stopped her struggles. The bald guard's knife had stuck in her father's boot.

"Can you see a knife in your right boot?"

"No. But I feel it. It's poking my big toe."

"Good. You be my eyes. Let me know if anyone's looking this way."

"Not directly."

"Good."

Hudson broke off a handful of leafy brush. Using it to camouflage her head and arms, she scooted just far enough to reach the boot with her left hand.

"I've got it," she said. "I'm going to pull it out."

"Do it quick."

"Okay. Three. Two. One." Hudson pulled, and the knife slid free. He sucked in a breath as she wriggled backward.

"Don't move," Father muttered. "Someone's looking."

Hudson held her breath and willed every cell to freeze. She waited.

"Clear," Father said.

Hudson scooted to safety and resumed sawing at the rope. "Get ready," she said. "I'm just about through."

Hudson felt warm breath on her neck and almost screamed. She spun, knife in hand, and came face-to-face with a big hairy nose.

"Chewed Ear," she whispered as the mule nuzzled her neck. Stunned, all she could thing was, perfect timing.

Then she noticed Ned. Against all odds, he'd actually managed it; he'd tracked down Chewed Ear. Not only that, but he'd followed her instructions to the letter: he was dressed like a miner—from the boots to the slouch hat. If they were spotted, he'd blend in.

"I'm glad I saw Chewed Ear first," she whispered. "The way you look, I might have hurt you."

"Or not," he said.

"You look even more convincing than I imagined." She turned to finish cutting the rope. "Did you set the fires?"

In answer, he glanced toward the miner's camp.

Red Duncan was the first to smell the smoke. He spun to stare at the tent village, his mean face frozen in horror.

Flames licked up the nearest canvas flaps.

"We're under attack!" Red Duncan screamed, his voice laced with fear. "The Indians, they've come for us. We're under attack!"

All chaos broke loose.

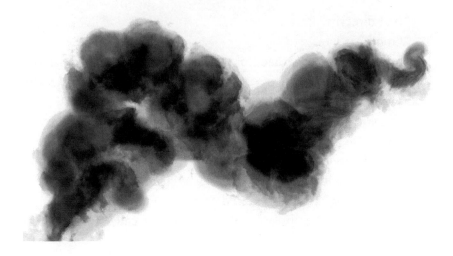

"Father, we're ready. Ned's disguised, so don't get excited when you see him. It will help us escape without being noticed. I'm going to make the final cut on the rope. He'll be there if you need help standing."

"And walking?" She heard the smile in her father's voice. "I suppose you have a solution for that, too."

"You'll only need to take a few steps. Chewed Ear will do the rest. Ready?"

"Do I have a choice?" her father replied.

"No. You're stuck with me."

Hudson made the final cut, and the rope dropped to the ground. Ned half-carried her father into the forest and helped settle him onto the mule. She climbed on behind him and wrapped her arms around him to hold him in place.

"No more talking until we're long gone," Hudson said.

She nudged the mule's flank, and Chewed Ear moved forward. Her father leaned against her, and she held him tight.

The plan was to head into the mountains, to ride the ridge before dropping back down to the main trail where Jason waited.

She still had no idea how they'd transport her injured father and Jason with his broken leg using a single donkey.

She startled when a second mule brayed behind her. It was black and marked with brutal scars. "It looks like Ned Duncan's poor mule! Ned, where did he come from?"

Ned didn't answer. "Hurry, we must go."

Why had Ned stolen it? It gave Duncan one more reason to come after them. Behind them, the fire burned higher and the shouts more frantic. Men were desperately trying to salvage their possessions and, no doubt, their gold.

Ned climbed onto Blackie's back and clicked his tongue. Soon they were riding side-by-side up a wide ravine.

Once out of voice range, Hudson demanded answers.

"Why did you steal Duncan's mule? That wasn't part of the plan. He'll be furious."

"One old mule will not add much to his anger."

"But then we're just as bad as he is. Taking what doesn't belong to us." She could feel her father tense.

Ned shook his head. "I did not take Blackie."

"You're riding him. Explain that."

"Chewed Ear made a new friend. Blackie followed us." Ned stroked the mule's neck. "I could not stop it."

"Seems to me," Father said, sounding a little stronger. "We're not the only ones wanting to escape Red Duncan."

Hudson smiled and hugged her father a little tighter. If he could joke, she knew he'd be okay. "Let's pick up the pace. We have a lot of miles to put between Red Duncan and us before daybreak."

CHAPTER TWENTY-FIVE

Three days later, Hudson sat on a log and watched Ned. He held a deer horn in one hand and an obsidian shard in the other. Volcanic glass chips formed a pile at his feet.

It was early morning. The sky was blue. The air fresh. The trees green. Her father had grown stronger with each passing day. He was almost back to normal.

Best of all, there had been no sign of Red Duncan or his men.

Nearby, Chewed Ear and Blackie lapped water from the clear stream. They'd made camp for the night behind a stand of young pepperwood. The trees gave off a sweet, spicy scent that reminded Hudson of Aunt Gertrude's kitchen.

"I'm sorry I broke your knife," she told Ned. "I wish *I* could make you a new one. Can you teach me?"

"Knapping is for boys and men." He was grinning but kept his eyes on his work. "Gathering roots and nuts is for women and girls. Like you."

She crossed her arms, her mouth hanging open. "How did you know?"

He kept grinning.

She said, "And by the way, I can do anything a boy can do, and better."

He laughed.

"Quit laughing. You better not tell anyone, I promised Father."

"Do not worry. Your secret is safe with me."

"What gave me away?"

"I knew from the first." He looked up. "Because you chatter and laugh like my sister. You remind me of her."

"Is Kachakaâch her name?"

He laughed again. "No. I believe it is your spirit animal. The bluebird that chatters all day to anyone who will listen."

"Hey! I am *not* a chatterbox!"

"A box? I did not say you were a box. I said, you are like a bird. A pretty bird the color of the ocean on a beautiful sunny day. I will miss your bird song."

"Oh." Hudson's face grew hot, and she hoped Ned hadn't noticed. Awkwardly, she said. "Aren't you coming with us?" When the words were out, she knew she wished he was.

He toyed with his knife and finally sighed. "No. I must return to my people downriver. It is where I belong."

"Hudson," her father called.

She jerked upright, pulled from the moment. "Yes?"

"Come over here. Jason has something to say to you."

Hudson rose, brushed off her pants, and joined them.

Jason faced her, hands fidgeting. In a rapid burst, he said, "I'm sorry for everything, I really am. I only did it because Red was going to kill me—he swore he would. No one's ever beat him, no one except you. You're smaller, but you're a better boy than me. You rescued your father from all those miners. And even though I was mean to you, you rescued me." Finally, he caught his breath and offered a trembling hand. "Truce?"

It was a big fancy speech, but could she believe him? She wanted to, and he did look sorry. She scuffed her feet in the dirt. What if Red Duncan had been her guardian? Fear was a powerful thing. Jason had been trying to survive. It's not what she would have done. When push came to shove, she would have run away.

She held out her hand. Jason took it and pumped her arm up and down.

"I forgive you, Jason," she said and meant it.

"I'm sorry about everything."

"No more apologies. We're good."

Hudson was uncertain about her future, but at least she wouldn't have to carry on being angry with Jason. It felt like dropping a heavy weight from her shoulders.

Now only one burden remained. Would her father let her stay with him? Or would her dream of being a family slip away?

CHAPTER TWENTY-SIX

Hudson and the others broke camp and continued on their trek.

Hudson's father broke the silence, "I'm still planning to go see Redick McKee, and maybe even the governor himself. He needs to hear about Red Duncan's attacks."

Hudson nodded. "I know. It's the only way to stop Red Duncan from hurting more people."

Still, she couldn't shake the dread that her father would send her back to Aunt Gertrude. After all, she'd cost him his place on the river. They were destitute. He didn't even have two buckets to his name.

Then her eyes brightened.

The nugget!

She had forgotten all about the nugget in her pocket.

After carrying it for so many days, the lump felt like a normal part of her clothes.

"Dad, I need to tell you something."

"What's wrong?"

She pulled out the gleaming lump and held it in her palm. The gold glinted in the sun.

"Eureka!" he gasped.

"I tried to tell you, before, when it all started. But then you got hurt and . . . I forgot." She sighed. "I'm not sure how I feel about all the trouble it's caused. Maybe, though . . ." She raised her eyes to his. "Maybe it's worth enough for us to make a new start?"

Her father was speechless. Was he angry?

"It's for you," she whispered.

"A lucky strike for us at last." He dropped down on one knee and squeezed her shoulders. "Hud, I'm proud of you. You've saved my life twice and now once again. All I've ever wanted was to make a life for us, to make enough to come back and get you and be a family."

"You . . . are you saying . . ."

"I'm saying that you've done what I couldn't." His eyes grew damp. "We're free. You've found us the riches to live a good life."

Her heart lurched. Was he saying what she hoped he was? "We? As in you and me? Together?"

He nodded and scooped her into a hug.

"Father, I love you," she said and hugged him back. "I promise to never let you down. Take the nugget, it's yours."

"No. You keep it for now," Father said, releasing her. "We'll cash it in and buy us a store. What do you think? Is that a plan?"

"It's a wonderful plan. What about Aunt Gertrude, what will you tell her?"

"That it's time I took care of my own."

Ned approached. "Where will you go?" he asked Jason.

Jason frowned. "I don't know. I don't have any family."

Father hesitated. Hudson had a terrible feeling he'd offer to let Jason join their newly-forged family. She might have forgiven Jason, but that would be awful. She'd never truly trust him.

Father cleared his throat. "My sister Gertrude in San Francisco will take you in. She is not an easy woman to live with, but I think you could manage it."

Hudson opened her mouth, surprised. Then again, Father was right. Jason was a big guy. Aunt Gertrude wouldn't dare take the whip to him. Instead, she'd put him to work running deliveries, she'd make sure he learned his manners, and with all her contacts, she might even find him a good job.

"That's an idea," Hudson said.

"Thank you," Jason said.

Her father settled his hand on the boy's shoulder. "Son, I suspect you might both be a benefit to one another."

Jason beamed.

Ned said, "It has all worked out well."

Hudson laughed and hugged her father. "We did it," she told him. "I can hardly believe it. I feel invincible. We found each other. We beat the odds. We escaped Red Duncan. We escaped the Gold Rush Massacre!"

———

THE END
Turn the page for amazing facts about
The California Gold Rush and more!

10 Fast Facts About the California Gold Rush

1. When the first miners arrived on the Klamath, the Karuk acted as helpful guides.
2. The Karuk lived in short, wooden houses built over underground basements, not in teepees.
3. The Karuk's friendliness faded when droves of miners arrived from all over the world and took control of the Klamath River.
4. Tensions exploded when some miners' cows ate poisonous Klamath weeds and died.
5. The miners claimed the Indians killed their cattle and burned Karuk villages in retaliation.
6. The surviving Karuk fled to the mountains.
7. According to history, local American militias were overly violent in taking revenge on natives for "crimes" the Indians supposedly committed.
8. Government official Redick McKee wrote to the governor of California, reporting that miners had murdered 30 or 40 innocent Karuk.
9. Prospecting gold was a gambler's life. Many got rich. Many went broke.
10. There is still gold to be found in California

CALIFORNIA GOLD RUSH QUOTES

The whole country . . . resounds with the cry of 'gold, GOLD, GOLD!' while the field is left half planted, the house half built, and everything neglected but the manufacture of shovels and pickaxes.

— FROM A CONTEMPORARY
NEWSPAPER

". . . the glimpse of something shining in the ditch. I reached my hand down and picked it up; it made my heart thump, for I was certain it was gold."

— JAMES WILSON MARSHALL

"It appeared only an easier way of making a living for a few of us."

— ADAM WICKS, A GOLD PROSPECTOR

The rush to California . . . reflect the greatest disgrace on mankind. That so many are ready to live by luck, and so get the means of commanding the labor of others less lucky, without contributing any value to society!

— HENRY DAVID THOREAU

Talk like a Gold Miner!
WORDS MINED FROM THE GOLD RUSH

Paydirt: Gold miners called dirt that was full of gold paydirt. Today paydirt means something is financially beneficial.

Panned Out: If a pan was filled with gold, it panned out. Today panned out means something worked out well.

Eureka: An expression like WOW! that a miner said or shouted when he found gold. Today, it can mean 'I've found it.' Eureka is California's State motto. It's also a city in California's Gold Rush region.

Lucky Strike: Means that a miner found gold. Today it means a person has had a streak of good luck.

Forty-Niners: The nickname given to the 300,000 migrants who came to California to find gold. They were named "forty-niners" because they began to arrive in 1849. Today the 49ers are a football team in San Francisco. They've had gold rush luck because they've been to the super bowl seven times and have won five times.

Motherload / Mother Lode: A motherload is a large vein of gold or gold ore that's worth a lot of money. Today if you hit the motherload, you've hit a jackpot of great value.

DID YOU KNOW?

THE CALIFORNIA GOLD RUSH

Gold was first discovered in California at Sutter's fort in 1848. The following year gold was found in the Klamath and Trinity rivers in northern California.

Can you imagine wading in a river, looking down, and seeing gold at your feet? That's how it happened!

AMERICA'S FIRST GOLD RUSH

Here's something you might not know: America's first gold rush happened on the east coast. 50 years before the California Gold Rush began, prospectors discovered gold in Cabarrus County, North Carolina. The state even minted a coin to commemorate their gold rush.

MINERS CAME FROM ALL OVER THE WORLD

California's first miners came from Oregon, Mexico, and the Sandwich Islands (present-day Hawaii).

In the beginning, finding gold was pretty easy pickings. It was still plentiful, and there were fewer miners to share it.

Those first arrivers got a real jump on the thousands of people who came later—from Europe, Australia, China, and Latin America. By then, claims had been staked, the easy pickings were gone, and mining was just plum hard work. Still, if you were one of the lucky ones, you got rich. And that kept people coming.

At the height of the gold rush, 13 prospectors died while crossing a desert valley in eastern California. After the incident, the area received its name: *Death Valley,* which is still used today.

WHO GOT RICH?

Most would-be miners lost money during the Gold Rush, but the people who sold them picks, shovels, tents, and supplies became rich.

With so much gold available, basic supplies became expensive. A single egg could cost $25 in today's money, a cup of coffee went for more than $100, and replacing a pair of worn-out boots could set you back more than $2,500.

Samuel Brannan, a *shopkeeper and newspaper publisher*, was considered the wealthiest man in California during the Gold Rush.

Another Gold Rush success was Levi Strauss, who made and sold heavy-duty work pants to miners called (drum roll please) *jeans.* At first, the pants were made of thick canvas. They were hard to sew and probably uncomfortable to work in. He switched to blue denim, and the rest is history.

WHO LOST THE MOST?

The Klamath River is home to three main Indian tribes—the Karuk (pronounced Ka-rook), the Hupa (pronounced Hoopa), and the Yurok (pronounced Your rock).

The Klamath River was the lifeblood of the Native Americans, who relied on its salmon and trout for food. Klamath comes from the Indian word "Tlamatl," which means "swiftness."

Local Native Americans depended on traditional hunting, gathering, and agriculture. The arrival of the miners changed everything. With more arriving every month, it probably felt like an invasion.

The miners blocked the Karuk from accessing their land since they got in the way of gold extraction. The natives were told to "move on." Villages and sacred ceremonial spaces were replaced with mining camps.

The miners dammed the Klamath and diverted water for mining purposes. This destroyed habitats for fish and game.

Sadly, after only three short years, over half of the Karuk tribe had died from disease, starvation, or murder.

EFFECTS OF THE GOLD RUSH

The Gold Rush affected San Francisco, too. Beginning in 1848, it took just 4 short years for San Francisco to grow from about 200 residents to over 36,000!

Once settled, it kept growing. Its population in 2021 is 883,255.

By the time the Gold Rush ended, California had gone from a thinly populated ex-Mexican territory to a state.

Reportedly, almost 92% of the people prospecting for gold were men.

Agriculture and ranching expanded throughout the state to meet the needs of the settlers.

With so many miners, the easy picking soon dwindled. Americans began to drive out foreigners. After two years of mass immigration, the new California State Legislature levied a foreign miners' tax of $20/month ($600 per month as of 2019).

New methods of transportation developed as steamships came into regular service.

By 1869, railroads were built from California to the eastern United States.

GOLD MINING TECHNIQUES

GOLD PANNING
Early miners simply panned for gold using a large metal pan along rivers and streams. Panning cannot be done on a large scale. Try your hand at gold panning using the activity in the next section.

DIVERTING THE RIVER
Miners build dams and channels for easy access to the riverbed.

SLUICE BOXES (cradles, rockers, and long-toms)
These were developed to process larger volumes of gravel. They separated the gold from dirt using water and movement. How? Gold is heavy and settles to the bottom.

HYDRAULIC MINING
Miners aim a high-pressure water stream at gold-bearing gravel beds on hillsides above the rivers or streams.

DREDGING
Developed in the late 1890s, dredging allowed miners to dig and process large quantities of gravel at one time.

HARD-ROCK MINING
Miners blast gold veins from 'host rocks' containing gold (usually quartz). These host rocks are brought to the surface and crushed. The gold is then leached from the crushed rock with arsenic or mercury. Unfortunately, this method causes extensive environmental damage. The hard-rock mining technique produced the most gold from California's Mother Lode.

TRY YOUR HAND AT MINING WITH
THIS GOLD PANNING ACTIVITY
Recommended as an outdoor activity

MATERIALS
Quantities will depend on the number of kids participating.
• metal pie tins (*Marie Callender pie tins work the best*)
• a mixture of dirt, sand, and gravel
• small garden hand trowel
• 2 large tubs
• 1 small bottle or zip-lock bag to keep the *gold* participants find
• a scale (*to weigh the gold participants find*)
• 'gold' - using one of the suggestions below

GOLD OPTIONS:
• Iron Pyrite, a.k.a. *fools gold*
• Paint pea gravel with metallic gold-colored paint

SET UP YOUR GOLD FIELD
1. Chose a workable and safe location.
2. In one tub, mix your "gold", dirt, sand, and gravel.
3. Fill the second tub with water. You might want to have a garden hose ready to refill the tub if necessary.

THE TECHNIQUE
(*If doing this as a group activity, you may want to practice this before you gather up your group.*)

1. Using a garden trowel, shovel "pay dirt" into a pie tin.
2. Dip the edge of your pan of dirt into the water and fill it WITH JUST ENOUGH WATER TO BE ABLE TO SWIRL THE DIRT. Don't spill the dirt mixture into the tub. KEEP YOUR WATER CLEAN.

3. HOLDING YOUR PAN WITH BOTH HANDS, step away from the water tub and squat over your pan.
4. Shake your pie tin pan until the water looks dirty. You can also use ONE hand to stir up the dirt.
5. Carefully tip out the dirty water without losing any rocks.
6. Pick out any large rocks that aren't "gold."
7. Add fresh water and repeat. Do this as many times as it takes to wash the dirt away and the water is clean.
8. Once the water is clean, squat over the water tub and rotate the pan in a circular motion, letting the gravel bits dribble into the water. As soon as you spot a "gold nugget" in the pan, remove it and place it in a bottle or zip-lock.
9. Continue to pan until your pan is empty.

GATHER YOUR GOLD MINERS AND START MINING

1. Begin by demonstrating how to pan for gold.
2. Give each child a pie tin and bag or bottle for their gold.
3. One at a time, let participants fill their pan from the "pay dirt" pile. Don't let them try to find the gold in the tub. To avoid this happening, an adult or assigned group leader can fill their pans.
4. Let participants pan, giving advice when needed.
5. The number of kids that can pan at one time will depend on the size of your gold field.
6. At the end of the activity, each child weighs their gold.
7. BONUS IDEAS: Turn this into a math activity. Based on the week's current gold price, figure out how much their "gold" would be worth if it was real. You could also set up a "store" where they could buy things with their gold.

I ESCAPED
THE
KILLER BEES

THE BESTSELLING KIDS SURVIVAL SERIES

SD BROWN + SCOTT PETERS

I ESCAPED THE KILLER BEES

CHAPTER ONE

Marana, Arizona
September 2021

Thirteen-year-old Carlos Mendoza tried to open the front door, but
the knob didn't turn. He wrenched it again and realized it was
locked. Fear trickled down his neck like a stream of Mama's
jalapeño honey.

"Mario," Carlos said, trying to sound calm. He didn't want to
frighten his little brother who was only nine and had a broken leg.
"No more jokes. Toss me the house keys. Now."

"I don't have the keys," Mario said, not taking his eyes from his
Spiderman comic. "They're inside."

"You locked the door?" Carlos tried not to sound upset—or as
scared as he felt. It would only make things worse.

Mario shrugged. "Leave me alone. I'm reading."

Carlos whipped his gaze back toward the bee cloud hovering
over the rake at the side of the house. Sweat streaked his face. He'd
been digging up a clump of bunchgrass when he'd disturbed a
hidden hive of underground bees.

Mouth slack, he sucked in air and watched the growing swarm rise from the ground. They had to get into the house before the bees found them. For some strange reason, the bees hadn't followed him... not yet, anyway. Had they identified the rake as the enemy? That wouldn't last long.

He started to hyperventilate.

The insect cloud grew twice its size in seconds. There had to be hundreds of bees. And more were coming out of the ground. What if these bees were Africanized killer bees like the ones in the Channel 4 news that morning?

He had to get his brother to safety.

"Come on, Mario. Put your book down. We have company," Carlos said, pointing to the swarm.

Mario's eyes went wide and his comic book slipped to the ground. "What are we going to do?"

Carlos whispered, "We have to find another way inside before they notice us."

"What if we don't?" Mario's voice squeaked.

"We will," Carlos said it like he had a plan when he had none. Shoot. Mama had left Carlos in charge, and he didn't know what to do.

Think Fast!

"Cover your head with your shirt. Follow me."

Carlos tiptoed to the kitchen window and tried to push it open. But like the door, it was locked.

"Carlos! The bee cloud is moving." Mario sounded scared. "It's by the giant saguaro cactus next to the driveway. "And headed this way."

That left one option. Not a great one. But the best one Carlos could come up with. "Run for it. Go."

"I can't," Mario whimpered. "My leg." He turned to face the swarm, raising his crutch like a baseball bat. "I'll swat 'em."

"Forget that." Carlos grabbed the crutch, threw it down, slung Mario over his shoulder, and ran for the garden shed.

"Hurry!" Mario screeched. "The swarm looks like a giant fastball. It's coming straight at us."

"Shut up," Carlos panted. Mario was heavier than he looked. "You're making things worse."

Mario's grasp tightened and Carlos's foot twisted. He almost fell. Pain raced up his shorter leg but he kept going. He had to get Mario to safety. They were almost there. Just another six feet to go. Five. Four. Three. Two.

They'd reached the shed.

He dropped Mario onto his feet and yanked open the door. The blood pumping through his heart had given him super strength— too much. He ripped the door right off its hinges.

"Why'd you do that?" Mario said.

"I didn't mean to."

A sharp stabbing sensation pierced his neck. No. The first bee had reached them. Without looking, he knew the rest of the swarm was close behind.

Time was running out.

The sting throbbed a million times worse than any sting he'd ever had. And it wasn't his imagination. These weren't regular bees. These were killer bees!

"Quick. Drop flat on the ground," Carlos ordered. "And keep your face covered."

"We're going to die," Mario cried. "They'll swarm us and sting us all over. And we'll die."

Carlos shoved Mario down. "Just do what I tell you. Lay flat. Don't move. I've got a plan."

CHAPTER TWO

2 1/2 hours earlier

Carlos sat at the kitchen table wolfing down a serious pile of pancakes slathered in butter, whipped cream, honey, and topped with a dust storm of cinnamon-sugar.

Today was Wednesday and the Marana School District had scheduled a district In-Service Day. No school. No teachers. No books.

His mom had the day off, and Carlos had plans—no watching Mario, his nine-year-old brother. Carlos was headed to the BMX Ranch.

"Slow down, mijo," his mother said, flipping another batch of pancakes on the small electric grill. "Eat too fast and you'll be sick. You can't win races that way."

"I can't be late, Mama. All the guys will be there."

"Well they won't be impressed if you lose your breakfast on the track. Now go wake your brother. He's slept long enough."

Carlos shoved half a pancake into his mouth and mumbled, "The BMX Ranch is already open for practice. Coach is running time checks to decide who races in what divisions on Saturday."

"Don't talk with your mouth full." Mama shook the spatula at him. "Wake your brother. Now. Or you will go nowhere today."

"Okay. Okay." He noisily slid his chair across the cracked tile floor. "I'm going."

Carlos limped toward the small bedroom he shared with his little brother. Mario perched on the edge of his bed in his Spiderman pajamas. Feet dangling. Swinging his broken leg with its blue strap-on cast. His thick wavy hair was in bed-head mode. He was messing with Carlos's cell phone.

"Hey." Carlos grabbed his phone.

"Please?" Mario said. "Just let me use it. For a little while?"

"What? And let you flush my phone like you did yours? I don't think so."

"Mama said we're brothers and should share." Mario grabbed for the phone.

Carlos stepped back and shoved it into his back pocket. "What Mama said is for you to get up. Or you won't get breakfast."

"Mama!" Mario shouted. "Carlos bumped my leg. He hurt it."

"He's fine," Carlos called out just in case she heard and then lowered his voice. "Don't be a brat."

He rushed into the living room, flipped on the television, and turned it up loud enough to drown out Mario if he started again. A commercial for tortilla chips blared. "Get your CRUNCH on."

"What's that?" Mama called. "I can't hear you over the television.

"Nothing," Carlos shouted.

He plopped on the couch and checked his text messages. Last time his little brother "borrowed" his phone he'd sent a bunch of stupid texts to Carlos's friends. Not cool.

Usually, Mario wasn't such a pain. But ever since he'd broken his leg, he thought he deserved special treatment. He'd slid into home plate at a Little League tournament. Now he acted like he was a hero for scoring the winning point—sacrificing his leg for the team.

Carlos glanced at the row of his brother's baseball trophies running across the top shelf of the bookcase. There was enough to open a store. He frowned. It wasn't fair he'd been born with one shorter leg than the other. Then he'd have a row of trophies instead of just the one—BMX Hot Shot Rider. "I guess one's better than none," he muttered.

"News 4 Tucson," the TV blared.

Mario hobbled in from the bedroom with one crutch and flipped down the TV's volume. With his strap-on cast, his limp matched his brother's. "No wonder your old friends think you're a loser. Only old guys watch the news."

"It's not my fault you broke your leg," Carlos shot back. "Or my fault your friends are too busy texting each other to remember you exist." As soon as the words slipped out, Carlos regretted them. Mario was just a kid and he was extra grumpy because of his broken leg. "Hey. You up to riding double on my bike?"

Mario's eyes lit up. "You mean I can hang with you today?

Carlos nodded. "If Mama okays it. The BMX Ranch opens at eleven. Can you be ready by then?"

"Sure." Mario headed for the kitchen. "Mom!"

Carlos was reaching to turn off the television when a news alert banner popped up.

"Breaking news," said the anchor. "We've received a report of a major bee swarm attack in Douglas this morning."

Carlos's mouth went slack. He'd take a diamondback rattlesnake strike over a bee swarm sting attack. He didn't know why bees terrified him. He hated it but he couldn't help it. He was beyond afraid of bees. And everyone made fun of him for it—especially his kid brother.

"About eight this morning a man tried to remove a beehive from an old swinging bench in his backyard. The bees reacted instantaneously and chased the man onto his front porch where he collapsed. Luckily his neighbor witnessed the incident and called 911. The man was stung 100 times and has been hospitalized. Emergency crews dispatched have contained the bees. One lesson from this incident is to leave bee removal to the experts.

"Up next is John Marshall from the Arizona Department of Agriculture with tips on what to do in a bee attack."

Mario came back from the kitchen, scowling.

"What's the matter?" asked Carlos.

"Mom says I can't ride on the back of your bike. She says my leg hasn't healed."

Carlos knuckle-rubbed Mario's head. "Sorry, brother. Maybe next time."

"You still watching the stupid news?"

"Yeah. There was a bee attack In Douglas."

Mario grinned. "Buzz, buzz, buzz." He flapped his crutch-free hand in his brother's face.

"Cut it out," Carlos said, swatting his brother. "You're not funny."

"Don't think so? How about this? Roses are red, violets are blue, killer bees are coming for you." His laugh sounded like a tickled pig with hiccups. "Did you know that bears without ears are commonly referred to as B's?"

Carlos groaned.

"You smiled. I saw it."

The news was back on. "If you notice a swarm," said the Ag guy, "get inside. Close the doors and windows—"

"I have a better one," Mario said. His laugh drowned out the TV. "What do you call a bee that won't stop eating? A chub-bee."

"Buzz off. I want to hear this." Carlos turned up the volume.

"If you can't get inside," the man was saying, "pull your shirt over your head and run as fast as you can. Africanized Honeybees can fly ten to fifteen miles per hour and will chase you the length of two football fields."

Carlos's knee started to bounce. He was a lousy runner. Maybe Mama would let him keep his bike in the house instead of the shed. On his bike, he'd have a chance to outrace them.

"What shouldn't you do if attacked?" asked the news anchor.

"Don't play dead. Don't swat at the bees."

A cramp crawled up Carlos's knee. The phone rang in the kitchen.

"Turn down the television," Mama called.

"Most important, never jump into a pool or underwater. The bees will wait until—"

Mario grabbed the remote and hit the power button.

"Hey!" Carlos said. "She said down, not off. Now I've missed it." He grabbed a couch pillow and swung it at Mario.

Mario grabbed another pillow, and the fight was on.

"mijos!" Mama stood in the doorway with her hands on her hips. "Stop this instant—before something is broken."

The boys stopped mid-swing, dropped the pillows, and did what they always did. Fake hugged. Mama fell for it every time.

"What's up?" Mario asked, grinning.

"Who called?" Carlos asked.

"Sorry. It was work. I must go in. They're short-staffed and we need the money. Carlos, you have to stay home with your brother."

"But, Mama," Carlos said, his stomach sinking. "You promised. Coach is expecting me. If you make me stay home, everyone else will get to try out the new starting ramps except me. I'll have a disadvantage on Saturday. Probably lose." He didn't add, it's not fair.

"I know," she said, "but everything costs more these days. I'm sorry, mijo. It's time for you to grow up. Paying the bills is more important than winning another bike trophy. Besides there's plenty of yard work that needs to be done."

How could she say that? Didn't she remember being thirteen? Middle school was brutal if you weren't good at something besides getting straight A's. BMX racing was the one thing he was good at. Winning made him cool. Racing trophies meant everything.

Carlos stomped outside. Why couldn't he be an only child?

He looked at their yard. Mama was right. It didn't look much better than the lot next door with its abandoned old Winnebago and condemned notice. Both yards were overgrown with scraggly weeds, had piles of uneven gravel, and looked neglected.

Even their garden shed looked junky. Summer was over but the blow-up plastic pool still rested half-in-and-half-out of the open door like someone was too lazy to take care of it properly.

He felt heat creeping up his neck.

He should help out more. His dad lived in Nogales with a new family. Carlos was the man of the family now.

Okay. He'd put things in order. It wouldn't be as nice as the Smiths'—a house with a real swimming pool across the street. Sometimes they paid him for yard work and let him swim in their pool.

He used the money to buy an old used adapted Schwinn Stingray. It wasn't even close to the top of the BMX line, but it was a start.

His friend Luis had a Haro Pro XL that Carlos would die for.

Carlos had won his trophy racing against Luis. But if Luis got to practice on the new starting ramps and Carlos didn't, Luis would be the one coming in first.

Carlos would probably end up last. He gritted his teeth. He hated being a loser. There had to be something he could do.

But what?

CHAPTER THREE

Carlos looked down the dirt driveway to the street. Coyote Drive wasn't paved even though they were in a suburb of Tucson, Arizona. And that's how the locals liked it. The lots were large and covered in desert scrub. You had privacy. If you sneezed or did something else impolite, no one heard you. It felt like they lived in the country and not a city.

His gaze shifted.

Every lot had its own private desert—Palo Verde and Mesquite trees, thickets of Quail bush, Hackberry, Acacia, and bunchgrass. Plus, there were at least six different kinds of cacti to avoid bumping up against.

"Carlos!!"

His gaze swiveled to the driveway.

It was Luis. He was peddling a brand-new GT speed series black BMX bike. Back in grade school, Luis had been Carlos's best friend. Middle school changed everything. They hardly hung out at all now. BMX biking was the only time they did things together and not too often.

"Check out my new ride," Luis said, skidding to a stop. He was dressed in the most expensive bike gear. Bike pants, a helmet, and gloves. "It's fast and light and really handles."

Carlos pretended to smile. "It's cool. But what was wrong with your Haro Pro? I thought it was your baby."

Luis shrugged. "Time for an upgrade. You should, too. Your old Schwinn has seen better days."

"It's okay. I've got it modified the way I like it."

Carlos didn't add that Luis didn't get it.

Luis's family had money. They didn't have to watch every penny spent.

Luis lived only a half-mile away from Carlos's house in a gated subdivision across Twin Peaks Road. It was a planned neighborhood and a whole different world. The fact that Luis came from a rich family and Carlos was poor hadn't mattered until they hit Middle School.

Their friendship had changed. Carlos was a nobody. Luis had become super popular with the guys and the girls.

Stuff that hadn't mattered before now mattered big time.

Like how there was no way Carlos could afford an $800 bike. Or that Luis played first-string baseball, basketball, and soccer, ran track, and had lots of new friends. Which meant he didn't have much time for Carlos.

Mama came out dressed in her Cracker Barrel uniform. "Hi, Luis. Almost didn't recognize you. You must have grown a foot overnight. How's your mom? Haven't seen her in ages."

Luis smiled. "She's good. Dad bought her a convection oven and she's baking up a storm."

"That's nice. Well, it's off to work for me." She got into the car and rolled down the window. "Carlos, after you get the weeds cleared and the yard raked, clean out the shed." She smiled and winked. "It's nice having a man in the family. One I can rely on."

"Okay," Carlos said, wishing Mama was right. He was the man of the family. He should help out more and not complain. He'd go to the track early on Saturday and get in some practice. He couldn't win if he didn't give it his best shot.

Mario hobbled out of the house and waved his crutch at Luis. "Cool bike."

"Yeah. Can't wait for Coach to see it." Luis grinned. "Plus, Coach is bringing someone special to practice." He lowered his voice. "It's a surprise but Dad told me it's a rep from Wolf Racing. They're looking for a rider to sponsor in a new ad campaign."

Carlos's stomach dropped to his toes. Of all days, it would have to be today when he had to stay home. Life was so unfair.

"You ready to go?" Luis asked. "We'll have an hour to warm up before practice starts."

"No. I got to stay with Mario."

"Too bad. It's a one-day shot at becoming rich and famous."

Carlos shrugged and pretended he didn't care. "Mom got called into work and left me in charge."

Luis laughed. "The blind leading the blind, or as in your case—the gimp leading the gimp." He looked from one brother to the other.

Luis said it like it was a friendly joke, but Carlos knew it wasn't. It's probably what all the guys said behind his back.

Carlos pretended to laugh. "At least you have a shot at the sponsorship now."

Now it was Luis's turn to laugh awkwardly. He looked uncomfortable and stared at the open shed door with the inflated pool. "Hey, nice kiddie pool."

"Mom got it for Mario for his broken leg to do his therapy exercises." Carlos didn't add that on hot days it was great for cooling off. "Anyway, maybe I'll show up, you never know."

Luis said, "Well, don't forget Coach's rules. Text him either way or you're off the team."

Coach had put his foot down a couple of months ago when kids were showing up late or not coming to practice. He said unless his riders were serious, they were out. So now everyone had to text Coach to let him know whether they were coming or couldn't make it. And you only got one late pass. Coach had already cut two riders.

"I know," Carlos said. "I'll text him."

"Okay. See you later." Luis pushed off like he was already on the BMX Ranch track and sped down the driveway. Brutus, the neighbor's Rottweiler, appeared and raced along, barking.

Carlos grinned. For some reason, Luis was afraid of Brutus which was crazy. The old mutt just liked the attention.

"Why did you lie to Luis?" Mario asked.

"I didn't."

Mario frowned and shook his head. "Momma got the pool for us to cool off on hot days."

"Not really. She got it mainly for your physical therapy leg exercises."

"But you use it too," Mario said. Pause. "I thought you and Luis were best friends."

"We were. He has cool friends now. And I didn't lie. Just bent things a little."

Mario rolled his eyes. "Don't be mad at me. It's not my fault."

"This time it is," Carlos said bitterly.

"What did I do?"

"You were born."

Mario's face went white.

"Sorry," Carlos said. "That came out wrong."

"You hate me?" Mario's lower lip quivered.

"No, I don't. You're my brother—my best friend for life. I didn't mean it. I'm just mad. Hey! Give me five!" He held up his hand.

Mario nodded and slapped it. "I'll help with the yard. Then you can go to the practice."

Carlos shook his head. "Mama would kill me. Luis will get the sponsorship like he gets everything else. I probably didn't have a chance anyway. He's got the new bike, the looks, and a rich father."

"But you're a better rider."

Carlos grinned. "There's one thing he doesn't have. An awesome little brother like you who's really funny."

"Does that mean you want to hear another joke?"

"Sure."

"How do bees style their hair?"

"Bees don't have hair."

"With a honeycomb." Mario punched the air and gave a coyote howl.

Carlos groaned. "Hey. I need to call Coach. Can you go get my phone? It's on the couch."

"Sure." Mario headed for the house.

Carlos went to the shed where the oversized inflated pool blocked the doorway. He'd have to pull it out to get to the weed whacker. Easier said than done. By the time he'd wrestled it out the door and propped it up against the side of the shed, he was drenched in sweat. Panting, he stared into the shed and frowned.

What a mess! Cobwebs clung to the walls. Dust motes drifted aimlessly in the air. Except for his modified Schwinn bike hanging on the wall, it looked like a bomb had gone off. Carlos glanced at the broken window in the back wall. A shiver trickled down his neck as he tried to block the memory of his father smashing the glass in a fit of rage.

The shed hadn't been cleaned since. It felt like yesterday instead of two years ago.

"Shake it off," he muttered. "I am the man of this family now."

He glanced at the house. What was taking Mario so long? He must be getting a snack.

"Mario!" he shouted. "I need my phone. Stop whatever you're doing and bring it to me."

Carlos gingerly stepped into the shed and froze the instant he heard the low thrumming hum. Buzzing? Near the broken window on the back wall? Did it come from inside the shed or outside?

Holding his breath, he strained to listen but suddenly it was silent.

Had it been his imagination? The TV news story had him all freaked out.

Sweat trickled down his back and he shivered, imagining a bee crawling under his shirt.

The buzz, buzz, buzz started again, a little louder this time—a warning?

Eyes glued on the window, he stepped sideways. His foot landed on a fallen hammer and he stumbled onto the rake's tines. Its handle flew up and thwacked him in the back of the head.

"Aaaaaaagh" he yelled.

CHAPTER FOUR

Carlos grabbed his throbbing head and kicked the rake.

"Stupid rake!"

Suddenly the shed seemed hotter and stuffier. His rake dance had stirred up the dust making his nose twitch. He sneezed—rubbed the back of his head.

"Buzz. Buzz. Buzz."

The loud buzzing morphed into hiccuped laughter.

"Mario!" Carlos spun and stumbled on the rake. Again. Arms windmilling, he fought for balance. He landed on his knees—half in and half out of the shed door. He scrambled to his feet, his heart beating like a steam pump.

"You're going to be sorry," he shouted. Race-limping, he charged around the outside of the shed.

Mario leaned against the back wall, armed with the crutch in both hands and ready for battle. He jabbed the pseudo-weapon in the air as if warding off a rabid coyote. "You can't touch me."

"Want to bet?"

"Mama will be mad if you hurt me."

Carlos grabbed the crutch, wrenched it free, and tossed it on the ground. He stepped closer. "Who said I was going to hurt you? We're going to play tickle monster."

"No!" Mario held out his hands and started to inch away.

Carlos kept a frown on his face but inside he was grinning. He might be afraid of bees, but Mario hated being tickled. "I'm the monster and you are my prey."

"Please? Don't tickle me," Mario begged. "I won't do it again. I promise."

"Never ever?"

"Never ever."

"How do I know you're just not saying that?" Carlos said.

"I won't do it again. I promise." Mario held up two fingers. "Scout's honor."

"You're not a scout."

Mario shrugged. "Please don't tickle me."

"Okay. You don't buzz and I won't tickle." Carlos grabbed Mario by the waist, lifted him, and spun in a circle. "But it's washing machine time."

At first Mario giggled and whooped. But then he cried, "Stop. I'm going to be sick."

Carlos set Mario on his feet.

"Can I ask you something? And you don't get mad?" Mario asked.

"What?"

"Why are you afraid of a tiny little bee. You could squash it in two seconds."

"And it could sting me in a nano-second. Their stingers are full of venom. People have died from bee stings."

"Have you ever been stung?" Mario said. "Mama says if you leave them alone, they'll leave you alone."

"Well I've been stung. And it hurt." Carlos held out his hand. "My phone."

Mario's smile faded. "Uh, I forgot. I'll go get it."

Carlos went back into the shed. It was still a mess. Dusty and disorganized with junk everywhere. He grabbed the weed whacker and leaned it up against the pool outside. At least the shed would look good when it was all done. He could already picture it.

He shouldn't let his little brother get to him. Mario was just a kid and as bored as Carlos was. The fact that mom had to work was neither of their faults.

If only he could get a real job and help with the bills.

He thought about the man from Wolf Racing Luis said was coming to the practice. If Carlos could get the sponsorship, not only would he have a new bike and cool new gear, but he could also help his mom with the bills. She wouldn't have to work double shifts or go in on her days off.

That left one choice: make it to practice and wow the guy. But how could he do that if he was stuck at home with Mario?

He grabbed the broom and started sweeping. By the time the

floor was clean, he had the answer. He'd bribe Johnny to come over and play video games with Mario while he was at the track.

If Mama found out, she'd be mad. But she'd get over it—if they gave him the sponsorship. The commercials alone could earn him thousands of dollars. And Mama wouldn't have to work so hard.

He still had a lot to do and only one hour before he had to leave for the track.

Carlos turned into a whirling cleaning machine. He tossed screwdrivers, hammers, and wrenches into a toolbox. It went on the shelf next to some plant clippers. Then he rolled the hose in big loops and hung it on the wall.

By the time he finished, the shed looked pretty good. Not perfect but better.

The plastic inflatable pool leaned up against the outside wall. It'd be easier to store for the winter if he let the air out. For that, he'd need Mario's help.

Where was Mario?

Carlos started for the house and spotted Mario hunched in a lawn chair by the front door staring down at his lap.

"Mario! Whatever you're doing, stop. I need your help."

"In a minute." Mario waved, looking totally guilty. He slid lower in the chair like he was hiding something. "My leg hurts."

Carlos gave up on deflating the pool and went back into the shed to grab the weed whacker.

CHAPTER FIVE

Carlos grinned. Mama would be happy when she saw the shed.

His chores were half done. If he kept up this pace, he'd definitely make it to practice. Wait. He still hadn't texted Coach.

His grin morphed into a frown. Mario was supposed to bring him his phone. He'd better not be running down the battery playing some stupid game.

"Mario! Where's my phone?" he yelled, striding toward the house.

Halfway there, a bee dive-bombed him. A real bee, one with wings whirling—not one of his brother's pranks. Carlos's heart began to pound.

What had the news reporter said?

Cover your face and head. And run.

He yanked his T-shirt over his head and ran for the house. By the time he reached Mario, he was panting.

"Why is your shirt on your head?" Mario asked. "You look weird."

Carlos checked that the bee was gone, pulled down the shirt, and held out his hand. "My phone. Now."

"You don't have to be a jerk," Mario said. "Take it." He tossed the phone.

"Hey!" Carlos dived but his fingers grabbed air. His Samsung cell clattered on the concrete porch.

Mario's eyes went wide. "Oops. I thought you could catch."

Carlos saw red and lunged. "I asked you for my phone and you just tossed it on the cement!" He caught his brother's shirt, pulled hard. It ripped in the scuffle, but Carlos didn't let go.

"I'm sorry," Mario gasped. "I didn't mean to. I'll never touch your phone again."

"You better keep that promise." Carlos stepped back, heard an awful crunch, and felt his future disappear.

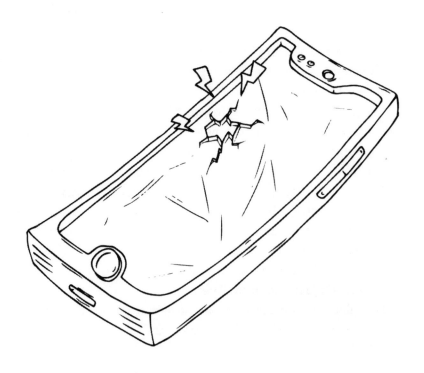

Mario's face went white. He scooted inside, shouting, "I didn't do it. It's not my fault."

With a groan, Carlos picked up his phone and heard the door slam shut. The cell's screen was black and cracked. He shook it and a piece of glass fell out.

"No. No. No. This can't be happening."

Frantically he tried to turn it on, a million thoughts racing through his head. "Please. Just work long enough for one message."

He shook the phone.

Nothing.

He collapsed into the lawn chair, defeated. This was the worst day ever. The Samsung was junk, and his life was ruined. There was no way he could text coach now. He was done—off the team for good.

Not only would he lose his spot, he'd be the only guy in middle school without a phone. Not just the kid with the limp—but a two-time loser.

His future was over. No friends. No texts. No games. No videos. And worst of all he'd miss the most important opportunity of his life if he didn't contact Coach.

On top of that, Mama would be furious. She'd spent a month's worth of tips to buy it.

"I'm done," he muttered. "Unless . . ." He breathed deep, hope lighting a tiny flame in his chest. He leaped up.

He'd use the landline to call both Coach and Johnny. He was pretty sure he had their numbers written down somewhere. Whatever it took, he was getting that sponsorship. Then he could buy the hottest cell phone. And maybe one for Mario, too.

But what if Luis won the endorsement? *Don't go there.*

At least that stupid bee was gone.

He tried the door. It was locked. Great.

"Open up," Carlos shouted, jiggling the handle. "I need to use the landline."

From inside, the television blasted cartoons.

Carlos pounded harder. "Come on. Unlock the door. I'm not mad at you. It was a stupid accident." Pause. "I'm the one who stepped on it."

Fine. If he couldn't call them, he'd modify his plan. Practice started in half an hour. He'd finish the chores, ride to Johnny's house, and convince him to come over and play video games with Mario. Then he'd book it to the track and explain everything to Coach.

Hopefully Coach would let him off the hook for not texting this one time.

He fired up the weed whacker. It was loud and vibrated his arms.

The door opened and Mario stuck his head out. "You're not going to kill me?" he shouted over the whacker's engine.

"I'm still thinking about it."

Mario started to retreat.

"Wait!" Carlos shut off the machine. "I was kidding. It was an accident."

"So you're not going to kill me?"

Carlos shook his head. "Come back out and read your comic books."

"Okay." At least Mario looked embarrassed. He held open the door. "You can use the landline."

"When I'm done here." Carlos restarted the weed whacker.

Its whirling green string tore at yellowed bunchgrass, whipping up a dirt and grass dust storm. Carlos coughed. Why hadn't he thought to grab a facemask? Sweat streamed down his cheeks leaving gritty streaks.

He made wider sweeps with the roaring whacker. Rocks flew and bounced off the side of the house while Mario sat in the yard with his boot-cast propped up on a milk crate.

Carlos worked around the side of the house until the weeds were uprooted. Time to trade the whacker for the rake and scrape the grass into little piles.

When he'd raked the length of the house, he spotted a clump he'd missed with the weed whacker. Grabbing the clump with both hands, he pulled.

At first nothing happened.

"Stupid weed," he shouted.

He took the rake and beat at the roots like he was fighting off a rattlesnake. The ground began to crumble. That was weird. Little holes were appearing.

He squinted.

The dirt shifted. A bigger hole appeared.

And then a bee crawled out.

The striped, yellow creature looked angry. It halted near the hole's edge like a sentry and stared up at him. Two big black eyes glared, and its stinger vibrated as if ready to attack.

Carlos couldn't take his eyes off it. It was just a bee. One little bee. Standing motionless on the loose dirt.

The wings whirred. It lifted off and hovered over the open hole.

Carlos told himself not to freak out.

But then there were two. Three. Four. Shoot! He'd dug up a hive. Horror ricocheted down his spine.

Grabbing the rake, he frantically tried to cover the hole.

Panic-stricken, he stomped the ground to pack down the dirt. He had to trap the bees underground. But with each footfall, the ground crumbled a little more. Another bee pushed through the loose dirt.

"Shoot!" He was making things worse.

Carlos threw the rake down and ran for the front door. They had to get inside before the bees could swarm and attack.

"Into the house," Carlos shouted to Mario. "Move."

"Quit bossing me around." Mario turned the page of his comic. "I'm reading." He looked up and smiled. "I got you a glass of water."

Carlos looked back over his shoulder. More bees had emerged. They were forming a low, black buzzing cloud just inches off the ground. Soon they would be airborne. There wasn't time to argue. Carlos pulled but Mario didn't budge. His boot cast was snagged on the chair.

"Hey." Mario tried to jerk free. "That hurts. Are you trying to break my leg again?"

"No. I'm trying to save your life," Carlos said, panting out each word. "There's a swarm of bees. They're coming."

"A swarm of bees?" Mario laughed but when he turned his eyes widened. "BEES!" For the first time he looked scared.

Carlos grasped the doorknob, turned it, and yanked. And yanked it again. It was locked. He started to hyperventilate.

"Tell me you have the house keys in your pocket."

CHAPTER SIX

Carlos stared through the window. The house keys hung on their usual hook under the wall phone.

He whipped his head back to the bee cloud. It wasn't moving. Yet. But it was twice the size, hovering just over the rake he'd left in the dirt. There had to be hundreds of bees. Maybe a thousand. Or more.

For some reason, they hadn't followed him to the house. Didn't they see him run? Or had they identified the rake as the enemy?

"What are we going to do?" Mario squeaked.

"We have to find another way in," Carlos whispered. "Get low and cover your head. Be ready to run."

As Mario scrunched down and pulled his shirt over his face, Carlos threw his shoulder against the door to pop the lock.

The door didn't budge. He slammed it again. And again. After two more tries, his shoulder hurt and they were still outside with the bees.

Even worse, hitting the door had got the bees' attention. The dark bee cloud distorted into a noise-seeking missile. It swarmed toward where the boys huddled.

They had to get inside.

Carlos's mind raced. The windows. Maybe one of them was unlocked.

The swarm shot over the covered porch, scouring the air and searching for the enemy.

Carlos put a finger to his lips. Maybe if he and Mario moved super slow, they could get away.

The neighbor's Rottweiler started to bark. The swarm swooped toward the dog's howls.

Thank you, Brutus.

"Mario!" Carlos whispered. "I'll try the living room window. Keep low and don't move. I don't think they've figured out we're here."

Carlos crept along the side of the house and heaved up on the nearest window. It didn't budge.

What now? Should they run?

"The bees are coming back," Mario whispered. "Break the window so we can get inside."

"No, then they'll be able to get in, too. I'll try the kitchen window. Follow me and stay close."

He tiptoed to it with Mario hobbling behind. It was locked too.

Shoot.

The bee cloud had reached the giant saguaro cactus by the drive.

Think!

The house was out. That left one option. Not a great one but what other choice did they have?

"Run for it. That way. Go."

"I can't run," Mario whimpered. "My leg." He turned to face the swarm, raising his crutch like a baseball bat. "I'll swat 'em all."

"Forget that." Carlos threw the crutch down, slung Mario over his shoulder, and ran for the shed.

Mario's started screeching. "The swarm looks like a giant fastball. It's coming straight at us."

"Shut up," Carlos panted. Mario was heavier than he looked. "You're making things worse."

Mario's grasp tightened and Carlos's foot twisted. Pain raced up his shorter leg but he kept going. He had to get Mario to safety. They were almost there. Just another six feet to go. Five. Four. Three. Two.

They'd reached the shed.

He dropped Mario onto his feet and yanked open the door. The blood pumping through his heart had given him super strength—too much. He ripped the door open. Now the shed door dangled on one hinge. So much for his escape plan.

A sharp stabbing sensation pierced his neck. Uh oh. The first bee had located them. Without looking, he knew the swarm was close behind.

Time was running out.

The sting throbbed a million times worse than any sting he'd ever had. And it wasn't his imagination. These weren't regular bees. These were killer bees!

"Quick. Drop flat on the ground. And keep your face covered."

"No. We have to run," Mario argued.

"You're too slow and you're too heavy for me to carry." Carlos shoved Mario down. "Just do what I tell you."

"We're going to die," Mario cried. "They'll swarm us and sting us all over. And we'll die."

"Lay flat. Don't move. I have another idea."

Carlos scrambled to the side of the shed where he'd propped the big, rectangular, inflatable swimming pool earlier. It was semi-clear, and the sun shone through the red, white, and blue colors. The plastic pool might only be three feet deep, but it was wide enough to hold six.

"What are you doing?"

"Head down," Carlos ordered, grabbing the pool and flipping it topside over his brother like a giant shield.

The swarm buzzed like an air brigade, setting his heart racing. He took one last look and dove under the pool.

They were safe—for the moment.

"Carlos? Will the pool keep the bees out?"

"Yeah," Carlos said, hoping it was true. "I don't think they can chew through plastic." His skin prickled. Not plastic, but what about dirt?

"You better be right." Mario sucked in a big breath. "How long until they leave us alone?"

Carlos's stomach began to twist into knots.

The bees had built their hive in the ground. They knew how to dig and burrow. How far did their tunnels go? Were they safe hiding under this cheap swimming pool on the ground?

CHAPTER SEVEN

Carlos and Mario lay on their sides, sweat soaking their skin. They faced each other under the red, white, and blue plastic pool. It was like a sauna—hot and the air thick. Mario was still panting through his open mouth.

"Chill and breathe through your nose," Carlos said, wiping sweat from his face. "Or you're going to use up all our oxygen."

"When are they going to leave?"

Waiting for the bees to get tired and leave didn't seem to be working. Instead of going away, more had arrived. The bee-cloud looked larger and darker, and now he could clearly hear a buzzing hum. Several had settled on the pool and had become dark spots crawling across the plastic pool overhead.

"Are those bees?" Mario asked.

Carlos nodded.

Mario slapped the pool. The bees took flight.

"Don't," Carlos said. "You're only making them angry."

"I thought you said we're safe under here."

"We are." At least I hope we are, he added to himself. "And now they know we're still here."

"Oh." Mario fell silent.

The bees returned and resumed their search for the pool's weakness. More winged avengers joined them. The buzzing multiplied. Shifting shadows intent on revenge. They were like storm clouds morphing from one ominous image to another.

Carlos squeezed his eyes shut. Five minutes passed.

"I'm tired of being stuck under here," Mario complained. "The ground's hard. My leg hurts. This was a stupid plan."

"Maybe. But we're still alive."

"Why don't they go away?" Mario complained. "We've been under here forever. Maybe longer and I'm thirsty."

"It's probably only been ten minutes," Carlos said. "Waiting a little longer won't kill you." He didn't add, but the bees will. There was no point in getting Mario riled up again. Complaining Mario was easier to deal with than panicked Mario.

"How many stings do you have?" Mario said. "I have six."

"Ten. I think," Carlos said. "Not enough to be dangerous." He didn't add, and they're still throbbing.

A vehicle blasting with country and western music stopped at the end of their drive—engine idling.

"Wahoo," he shouted, hope bursting like fireworks in a Fourth of July night sky.

It had to be the mail carrier. He always listened to that kind of cheating-heart music.

Grinning, Carlos pushed Mario's shoulder.

They were going to make it.

"Yell. Get his attention." Carlos rose onto his elbows. "HELP! Bee attack! We're under the pool."

Mario joined in. "Call 9-1-1."

The mail truck's engine shifted into gear.

"Nooooooooo," shouted Carlos. His grin slipped.

"Don't go," Mario whispered. "We need help."

Carlos kept yelling. Louder. "Come back." He kept at it until his throat was sore and his voice croaked.

No one was coming.

He was mad at himself. Why hadn't he thought of the mail

carrier earlier? He and Mario could have crawled out to the road. Waited. Been rescued. But it was too late now.

Carlos realized Mario must be totally frightened because his little brother had rolled onto his side. He was chewing his lip and silent tears mingled with the sweat on his cheeks.

Above the pool, the bees were going crazy, stirred up by all the shouting. They seethed in a death dance atop the plastic. The swarm had grown into a blanket so thick that they blotted out the sun.

Lying in their shadow, Carlos felt ill. No one was coming to help. It would be hours before Mama got home. His next thought sent a chill into his heart. By then, the bees would have burrowed under the pool's edge and stung them a thousand times.

His hand slid over the swollen welts on his arms and face. He squinted through the plastic at the dark, ever-changing swarm. If there had been a thousand bees before, there must be ten thousand now. Their weight pressed down on the plastic, making it sag.

Carlos looked at Mario and dry swallowed, wishing he had a big brother to protect him. But that was his job. Mama expected him to take care of Mario and keep him safe.

Okay. Time to think. What did he know about bee attacks?

Bees can fly ten to fifteen miles per hour.

If you see a bee swarm, protect your face.

Run away as fast as you can.

Don't swat at the bees.

Don't play dead.

Never jump into a pool to hide underwater.

It all sounded easy unless you were a bee hostage.

All the advice in the world was no good if it didn't help. He and Mario were stuck under a plastic blow-up swimming pool, hot, thirsty, and with no help on the way.

It was time to man up. If they were going to survive, it was up to Carlos to come up with a real plan.

CHAPTER EIGHT

The hovering swarm cast an even larger and darker shadow over the pool. Carlos imagined there must be thousands of bees in the pulsating blob. He was confident the bees couldn't chew through the plastic shield, but now they seemed to search every inch of it, looking for a way in.

His gaze shifted.

Some bees had started crawling down the pool's outer wall, just inches from his face. How long would it take for them to discover a bee-sized crack between the plastic and the ground?

He shivered, his sweat burning like acid, and glanced at Mario.

Mario was on his stomach and focused on drawing a giant wasp in the dirt with his finger. Obviously, his little brother hadn't noticed the bees searching for an entrance along the ground or he'd be chewing his lip again.

That was good. At least drawing kept him busy, giving Carlos time to think. He started running through options, trying to devise a workable plan.

Escape idea one: wait for the bees to get tired and fly away. His jaw clenched. The swarm wasn't leaving. Some bees covered the pool's surface while others flew in frantic circles. It was only a matter of time before they wriggled under the pool's flimsy plastic edge.

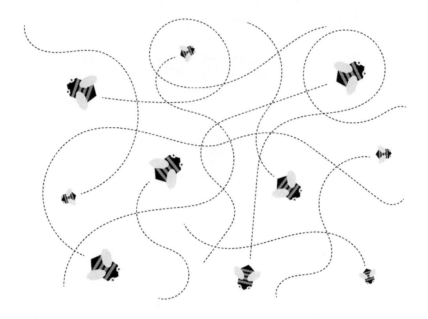

Carlos and Mario would be trapped in a stinging nightmare.

His teeth clamped together so tight it hurt. He forced himself to relax his jaw muscles and breathe deep. Focus on surviving not. . . the other.

Escape idea two: run like the news reporter suggested. Carlos shook his head. The instant they tossed the pool covering aside, the bees would be all over them like two massive blankets. Plus, Mario had a broken leg and Carlos was too slow with his shorter leg. He'd be even slower if he had to carry Mario. Running wouldn't work.

Escape idea three . . .

Nothing came.

Frantic, Carlos squinted at the droning enemy. The noise was unbelievable. How could the swarm be growing bigger? He dry-swallowed.

Think.

Think.

Think.

A memory popped into his head.

They were in front of their house. Mario was pitching and Carlos was swinging an aluminum bat. After twenty strikes, Carlos grand-slammed the baseball into the neighbor's lot. Cacti, brush, and Palo Verdi trees studded the ramshackle yard. The owners had abandoned it ages ago. The only sign they'd once lived there was an old RV camper.

The brothers hadn't found the ball, but the RV had been unlocked and they'd peeked inside.

Now, Carlos shook his fist at the bees. He had a plan.

They'd use the pool as a shell, play snail, and crawl to the rusty RV. Then they'd get inside and wait out the bees until Mama came home.

"Why are you grinning?" Mario asked.

"I have an idea. But it will only work if you do exactly what I say this time. Can I count on you?"

Mario stared at the dirt and nodded. "I wish everything wasn't my fault."

"It's not," Carlos said, even though most of it was Mario's fault, but that didn't matter now. "I stepped on my phone. You didn't."

"Yeah, but I threw it."

"And I stepped on it." Pause. "And worse, I weed-whacked the beehive."

"I locked the keys in the house," Mario sniffled.

"Forget it. We both messed up. Now it's time to be a lean, mean, bee-fighting team." He raised his fist for a knuckle bump.

Mario returned a half-hearted knuckle slap.

"We have amigo power. We're smarter than a bunch of bees," Carlos said. "I know exactly what we have to do."

"What?" Mario sounded a little less scared.

"Escape idea numeral tres." Carlos took a deep breath and hoped Mario wouldn't be freaked out when he heard the plan. It was crazy but it might just work. "Do you think you can crawl?"

CHAPTER NINE

"Are you sure this is a good idea?" Mario said, eyeing the heavy, menacing swarm. "Why don't they leave?"

Carlos wiped his forehead. "The news guy said killer bees stay in attack mode for a long time. Sometimes hours. This pool won't protect us forever."

"I don't want to go." Mario pinched his lips and hummed a long, single note in unison with the bees. *"Hmmmmmm."*

"Come on, buddy, we can do this." He tried not to look at the growing layer along the ground.

"It stinks being stuck under here." Mario's face was drenched with sweat and his hair was plastered to his head.

"That's why we need to get moving. I don't want to wait five hours until Mama gets home. Besides, the only thing that stinks is your armpits."

"Not funny." Mario bared his teeth like a pit bull. "Your idea is stupid. I'm hot. And I want Mama. And I'm dying of thirst."

"Think of something else. If you're thirsty we need to get moving."

Mario ignored him.

"I mean it. We need to go."

Mario pinched his lips and started to hum. "Hmmmmmm." At first, he was in unison with the bee chorus, holding onto a long, single note. It sounded eerie. The bees didn't seem to notice. Then Mario's head began to bob, and he hummed a loud bouncy rhythm. His shoulders rocked and his fingers tapped along.

The bees went crazy. The swarm split into chaos and then reformed to dive-bomb the pool. The impact vibrated the plastic.

Mario's mouth and eyes popped open in terror.

Carlos's pulse pounded in his ears. "Let's go. Grab your side. Keep it down. We need to get to the abandoned RV."

Carlos belly-crawled to the front of the pool. He glanced at his brother. Mario hadn't moved. He seemed petrified—his eyes were locked on the teeming mass of winged avengers.

"Mario! Snap out of it. We've got to move. Get on your stomach."

"The bees are everywhere," Mario whispered but did as he was told.

"We'll go slow. Make sure your side stays on the ground. I'll do the same."

Carlos kept his elbows on the hard dirt and held down the pool's front edge. "Ready?"

"Ready."

"Okay. Tell me if you need to stop. Uno. Dos. Tres. Now."

Crawling on his elbows, Carlos used his hands to inch the pool forward.

The swarm seemed confused. It soared upward in a massive black cloud. Then it resumed its deadly vigil, landing and busily searching the pool's surface.

The brothers kept moving.

They'd only traveled for about three minutes when Mario said, "How long will this take? We're moving like snails. And the bees are having no problem keeping up."

Carlos didn't bother answering. His brother's complaining was a good sign. It meant he wasn't as scared as before.

"Mama's not going to like this. My cast is filling with dirt."

"You can take it off and dump it when we get inside the RV. Just keep moving. Make sure no bees get in. If you see one, squash it."

"With what?"

"Your fist."

"Eew!" Mario said. "Are we there yet?"

"Almost."

Stones scattered under their hands and knees. They reached the property line. Carlos halted. Only twenty feet lay between them and the rusted Winnebago Minnie Winnie.

Unfortunately, those twenty feet contained screwbean mesquite, hackberry brush, and thorny cacti. There was no straight path. They were growing so close together, he felt sick.

How would they get through?

Everything looked distorted through the double layers of plastic. He knew well-worn animal trails looped right and left. Were they wide enough for the pool? He wasn't sure. Which was crazy. He'd lived his whole life next door to the lot but hadn't paid attention.

"Why'd you stop?" Mario asked.

"I'm deciding which way to go."

"And?"

"We'll turn right first and then double back. There's a wider path for the pool that way." He crossed his fingers and prayed he'd made the best choice. "It won't take more than an extra few minutes."

The killer bee cloud churned with their ominous, never-ending hum. They seemed to be waiting for him to make a mistake. They must smell them under the pool. He wished he'd never used the weed whacker and had woken them up. Why couldn't they just leave?

He spotted a wide gap in the desert scrub. What a relief. It was an old, rutted road, leading into the property. They eased onto it and scooted faster now that they had a clear path.

"Won't be long now," Carlos gasped and pushed forward, ignoring his scraped hands and knees.

The pool bumped into something.

"No!" The word escaped before Carlos could stop it. Not now. They were almost to the RV.

"What's that hissing noise?" Mario cocked his head to the side. A bee's shadow crawled over his face. "It sounds like a rattlesnake."

"No snake," Carlos assured his brother. "We got too close to a jumping Cholla cactus."

"What now?" Mario cried. The pool was deflating by the second.

"Keep going. Crawl a little faster."

"I am," Mario sobbed.

Carlos knew his kid brother's leg had to be hurting and that his palms and knees had to be shredded. "Almost there, you've got this."

Soon they were draped in a semi-clear red, white, and blue plastic shroud, which was blanketed with killer bees. The whole mass hung heavily on their backs.

They squirmed onward.

It was hard to see through the plastic, but Carlos spotted the RV just ahead—only five feet left to go.

Then, like some miracle, they were there.

The Winnebago might be an old, abandoned RV camper but it looked like a palace.

"I told you we'd make it," Carlos said.

"So did the bees," Mario squeaked. "I just thought of something. What if it's locked like the house?"

"It's not."

"How do you know?" Mario demanded suspiciously.

"We looked inside, remember?"

"But that was a long time ago, and—"

"Listen to me. We'll jump up as fast as we can. We'll keep the pool on us until I get the door open. Then we'll dive inside and slam the door. Got it?"

Mario bit his lip and nodded.

"Okay. Ready?" Carlos paused, praying they weren't stung too many times before they got into the RV. "Now!"

CHAPTER TEN

Together, the brothers threw the pool with its mass of bees backward and dove inside.

Chest heaving, Carlos slammed the RV door shut. He leaned up against the wall to catch his breath, gulping in the stale, musty air.

"We did it. That was close," Carlos gasped.

The brothers grinned at each other.

Mario limped a few feet, wincing, and plopped down on a paint can. Carlos pressed his raw palms against his legs to stop their burning.

They were in the kitchen. Everything looked half-sized, like it was built for a hobbit—a two-burner stove, a tiny sink, and a refrigerator barely large enough to hold a grocery sack.

Once, it must have been nice with its wood-paneled walls and built-in cabinets. Now it was a dump, littered with old stuff. Carlos counted eight bulging black plastic bags. He peeked in one. At least it wasn't rotting garbage. Just junk. Old tape. Papers. Broken odds and ends. And who knew what else.

"This place is a pit," Mario said. "Do you think the old guy was a hoarder?"

Carlos shrugged. "Don't know. Don't care. We're safe." He

pulled open the kitchen drawer and slammed it shut. It looked like mice had used it for a toilet. The cabinets weren't much better.

Mario stared at one of the windows. "You sure we're safe?"

Carlos nodded and hoped it was the truth.

Outside, the muted buzzing was a throbbing reminder that the bees were in attack mode. Did they ever give up? He knew the answer was no—at least not for a good while. That's what made killer bees so famous. And deadly. They darkened the windows, crawling and searching for cracks or gaps.

Carlos scanned the room to make sure none had gotten in.

The coast was clear.

Anyway, he'd know by now if they'd found a crack—they would have already attacked.

All they had to do was sit there until Mama got home.

"I thought your plan was stupid," Mario said. "But you know what? That was awesome."

"Stick with me and we'll be good."

Mario rolled his eyes, grinning. Then his grin morphed into a frown. "Wait, what if the bees are still here when Mama comes looking for us? They'll attack her."

Carlos shook his head. "She won't be home for at least five hours. The bees will be long gone before then."

Carlos hoped his words were true.

"What if Mama phones on her break to check on us?" Mario asked.

That would be a disaster. They couldn't answer and she'd think something was wrong.

"Don't worry," Carlos said, hoping he spoke the truth. "We'll be out of here by the time Spiderman comes on at three. I'll even watch it with you."

Of all days to break his phone? The one time there was an emergency, he didn't have it. They could have called for help. He could have texted Coach. Now Coach had to think he was a flake. He'd be off the team. And so much for impressing the Wolf Racing sponsor. He pushed the thoughts from his mind. The only thing to worry about now was surviving.

"I'm bored," Mario said.

"Already?"

"This place is small. I wouldn't want to live here. There's no bed."

"That's because the bedroom door is shut."

Mario's head swiveled. "Door? Where?"

Carlos pointed. "Right behind you. It's a pocket door. It slides into the wall."

Mario stood awkwardly on his cast and hopped toward the sliding partition. "Wow. It looks just like the wall. Sort of."

Carlos grinned. Mario was a mess—sweat-streaked, dirty, and scratched. A red welt had sprouted on Mario's cheek and another on his neck.

"What's so funny?" Mario said, plopping down on his paint can.

"I wonder if I look as bad as you do?"

"Worse."

They both laughed.

Now that the danger was over, his adrenaline rush faded. He winced. Throbbing pain sprouted on his forehead, arms, belly, and legs.

"How many?" Carlos rubbed his arm and flinched.

"How many what?" Mario said, suddenly looking like he was going to barf.

"How many stings do you have?"

Mario grew pale and peeled up his shirt. "Oh no. One, two, three, four, five, six. Am I going to die?"

"No. But you didn't count the one on your face and neck. Seven." Carlos tried to put on a brave face and examined himself. "Beat you. I have ten and I'm not dead."

The welts hurt but not as bad as when Carlos had wrecked his bike and road-rashed his whole leg. "Don't worry. We'll be fine if we don't get stung again. They aren't swelling, are they?"

"No, but they hurt," Mario said.

"They'll stop hurting soon. Promise."

"Do you know the worst part about getting stung by bees?" Mario said, looking serious.

"The itchy pain?"

"No," Mario giggled. "Now we have to take care of their hives."

Carlos stifled a snort and wondered if bee venom had messed up his little brother's mind. "What are you talking about?"

"It's a joke. Don't you get it? The little red bumps that look like zits where the bees stung you. They're hives. We've got them. And we have to deal with them."

Carlos groaned and rolled his eyes. At least Mario was back to himself, corny jokes and all. "How's your leg?"

Mario shrugged. "It's okay." He held up one arm. "But my arm is covered in dried blood and dirt."

"Maybe I should take the first shower tonight because all your dirt will clog the pipes," Carlos said. "And Mama will have to call a plumber. And I'll have to wait for morning to get cleaned up."

"At least my jokes are funny," Mario said, smiling. He rooted through a pile and held up a huge, twisted ball of wire and a Marie

Callender pie tin. "Why did they leave all this junk? It's just garbage."

"That's why. They didn't want to take it," Carlos said. "But hey, there is some good stuff. Duct tape. Lots of old newspapers to read."

Mario made a face.

"With comic strips."

"Hand 'em over," Mario said.

Carlos grabbed an armful, dropped them next to Mario, and went back to rummaging.

"Cool. This is something we really need." Carlos held up a deflated soccer ball. It was flat as a pancake and just as floppy. "Want to play soccer?"

"I don't know," Mario said with mock seriousness. "We're not supposed to horse around inside 'cause something might get broken." He grinned. "Plus, I can't kick the ball with a broken foot."

"Yeah, but you can bounce it off your head." Carlos flung it like a Frisbee. It sailed past Mario and hit the pocket door.

Thwack. The door shifted. A tiny crack appeared.

The bees outside went wild. The window crawlers took flight.

The buzzing grew louder. Closer. Like the bees were in the Winnebago with them.

Weird.

"Carlos?" Mario's voice sounded strained. "Look."

On the floor, a single bee was crawling through the tiny crack in the pocket door.

CHAPTER ELEVEN

The bee didn't hesitate. Before Carlos could react, it shot straight at him. Adrenaline kicked in and Carlos grabbed a filthy red handkerchief and shoved it into the crack. Ignoring the sharp sting on his neck, he kept working until the crack was filled.

"Ouch!" Another sting. Carlos slapped his cheek fast and hard. In his palm, the bee was smashed. He shook it off and stepped on it. He knew that crushed bees gave off an alarm scent that sent other bees into a frenzy, but he'd had no choice.

"Carlos," Mario cried. "Something's in my cast. Ow. Ow! It stung me."

"Should I take off your cast?" Carlos said. The temporary boot cast was supposed to be on for one more week.

"Get it off. Get it off." Mario was freaking out big time. His eyes were wide with terror, and he kept slapping at his leg.

"Okay. Give me a second." Carlos dropped to his knees and pulled on the Velcro straps holding the boot cast in place.

"Hurry," Mario said, wincing at the ripping sound. "Before it stings me again."

Carlos peeled the temporary boot cast open. Mario's leg looked awful pale and skinny. Getting the bee without re-injuring his brother would be tricky.

Mario started hyperventilating.

"Where is it?" Carlos asked.

"Under my knee." Mario's leg jerked. "Ow. It stung me again." He swatted his leg with both hands.

Carlos grabbed Mario's arms. "Stop. I'll lift your leg and see if I can knock it off."

Tears flooded Mario's face.

The bee crawled onto Mario's kneecap.

"Don't move," Carlos said. "I'll get it."

Cupping his hand over the vibrating bee, he swiped it to the floor. Then grabbed an old tennis shoe and hammered the bee like he was driving a nail. The bee was history.

"You okay?" Carlos said.

Mario nodded. "But my leg hurts."

"Sorry, I didn't mean to hurt you."

"You didn't. The bee did." He rubbed his hand over his knee. "I think it got me three times before you knocked it off."

"Well, it won't ever sting you again."

Mario half grinned through his tears. "Hey. Look at the windows. The bees are gone. They gave up!"

"Maybe," Carlos said, breathing deep and letting it out slow. "Or they got tired after we outsmarted them and buzzed off. Either way, we're safe. No more running. No more crawling. Best of all, no more stings."

"So, we can get out of this dump, pronto," Mario said, struggling to stand.

"Not yet," Carlos said. "Sit down."

"What do you mean? Not yet?" Mario's lips pinched into a line.

"Let's give the bees plenty of time to retreat to their hive."

"You said they can fly ten miles an hour. If that's true, they should already be there."

"Yeah, but what if there's a straggler? It would only take one bee to raise the alarm and bring back the whole swarm. We need to wait at least fifteen minutes. Maybe more. You don't want to be stung again. Do you?"

Mario plopped down on his paint can, rubbing his sore leg. "What are we going to do for fifteen minutes?"

"I don't know," Carlos said. "How about you tell me a joke." Telling jokes were guaranteed to keep his kid brother distracted.

Mario's eyes sparkled. "Got one and I bet you can't guess it. Why did the bee lose his job at the barber shop?"

Carlos forced his eyes not to roll. "Don't you know any jokes that aren't about bees?"

"Because the bee only gave buzz-cuts." Mario giggled. "Even to the girls. Can you imagine Maggie Titus with a bald head?"

The joke was bad. Corny. Juvenile. Maybe it was the adrenaline. Laughter burst from Carlos's lungs, loud and raucous. He couldn't stop. Mario joined and the two of them howled like a pair of coyotes celebrating a full moon.

As quickly as it had started, it stopped.

Mario spoke first. "I told you it was funny. Can we go now?"

"Wait a second," Carlos said. "Shh, I think I hear something."

A sickly sensation of bees crawling in his hair sent prickles of fear racing to his toes. He could hear them. Maybe he was paranoid.

"What is it?" Mario demanded.

Carlos held up his hand.

The old red handkerchief stuffed in the crack seemed to quiver. Was it his imagination or was the rag alive? Then it stopped. Breathing in and out. But that was impossible.

"Did you see that?" Carlos said.

"I didn't see anything."

"I don't think they left. I think they're all in the front room of the RV—on the other side of the pocket door."

Like something out of a horror movie, the handkerchief popped into the room. Two winged intruders slipped through. Carlos leaped to his feet and plugged the hole.

"Toss me that duct tape," Carlos said. "Hurry."

"Where is it?" Mario said. "I don't see it."

Carlos frantically pressed the handkerchief over the hole, ignoring two sharp stings to his neck.

"Behind you. On the floor."

"I found something better. Hey, mean old bees," Mario taunted. "Come this way. Over here."

"Just give me the tape," Carlos shouted.

Mario tossed it and Carlos snagged it mid-air, ripped off a length and spun back to the door. "Cover your face, Mario. Quit messing around."

The tape was old and a little gooey sticky, but it would work. Carlos slapped the tape strip over the rag and tore off another piece. Another strip and another until silver tape completely covered the red handkerchief. Almost done.

A *psssssst* sound came from behind his back, accompanied by the scent of oil. He ignored it and focused on pressing the tape's edges to the door. Finally, the dangerous gap was sealed off.

That should hold them for a while.

Dreading what Mario had been up to, Carlos turned to look at his little brother.

CHAPTER TWELVE

Expecting the worst, Carlos stared, his worry morphing into a grin.

Mario held a blue and yellow can of WD40.

"That's what I smelled. What were you doing with it?"

"I sprayed the bees," Mario said, "and they just dropped. See?" He poked at two oil-drenched bees on the floor with a broken pencil. They weren't moving. Mario slammed the can down on them for good measure. "Take that. Your stinging days are over."

"Good job," Carlos said. "We're safe for now. Let's put your walking cast back on. Might as well be ready if we have to run."

"Run? Why? You just said we were safe."

"We are if the bees stay on their side of the door."

Mario scowled. "Stupid bees. How did they even get inside?"

"I think I know. Remember when I hit a grand slam off your pitch?"

"When you lost my best baseball with a lucky hit? Yeah."

"I searched all over," Carlos said. "Except for in this RV's front room. I bet you twenty pancakes it's in there."

Mario groaned. "Can't you close the pocket door tighter?"

Carlos shook his head. "Something's wrong with it. And if I try to fix it, I'll probably make things worse. I'll help you put the cast back on."

"Do I have to?" Mario said. "We're just sitting here and it kind of feels good to have it off."

Carlos nodded. "Mama would want you to."

Mario made a face but grabbed the cast and put it on.

"Happy now?" Mario said.

"Think you can stand on it?" Carlos said.

"I think so."

"I'll help and you can see if it feels right. Okay?"

Carlos helped his brother up.

Mario put his weight on the walking cast and winced.

"Too loose?" Carlos said.

"No. The cast is rubbing my bee stings. Now they itch and hurt at the same time."

"Think of something else."

"Like what? The bees buzzing in the walls and up there?" Mario pointed at the ceiling.

The low hum coming from the walls and overhead seemed louder.

Carlos noticed a metal air vent set into the ceiling and gulped. Its little slats were the perfect size for killer bees to crawl through. The vent looked closed but everything else in this RV was broken. What if it was busted, too? What if the bees discovered it?

Scrambling, he piled a rusted metal crate on top of another one and climbed up. "Toss me the Tape. I need to get this sealed."

In a few minutes, the vent matched the door. Duct-tape Décor by Carlos!

He hopped down and put his ear to the wall. The buzzing vibrated and sounded even more ominous. Was it his imagination, or were they gnawing the wood paneling?

271

They couldn't stay there. Eventually, the bees would get in.

Carlos grabbed one of the full garbage bags and dumped it on the floor.

"What are you doing now?" Mario asked.

"I'm forming a new plan. A better one." Carlos crossed his fingers and prayed it would work. It was a long shot.

"Another plan?" Mario whined. "Let's just wait here. I'm tired of new plans."

Carlos stirred one foot through the garbage. It was a real pile of junk, like you'd find at a dump. Empty oil cans, squashed boxes, discarded brushes, old clothes, shoes, and hats. Broken pencils and pens, yellowed newspapers and magazines, squashed soda bottles, stuffed toys, tools, batteries, balls of wadded tin foil, and who knew what else.

Mario said, "Your plan better not be running. My crutches are back at the house."

Carlos looked at his little brother.

Mario wore his stubborn frown. "The bees can fly ten miles an hour. I can't run that fast even if I had crutches. And neither can you."

Carlos stopped rummaging. "You won't have to run."

"Well, I vote to stay here." Mario crossed his arms. "Humph."

"We can't fight off the bees if they get in." Carlos tried to sound patient. "I think they crawled into the ceiling. If they can chew dirt, they can chew wood paneling."

Mario's eyes darted upward and he paled.

"We're getting out of here." Carlos returned his attention to the garbage. "But we've got to be smart about it."

"By going through garbage?"

"We need supplies. Stuff we can use to escape."

"Like what?"

Carlos grabbed a full bag, untied its top, and dumped it in front of Mario. "Look for something we can use for a knife."

Mario used a white-stained paint stick to stir through the pile. "How about this?" He handed Carlos a broken scissor.

"Perfect." Carlos sliced the garbage bags into four large sheets and set them aside.

"What are they for?"

"Bee armor. Look for anything that might prevent bee stings." Carlos held up three Chobani yogurt cups. "These can keep bees out of your ears."

"Gross!" Mario held up a large, faded-pink-camo baseball cap. "I'll use this."

"Okay. Keep looking for more stuff."

His plan was coming together. It was risky but could work if Mario didn't freak out. And if he could trick the bees into thinking they were still inside after they slipped away.

At least long enough to make their escape.

Under the next bulging bag, Carlos found a big box coated in grime. Sitting it on the sink, he opened it and smiled. With a little luck and perhaps a prayer, this could be the plan's missing link.

CHAPTER THIRTEEN

"So what's this big plan?" Mario asked.

"I'll tell you the details when you need to know," Carlos said. It was risky and there was no point telling his brother too soon. He'd be freaked.

"That's what I thought. You don't really have one."

"Just keep looking."

Carlos pulled the ancient radio from the dusty box. It was ancient—like from the 90s with round knobs. Turning one produced a click. But no sound. He tried again. Shook it. Still nothing. Flipping it over, he found the empty slot for AAA batteries.

"Mario. Did you see any batteries?"

Mario shrugged. "I don't know. Maybe. I wasn't looking for batteries. You said to find something useful like more tape or another hat. You didn't say anything about batteries."

"Look for some," Carlos said, trying not to sound desperate. "I'll check the cupboards and drawers. Again." This time his search had a purpose. Earlier when he'd looked it had been curiosity.

The kitchen drawers were empty, except for mouse poop. Good thing he didn't have to stick his hand in there.

The cupboards were next. He put his ear to one little door and listened for buzzing.

"What are you doing? Mario asked.

"Listening for bees."

"And?" Mario bit his lip.

"Don't hear any." Carlos opened the first cupboard door. "Keep looking for batteries."

While they searched, Carlos kept an eye on the duct-taped door and vent.

"I found one," Mario shouted, holding up a D battery. "It looks too big for the radio."

"It's a start. Keep looking."

Carlos opened the last cupboard. Inside was a stuffed bear clutching little brass cymbals. This toy was going to be worth its weight in gold. Luis had one in kindergarten. Carlos had been jealous. It wobbled and banged the cymbals to kiddy music when you turned it on.

"Wahoo," Mario said. "Check it out. JACKPOT." He dumped a pile of batteries onto the floor. Big ones and little ones.

Carlos set the bear in the sink and studied the batteries. Some had gray dust and had started to corrode. Hopefully, they weren't all dead. He sorted out the AAA's and came up with eight.

"All we need are two good ones," Carlos said, trying to sound upbeat. The first four were useless. "Four down and four to go. Cross your fingers, Mario."

Carlos slid the next two into the slot. Magically the radio blared Mariachi music.

Mario started shoulder-dancing and humming to the music.

Carlos shut off the radio.

"Why did you turn it off?"

"We don't know how long the batteries will last. Plus, the noise attracts the bees." Carlos opened the back of the toy bear. "This guy takes C batteries."

Mario handed him six.

Carlos went through the same trial-and-error process. He was down to the last two batteries when the bear came to life. It banged the cymbals in time to the song, Who let the dogs out? Woof. Woof, woof.

"Cool." Mario continued to sing after the bear stopped.

Carlos did a quick inventory. Six black plastic sheets, two-and-a-half rolls of silver duct tape, three pie tins, plastic cups, the gross Chobani yogurt cups, one baseball cap, a squashed cowboy hat, and gloves.

"We're ready for phase two," Carlos said.

"What's phase two?" Mario said.

"That's when we armor up."

CHAPTER FOURTEEN

Carlos grabbed two black plastic sheets and pointed to the rusty crate. "Sit on that and stretch out your legs."

"Why?" Mario asked.

"Just do it." Carlos knelt and wrapped one plastic sheet around Mario's good leg. "Hold this until I get it taped."

He wound silver tape around the leg, sealing the edges.

"Hey, you're turning me into a garbage bag mummy and it's not even Hallowe'en," Mario joked.

Carlos rolled his eyes and sealed off any holes with more tape. He took extra care with Mario's injured leg. "Legs done. Hold out your arms."

"I hope nobody sees me," Mario said, laughing. "I look stupid."

"This is the perfect armor to ward off a bee's stingers. If it makes you feel any better, I'll look just as stupid."

"I'm already sweating. Why didn't you go first?"

Carlos ignored the whining and finished his brother's garbage armor. "It's a good thing we've got lots of supplies."

Once Mario's anti-sting armor was complete, Carlos started on himself.

Mario started pawing through the garbage pile again.

"What are you looking for?" Carlos asked.

"This." Mario held up a broken hand mirror. "Wow. I look even weirder than I thought." He stuck his arms out straight and started making groaning mummy noises.

"You look fine. Help me do my arms."

Mario's eyes danced. "Yeah. Together we will be the trash dead."

"Just don't waste the tape. We need every inch of it."

Concentrating, Mario's face scrunched. Finally finished, he grinned. "Now we look like mummy twins. There's still one trash bag left. Can I have a cape?"

"Sure," Carlos said. "And a helmet. You want the baseball cap or the cowboy hat?"

"You have to ask?" Mario grabbed the cap and slapped it on his head. "I'm the baseball star."

"Okay. Put on the gloves and sunglasses."

"Where's yours?" Mario asked.

"I don't need them," Carlos lied. They only had one pair. "I need to see clearly."

Carlos put the sunglasses on his brother and attached the yogurt cups over Mario's ears. Then he tied rags over both of their faces like banditos.

"Then take the gloves," Mario said, starting to pull them off.

Carlos shook his head. "Put them back on. I need my hands bare."

"Because?"

"Because I said so." Carlos turned on the radio and found a talk show.

"Hey," Mario complained. "I liked the music. The bees do, too."

Carlos turned up the volume and set the radio on the floor by the pocket door. There still weren't any bees at the window. But they could hear the steady hum from the other room.

"Here's my plan," Carlos explained in detail. "I'll carry you piggyback. Once I open the front door we've got to move fast. And quiet. You ready?"

Mario nodded, his face hidden under all his gear.

"No improvising. Do exactly as I say. Got it?"

"Okay."

Carlos set the bear by the front door and slipped outside. He turned, motioning for Mario to climb on his back.

Mario wrapped his arms around Carlos's neck.

"You're choking me," Carlos whispered, trying to adjust Mario's weight. "Hang onto my shoulders. Not my neck."

Carlos reached for the toy bear and flipped its switch. The bear clanged its cymbals and sang over the talk show noise.

Gently, Carlos closed the Winnebago door, sealing the clanging bear and the blaring radio inside.

Gripping Mario's legs, he staggered toward the giant Saguaro cactus. Even though it lay only twenty feet ahead, it felt like a mile.

The garbage armor crinkled with each step. Please. Don't let the bees realize we've escaped, he prayed.

A muffled, "Who let the dog out? Crash! Crash! Crash!" mocked every step.

The sun beat down like a furnace.

On Carlos's back, Mario squirmed. More crinkling. The plastic armor felt like a super sauna. Sweat pooled inside and Mario's hot breath tickled Carlos's neck.

The Saguaro loomed skyward. Up close it was huge. It had at least eight arms. Desert willow and bunchgrass surrounded its base. It was the perfect hiding place to catch his breath. If they could just reach it without alerting the bees—part one of his escape plan would be complete.

CHAPTER FIFTEEN

Carlos helped Mario into a seating position on the ground, sheltered behind the huge cactus. The trick had worked, and the bees hadn't followed. The RV was less than twenty feet away. But the swarm wouldn't realize he was there if Mario stayed quiet.

Carlos leaned close and whispered the rest of the plan.

Mario's brows pinched in a frown. He looked confused. Then his eyes shot open wide like soccer balls. "No. I'm not staying here alone."

"You have to. It won't be long."

Mario tried to rise but Carlos pushed him down, leaned close, and whispered, "You can do this."

"But you're leaving me." Tears formed in Mario's eyes. "By myself."

"I'll be back. Soon. And this will all be over." Carlos squeezed Mario's shoulder. "Promise. Remember, you're like the invincible Spidey Man."

Mario nodded.

Carlos kept the Saguaro between himself and the RV and crept away. The large cactus wasn't much of a shield, but better than nothing. He ran as fast as his short leg allowed—the duct-taped garbage bags crunching and crackling with every step.

Salty sweat stung his eyes. Swiping them only made things worse. He shot a frantic glance back over his shoulder as he retraced the short distance they'd crawled earlier under the inflatable pool.

Within seconds, he reached the garden shed. Nearby, the weed whacker lay abandoned near the clump of grass he'd torn from the ground. If only he hadn't yanked out that bunchgrass! But how was he supposed to know killer bees lived in his own yard? And how long did they have before the bees gave up on the Winnebago and came racing back here?

He was half-blind, roasting hot, and totally sweat-soaked. He knew the risk of a heat stroke and needed water but there wasn't time. Mario might get tired of waiting and do something stupid.

Carlos's guts twisted into a knot. Time to double hustle.

He grabbed his bike from its rack on the wall, rolled it out of the shed, and hopped on. This would be the race of his life. His well-trained muscles cranked the pedals up to speed. He flew over the dirt ground, sliding through uneven ruts, swerved around a prickly cactus, and skidded to a stop in front of Mario.

Mario clambered to his feet, looking spooked.

At the RV, the clanging toy bear had fallen silent, and a cloud of killer bees hovered around the broken window. A black mass hung along one outer wall, buzzing and swarming.

He was out of luck if he'd hoped they'd calmed down by now. They looked as angry as ever. Then again, killer bees stayed angry for hours—he'd even heard some stayed angry for days.

Roving sentry bees drifted in an ever-widening arc, on the alert for anything they decided was a threat within their hive's quarter-mile radius.

So far, they hadn't spotted the brothers.

"Let's go," Carlos whispered.

Straddling the bike, Carlos half-lifted his brother onto the bike's trick bar.

Mario clung onto Carlos's back—with all his weight on his good leg.

"Hang on." Carlos pushed off, leaning sideways to counterbalance Mario's awkward sideways drag. He pumped hard a few times, trying to get moving. "Can you lean to the left a little?"

Mario shifted.

"Good. That's perfect."

Carlos panted through his mouth, slowly getting into gear. Riding with a passenger dangling a cast made it tricky. Especially cross-country over a dirt lawn studded with rocks. Right now, this was even slower than walking. But it was easier than carrying Mario on his back.

"Where are we going?" Mario gasped, sounding like he was in pain.

"Away. They'll lose interest pretty quick, as long as I keep riding."

"Wahoo!" Mario shouted. "Go faster, we're hardly moving."

"Shhhh! The bees." Carlos dug in, grunting as they bumped over clumps of dirt. "Look back. Are they following?"

"Oh no." Mario's voice was a hollow whisper. "They heard us. The swarm is coming."

Carlos went into panic mode.

"How close?" Carlos looked back and wished he hadn't.

The huge bee cloud detached from the RV wall and zoomed toward them.

Carlos pumped his legs. "As long as I don't stop, they won't catch us."

"How do you know that?" Mario said. "You said they can fly ten miles per hour."

"I pedaled faster than that in my last race," Carlos said. "I've got this."

"But you didn't have a passenger."

"Stop talking and hang on," Carlos said.

He left the lumpy yard and skidded onto Coyote Drive. The bike flew over a pothole, hit a rough patch of gravel, and sent both brothers flying. They hit the ground hard.

"Ow," Mario groaned as Carlos helped him to his feet.

They were out of time. The bees were closing in, and he needed a new plan, fast. They'd never get away down the dirt road. The riding was too rough with a broken-legged passenger clinging to Carlos's neck.

The Smiths' black iron gate was just across the gravel lane. The family was away but maybe they could get into the garage.

Carlos slung one arm around his brother and wheeled his bike up to the bars. The gate was electronically locked, but Carlos knew the code.

"They're getting closer," Mario said.

"Give me a sec."

Carlos punched 7- 4 - 6 -1 into the black box and waited for the gate to swing open. No response. Had he pushed a wrong number? Tried again. The gate didn't budge.

Had the Smiths changed their code when they left for vacation? They never had before.

"They're almost here," Mario yelled.

Carlos punched in the code a third time. Feeling stupid, this time he hit the star key.

The gate beeped, moving super slow—inch by inch.

"Get back on the bike!" Carlos told Mario. "Hurry!" The swarm was closing in. "Open, open, open!"

Carlos took off as soon as the space grew wide enough to fit through. The short driveway was paved—an easy ride if it wasn't uphill.

The bike careened upward.

"Faster. Faster," Mario cried.

Carlos pushed harder—they were nearly there.

The hill didn't slow the bees. It helped them. They shot up like helicopters in battle.

Carlos glanced at the garage with the sickening realization he'd never have time to open it, even if it was unlocked.

Glancing right, he saw the cool blue water of the Smiths' swimming pool. In the center floated a huge, inflated, pink flamingo—big enough to carry two adults.

Two recliner chairs blocked the way and forced him to slow.

The bees got closer.

Carlos slalomed between the chairs, past an outdoor table with an umbrella, and through scattered floaty noodles.

The swarm had almost caught up. The buzzing grew loud enough to vibrate the air.

"Hang on," Carlos shouted and felt a sting. He bit back a yelp.

"What are you doing?" Mario said. "Ouch! I'm stung."

"Take a big breath and hang on." Carlos aimed for the pink flamingo. Wrenching the handles, he punched down hard like in a takeoff at the track, and bunny-hopped into the air. The bike soared over the pool for two seconds before plunging into the water.

CHAPTER SIXTEEN

The chlorine water felt like a soothing blanket to Carlos's hot skin. Moving in slow-motion—every second stretched into a minute. The water pulled him to the bottom in a cool embrace. It felt so good. He could stay there forever.

Like he and Mario were fish. But by some miracle, he was still on his bike.

His eyes popped open. Where was Mario? He wasn't hanging on anymore. And Mario could hardly swim without a cast.

Still underwater, Carlos tried to kick away from the bike and couldn't. His foot was caught in the gear.

In total panic mode, he freaked. Pulled. Twisted. Tried to kick.

Bubbles escaped his mouth. Pinching his lips together, he tried to swallow the air in his mouth back into his lungs.

Looked up.

Mario floated under the big flamingo. Above the pool, bees skimmed its surface. Casting dark patches like storm clouds. Shadows shifting. Growing darker. Thousands and thousands of angry bees.

Mario had been smart. His head was in the air cavity under the flamingo's body, and he held on with both hands.

Carlos's lungs felt like they there were about to burst. A trickle of tiny bubbles escaped his lips.

Bending double, he squinted to see what was caught in the gear. It looked like the garbage bag armor. Frantically, his fingers tore at the black plastic. It shredded but the silver duct tape didn't.

The strip wrapped around his ankle had caught in the gear. He tugged at it, using both hands. It held tight.

Another tiny escape of air. Fighting the urge to suck in a deep breath, his fingers felt for the end of the duct tape. Peeled its end back. Gripped it. Began unwinding the tape from his calf and ankle.

Suddenly his foot kicked free.

Pushing off the bottom, he shot upward, kicking, and arms flailing. His head jetted into the small air space next to his brother. Open-mouthed. Gasping.

"What were you doing?" Mario said. "It's been forever. A lot of help you were."

Carlos sucked in precious air and let Mario complain. His little brother didn't need to know he'd almost drowned.

"You did fine without me."

"Nice bunny hop." Mario grinned. "Do you realize we're in a flamingo butt?"

Carlos started breathing through his nose.

"Why did that news guy say that if bees attack, you're not supposed to jump into the water?"

"I don't know. You turned off the TV," Carlos said.

Mario winced. "It's hard to tread water in this stupid garbage armor."

"Don't complain. It worked." Carlos said.

"You took yours off."

"Only one leg. And I had to because—" Carlos stopped. Mario had had enough drama for one day. "You're right. We don't need it in the pool. Let's get to the shallow end. It'll be easier to take off if we can stand."

They floated the flamingo to the shallow end of the pool.

In short order, the pool was littered with the remains of their bee armor. Black plastic floated like dead crows while Duct tape shimmered like skinned eels.

A real mess. Carlos would clean it out before the Smiths arrived home next week. They were nice people. They'd understand.

"Can I take my cast off?" Mario said. "I don't think it fits anymore. It's heavy. And hurts my leg."

Carlos shook his head. "Mama will kill me."

"Please?" Mario looked like he was about to cry. "I'm not kidding. It hurts. A lot. Like when I broke it."

"Maybe it needs to be adjusted."

Carlos began to remove the cast and blanched. His brother's leg was purple and swollen. He quickly refastened it without taking it off. He didn't want to see any more.

"We're leaving it on."

CHAPTER SEVENTEEN

"It's stuffy," Mario said. "How long do we have to stay under here?"

Carlos didn't answer. The plan needed a little tweaking. Mario couldn't swim with his leg looking like that. "I'll snag some noodles."

"Sounds good. I'm hungry."

Carlos rolled his eyes. "A floaty noodle. I'll grab an extra one for you to chew on. Hot pink, green, or blue?"

"Ha ha," Mario said.

"I saw some poolside by the three-foot mark."

Carlos piloted the flamingo to where the floaties had been abandoned.

"Hold the flamingo. Don't move an inch. I'll be right back."

Carlos took a huge breath, dunked under the water, and headed for the black number three painted on the pool's side wall. A cloud of bees followed.

A lime-green noodle dangled over the edge. Keeping his head underwater, he reached into the air to grab the noodle. Instantly his hand was covered in a live-bee glove—one full of stinging barbs.

He winced, tasting chorine.

Clutching the noodle, Carlos jerked his arm back into the pool.

The bees peeled off as they hit the water. Some escaped into the air. Some struggled on the surface. Others drowned.

Lungs bursting, he flipped off the side wall and swam to his brother.

Carlos popped up into the cramped airspace beneath the flamingo, huffing and puffing.

One look at his hand and he knew the bees had stung at least ten times. Felt like more. His fingers were already swelling into link sausages.

But getting the noodle was worth every sting. Mario needed the floating support. Who knew how long they'd be trapped under here? No one would be coming to save them now. No one even knew where they were.

"Ahh, what's that on your arm?" Mario said. The strain in his voice matched the fear on his face.

Carlos's skin rippled in terror as a soggy wet bee staggered toward his elbow. He slapped it hard. Lifeless, it dropped into the water. Lifting the edge of the flamingo, he flicked it under and away.

"Why did you do that?" Mario said. "It's dead."

"Dead, but its stinger can still sting."

Suddenly Carlos felt crawling sensations up his spine, in his hair, and even on his legs. It creeped him out. "See any bees on my back?"

Mario looked. "You're good. No bees."

Carlos sighed. "Okay. Ready to swim to the deep end?"

"Why?" Mario said. "I like it here. It's way better than under our plastic pool or the Winnebago. It's cool. And the bees can't swim." Pause. "Can they?"

"Don't think so."

Mario's face scrunched like he was trying to be brave and not cry. "I'm scared. Really scared. The bees are never giving up."

"We won't either," Carlos said. "Promise. Just one short lap and we win."

Mario didn't need to know that the air pocket would only last so long until the oxygen ran out. And if they let in air, it'd let in the bees, too.

They started moving. The bee cloud followed. To keep things light, Carlos said. "There are two unique things about this ool."

"Ool?" Mario's forehead wrinkled. "What's an ool?"

"It's what the Smiths call it."

"Why?"

"Because they don't allow any P in their ool." Carlos watched Mario's face morph from suspicion to surprise and into a lopsided grin.

"I get it," Mario laughed. "That's the first funny joke you've ever told."

"What do you mean? I tell jokes." Carlos breathed easier. Mario seemed less freaked out.

"Yeah, but they're not even close to funny." Mario chuckled.

"The second thing is that this is an indoor-outdoor pool."

Mario grinned again. "Is this another joke?"

"No. It's for real. I saw it the last time I was up here weeding. We're in the outside part of the pool. The indoor part is in the sunroom with the big windows."

"So, they have two pools."

"No. Just one. Half inside and half outside."

"Wow. That's fancy." Understanding lit his eyes. "How do we get in there?"

"We'll swim under the dividing wall and come up inside. There's a lounge area with a phone. We can call for help."

Mario chewed on his lower lip.

"Nothing can go wrong," Carlos said. "It's a short dive down and a short swim back up."

"I'll try," Mario said. "But my leg really hurts. I'm not sure I can do it."

"You don't have to. I'll tow you across the pool. You'll float." He grabbed the green floaty and realized his hand looked like a surgical glove blown up and ready to pop.

"Turn around," Carlos said, trying to hide his hand.

He wrapped the noodle under Mario's arms and tied it in a knot.

"Ready?" Carlos said.

"I guess so," Mario said.

Carlos started swimming, breathing hard in the enclosed space, with one hand on the flamingo and one hand on his brother. They passed the painted black three. Then the four. Then the five. Carlos spotted his bike twisted on the bottom—his stomach wrenched. He couldn't afford to fix the Schwinn. Not this season. His BMX racing days were over.

But at least he and Mario were alive.

They reached the glass wall when he had a sudden, sickening thought. He'd once asked Mr. Smith how they kept thieves from swimming under the wall and entering the sunroom. That's when he'd learned about the underwater security gate.

What if it was locked?

CHAPTER EIGHTEEN

Carlos said a silent prayer. God, let it be open. Please? I'll never call Mario a pest again. Or even think it. And if I do, I'll never say it out loud.

"Why are we just sitting here?" Mario sounded nervous.

"I'm resting before I do a scouting dive," Carlos said. "You doing okay?"

"Yeah." Mario's tanned skin looked pale. Sickly.

"Great. I'll dive down to check the gate."

"There's a gate? What if it's closed?" Alarm crept into Mario's voice.

"If it is, I can open it," Carlos lied. "I'll be back. Practice holding your breath."

He sucked in a deep breath and plunged. The stainless-steel fence loomed ahead. Up close, it looked like a set of prison bars bolted to the submerged wall.

Was the gate locked?

He pulled and then pushed. The gate didn't budge. He tried jiggling it. Still closed. His lungs began to ache. He needed air and swam toward the flamingo, bursting into the now stale air pocket.

"Was it open?" Mario asked.

"I'm not sure. I ran out of air. I'll try again. But first I have to catch my breath."

"I practiced holding my breath," Mario said, "but it made me dizzy. I'm up to thirty seconds. Will that be long enough?"

"Try for forty. Fifty if you can."

Carlos pushed the Flamingo forward until it bumped into the glass wall. "Second time's the charm."

"Isn't it *third time's the charm?*" Mario said.

I hope not, thought Carlos and dived again. He reached the gate and felt for a handle or a release on the other side. Nothing.

He pushed and pulled again. Still nothing.

Desperate, he smacked the gate with both hands. It shifted to the right. Hope flared. Did it open like the pocket door in the RV by sliding sideways? Nearly out of air, he gave it one desperate shove. A two-foot space opened just big enough to swim through.

Yes!

Nearby, a snap dangled from a loop. He used it to clip the gate open and resurfaced.

"It's open. Ready?"

"I don't feel so good," Mario said. "I tried to hold my breath for as long as you were underwater. I couldn't."

"It won't take that long. You'll do fine."

Mario shook his head, "You go in and call for help. I'll wait here."

Carlos grabbed Mario's hand. It felt ice cold. Then he noticed his brother's eyes looked glassy. A thousand thoughts raced through his mind.

Was Mario allergic to bee stings? Was he having an allergic reaction? How many bee stings were too many? Or was it the stale air?

Carlos didn't know.

Maybe Mario had hurt his leg? It was swollen and bruised. Was it broken again?

Carlos didn't have the answers. All he knew is that his brother needed a doctor. Soon.

"Come on, let's get the noodle off," Carlos said. "You'll hang onto my back, and I'll swim you inside."

Mario didn't argue. Or complain. He just followed orders.

Once the noodle was removed, Carlos said, "On three, take a huge breath. Ready? One, Two. Three."

Carlos waited until he heard Mario gulp in air before diving deep into the pool. Swimming like a porpoise, he skimmed through the underwater door and popped up inside.

The pool steps were just a few feet away. He plunged up, dragging Mario to the surface. Mario gulped air and started sputtering.

It was muggy hot in the sunroom, and the smell of chlorine was strong. At least they could breathe.

"Hold on, buddy," Carlos said.

He settled his brother on the top step next to a handrail. White-faced, Mario slumped against it. His breathing grew ragged between moans.

"We're safe, you're going to be all right." Carlos ran for the phone, which sat on a small table near a gas BBQ.

Mario groaned and slid back into the pool.

"Hey!" Carlos shouted, raced to grab his brother's shirt, and pulled him onto the floor. "Wake up. Wake up, little brother. You can't quit on me. I can't do this alone. I need your help."

Mario whimpered. His eyelashes fluttered open. "You need me?"

Carlos nodded, his throat too tight to speak.

Mario's eyes closed.

Carlos's face went numb. "Mario."

After everything they'd gone through, why was this happening? Now? All they needed was another five minutes. And they'd be safe.

Carlos laid his ear on his brother's chest and listened for his brother's heartbeat.

CHAPTER NINETEEN

Carlos hated to leave Mario's side, but his brother's heartbeat was strong. He limp-ran toward the phone and a horrible sight slapped him in the face.

"What? No! That can't be."

One of the sunroom windows was open. So much for security—not that there was much to steal in here. He zipped into high gear and slammed it shut with his swollen hand.

Outside, the flamingo floated on the pool, surrounded by clouds of bees. Circling. Skimming the water. Hovering over the floating lounge.

Carlos's heart slowed. The bees were outside. Everything would be fine.

He snatched the phone just as a stab of pain pricked his ear.

Carlos yelped, dropping the phone. It clattered on the floor.

Something crawled across his cheek. He saw it from the corner of his eye and froze. A bee. It crept onto the bridge of his nose—right between his eyes. Vibrating before sinking its stinger into tender skin.

"Aaagh!"

He slipped and fell hard on the wet concrete floor. Looked up.

Saw that his attacker wasn't alone. He counted twelve winged avengers, dive-bombing him in unison.

Carlos rolled onto his side and bumped into the BBQ. Frantic, he looked for something to cover his face and spotted a dishtowel on the bottom rack. He snagged it and slapped it over his mouth and nose.

That's when he saw the red canister strapped to the wall. A fire extinguisher. He crawled toward it.

The bees attacked from above, swarmed over his bare back, and stung. He ignored them and lifted the extinguisher from the wall with his good hand. He'd used one before and pulled the safety pin from its top. Squeezed the trigger.

White foam squirted from its nozzle.

Jumping to his feet, he held the extinguisher like he was Rambo. He aimed at the closest cluster of bees. The first foam blast took three down, covering them in sticky goo. They dropped. Wriggled helplessly.

He felt a sharp jab on his leg and sprayed it.

"Four down. Eight to go." Carlos's shout echoed in the room.

He jerked left. Jerked right. Slipping in the slimy foam. Aiming. Spraying. Managing to stay on his feet.

"Five down." Pause. "Six."

Another sting and he shot again, landing in an uncontrolled skid. "Seven. Eight. And nine down."

His short leg slipped and he landed flat on his back—the fire extinguisher clutched to his chest in a death grip. He aimed up and sprayed foam in a wild arc until the canister spewed only hissing air.

Three slimed bees dropped onto his torso. He flicked them to the floor and sat up, chest heaving. "Ten. Eleven. Twelve."

"Mario? Can you hear me?" Carlos grabbed the phone from the floor, punched in three numbers, and put it to his ear. "I'm calling 9-1-1."

The phone rang at the other end.

A calm dispatcher said, "911 emergency call center. What is your emergency?"

Carlos shouted into the phone. "My little brother and I were attacked by killer bees."

"Is there an adult I can talk to?"

"No. My brother needs a doctor," Carlos said. "Thousands of bees are outside."

"I see you're calling from 3197 Coyote Lane in Marana. Is that correct?"

"Yes."

"Emergency services will be dispatched immediately. Please stay on the line. I'll need more information."

Carlos took a deep breath and told her everything. Maybe not everything but enough. It felt like a miracle. Help was finally on its way.

"Carlos!" Mario called. "Come here."

"I've got to go," Carlos said.

"Don't hang up," the dispatcher said. "Stay on the line."

"I won't, but my brother needs me. He's only nine."

Mario had crawled to a lounge chair. "Can you help me up? The floor is hard."

"Sure." Carlos lifted him and propped him into a sitting position. "How does that feel?"

"Better. What happened to your face? It's all swollen. And so is your hand."

"While you were sleeping, I was in a bee battle." Carlos punched the air. "And I dominated."

"Looks like you lost. Does it hurt?"

"Not really," Carlos lied. Now that help was on the way, his arms, legs, and face felt like they had been used as a pincushion. "How about your leg?"

"I think I'll have to wear this cast for another six weeks."

Carlos raised his good hand. "High five?"

Mario slapped it. "Are the bees still out there?"

Together they turned and stared out the window. The bees had broken into smaller swarms. The largest swirled around the pink flamingo. Clouds of them skimmed the water. One mass hovered at the window. Others crawled on the glass.

"Do you think they'll ever leave?" Mario asked.

The faint screams of sirens grew louder until it sounded like they were next door.

The bees went crazy. Zipping left and right.

Emergency vehicles arrived in a burst of flashing red, blue, yellow, and orange lights. They raced through the open gate, up the short drive, and parked. Police Cars. Fire trucks. Sheriffs. Ambulances. Even a Channel 4 News van.

The bees gathered into what looked like a massive thundercloud and attacked.

The back doors of a big white truck were flung open. Men in hazmat suits swarmed into the backyard. They were armed with what looked like firehoses. Instead of water, they shot steady streams of foam exactly like he'd done with the fire extinguisher.

Carlos grinned at Mario. "I told you I had a great plan."

CHAPTER TWENTY

3 days later

Saturday morning, Carlos and Mario sat at the table. Bright sunlight streamed in through the kitchen window. They sipped hot chocolate while watching Mama finish cooking breakfast.

"You're lucky," Carlos said, fighting the urge to scratch. "You're not allergic to Benadryl. You look normal."

"You look normal, too," Mario said.

Carlos knew it was a lie. His face and right hand were still puffy and splotched. It was a small price. "Like the new cast?"

"Yeah. This one's cool because it's black."

"Who's hungry?" Mama said, setting a platter of steaming pancakes in the center of the table.

Carlos's stomach rumbled. Since the bee attack, he seemed to be starving all the time. Morning. Noon. Night. And in between.

Mario had already corralled the whipped cream, honey, and cinnamon sugar beside his plate. He leaned forward to stab a pancake with his fork.

"Hold on, mijo," Mama said, sitting down. "First, we say grace."

"Since when?" Mario complained.

"Since God saved you both from the bees."

"No, it was Carlos," Mario said. "He saved me from the bees."

"Mario," Mama's voice was stern. "Bow your head."

Mama said a short prayer of thanks for their family's safety and ended with an amen. "Mario. Don't take all the pancakes. Pass them to your brother."

Carlos loaded his plate and started eating.

"I love Saturdays," Mario said, talking with his mouth full. "Because we get cinnamon pancakes. And there's no school."

"Speaking of school," Mama said. "You both need to finish your assignments from the days you missed."

"That's not fair. Carlos and I are heroes. We shouldn't have to do make-up work."

Carlos grinned. Mario was back to his usual self.

Mama rolled her eyes. "Do you want to repeat the fourth grade?"

Mario frowned. "Can we talk about something else? Hey, I've got a new joke. What kind of bees can fly in the rain?" Pause. "The ones wearing yellow jackets." He giggled.

Carlos groaned. "I've heard enough bee jokes. Save them for your friends."

"Are you still afraid of bees?"

"I probably should be, but not really. At least not like before. I'm just tired of bee jokes."

"But I have to practice my timing."

The landline rang. Carlos hopped up. "I'll get it." He answered, listened, frowned, and covered the speaker. "Mama, It's your boss."

Mama took the phone and stepped away into the pantry.

Why did the boss always call Mama in on Saturdays? She deserved the day off. They could call someone else. He got that they needed the money and that sometimes doing the right thing wasn't fun. But every Saturday?

He'd have to spend the day with Mario. And today was race day —he'd planned to go and watch his team win.

Polishing off his last bite, he licked the honey from his lips.

Defeating the killer bees was a bittersweet victory. They'd ruined everything. His precious bike. The opportunity to impress the man from Wolf Racing. The chance of the sponsorship. The chance to help Mama with the bills.

It was all a lost dream.

Mario hobbled into the living room. The television came on.

Carlos set the dirty dishes in the dishwasher and joined his brother.

The TV was tuned to News 4 Tucson. UPDATE MARANA BEE ATTACK flashed across the screen in a red banner.

Mario turned up the volume.

"We have an update on the condition of the two boys attacked by a massive swarm of African Killer bees in Marana," the news anchor said.

"We're on TV again," shouted Mario.

Carlos and Mario's school pictures appeared on the screen. Then it cut to a video of Mario being wheeled on a gurney with Carlos, face swollen and limping at his side.

"The Mendoza brothers were released from the hospital yesterday. The heroic efforts of—."

"Haven't you watched that enough?" Mama said, shutting it off. "You've seen it a dozen times already." She shook the car keys. "Let's go if you want to make the first race."

"You're not going to work?" Carlos said.

"No. I told Mr. Baker I had a previous commitment. He'd have to find someone else to cover the shift."

"Thanks, Mama," Carlos said and gave her a hug.

They loaded into the car. Mario with his crutches, Carlos with a hat to hide his lumpy head. And Mama with a big secret smile. Twenty minutes later, they arrived at the BMX Ranch.

The races wouldn't start for another half hour. Still, the parking lot was jammed. They had to park in the back next to a big white travel van.

Luis slid to a stop by the car, all tricked out in his racing gear. "How's the hero? Everyone is talking about it at school."

"I'm okay." Carlos pulled his hat lower.

Mario got out and high-fived Luis.

"How many stings, little man?" Luis asked.

"Eighteen," Mario said. "Carlos got stung thirty-five times. The doctor said it's lucky he isn't allergic to bees."

Luis winced. "I can't imagine—"

"You don't want to," Carlos said with a grin.

"Come on. Coach wants to see you before the races start. He's over there by the bleachers." Luis looked at Mario and Mama. "You guys can come, too, and grab a seat."

Coach and the whole team were waiting. Plus, a bunch of strangers and Channel 4 News. Huge grins were plastered on everyone's faces. They clapped and cheered when they spotted Carlos. His face grew warm. He wasn't used to being the center of attention. Not like this. And definitely not with a puffy face.

Coach motioned for Carlos to join him on the track. He followed awkwardly until he stood alone by Coach's side. Everyone was watching. What was going on?

The crowd fell silent.

Coach put a hand on Carlos's shoulder and smiled. Then, he raised a microphone and said, "The team heard your bike didn't survive the killer bee attack, so—"

Sweat trickled down Carlos's neck. His heart pounded. Time seemed to slow. Standing in front of this many people staring at him, even if some were his friends, was almost as frightening as being chased by the killer bees.

Coach continued. "The team, community members, the BMX Ranch, Channel 4 News, and Wolf Racing joined together to present you with a new bike."

Carlos stared wide-eyed at Coach.

The crowd stomped their feet and started chanting, "Bee Racer."

"Look," Coach said and pointed.

Luis pushed the latest GT Speed series BMX onto the track. It had sleek lines and was painted a gun-metal green, Carlos's favorite color.

He could hardly believe this awesome bike was his. The team and all these people had actually pitched in to get this for him. Was this for real?

A huge grin split his face. "Wow," was all he could say.

That seemed enough, though, for the crowd broke into fresh cheers.

"Bee racer!" they chanted. "Bee Racer, Bee Racer!"

Luis slapped his shoulder. "You earned it."

"Thanks," Carlos said hoarsely, his gaze glued to the bike. It was perfect.

He couldn't wait to race it. But that would be after the pedal was altered to fit his shorter leg. He couldn't compete riding off balance. Then Carlos's jaw dropped. The pedal had already been modified.

"If you can tear your eyes off your new bike," Coach said. "Karl Ericksen from Wolf Racing has an additional presentation to make."

Coach handed the microphone to a tall, tanned man dressed in Wolf Racing gear. The man shook Carlos's hand like Carlos was an adult.

"So, you are the bike hero I've heard so much about," Mr. Ericksen said, handing him a Wolf Racing duffle bag. "Wolf Racing would like to recognize your bravery and present you with comfortable gear used by our BMX star racers."

The people stood, cheered, clapped, and stomped their feet.

Coach took back the mic and pointed toward Carlos.

Carlos leaned over and shouted out, "Thank you. Thank you so much."

"First race starts in fifteen minutes," Coach announced to the crowd. "Which gives you all time to visit the Snack Shak. All proceeds from today will go to the winning team."

"I'm looking forward to seeing you race today," Mr. Ericksen said. "Good luck."

Carlos wheeled the bike over to show Mama and Mario.

Mama was grinning.

"Mom, you knew?" Carlos said.

She nodded and hugged him. "You better get changed. Mr. Ericksen called me for your sizes. He said there's everything you'll need in the bag."

Mario was hopping up and down. "I bet it's a bunch of cool stuff. You're going to outride everyone. You can't lose. You're going to win."

Carlos laughed. "I don't know about that. What I *do* know is that I outrode the bees, we're safe, and that's what really counts." He gently knuckle-rubbed Mario's head. "Together, we escaped the killer bee attack!"

THE END

*Turn the page for amazing facts about
bees and more!*

10 Fast Facts About Killer Bees

----

1. Africanized honeybees look just like common European honeybees.
2. The average honeybee calms down in a few minutes. Africanized killer bees can hold a grudge and stay aggressive for hours. Also, killer bees respond to a threat in less than 5 seconds, while European honeybees take up to 30 seconds to react.
3. They nest in cavities—holes in the ground, tree trunks, discarded tires, or any crevice, like attic spaces.
4. A small Africanized beehive can have 40,000 bees.
5. Africanized bees can continuously sting their target over and over.
6. They're attracted to perfume or strong-smelling sunscreen.
7. They can fly 10 to 15 miles per hour. Be prepared to run up to the length of two football fields.
8. Bees attack where carbon dioxide is expelled. For example, your breath. Your face will be the first area to be stung.
9. If you jump into a pool, the bees will wait until you surface to attack.
10. If you are swarmed by Africanized bees, you have a 25% percent chance of survival.

KILLER BEE QUOTES

"The minute I got out of the car, I started getting attacked... All of a sudden it [the swarm] just attacked me on my face. I thought I hit a tree."
  - Steve Gluskin told 12 News

"People mustn't bother a bee . . . [here in Arizona] They have a little bit of African in them and a little bit of European, so you never know how to mean they could be."
  - Elliot Ginn, Beekeeper

"There is no way to tell the difference between bees, so all bees have to be handled with caution."
  - Dan Armijo, Exterminator

"As soon as the bees start stinging it's time to leave, and it's time to leave fast. And don't stop."
  - Scott the Bee Man

"I've been with the fire department for 18 years now and responded to several bee incidents. But never to this magnitude ... The bees were very aggressive."

  - Lisa Derderian, Pasadena Fire Department Public Information Officer, February 22, 2020

"They'll continue to go after you."

  - Jeff Pettis, United States Department of Agriculture's Bee Research Lab

"There were up to 500 stingers in her. She swelled up and has been intubated ever since [ten days later]."

  - Jerry Nassif, whose wife was stung by hundreds of Africanized bees

"Several people were injured and one person passed away due to their injuries."

  - Marana police officer, July 30, 2021

DID YOU KNOW?

READ ON FOR MORE FASCINATING FACTS ABOUT BEES

BEES ARE IMPORTANT!

Bees give us more than honey. In fact, most bees don't make honey. The ones that don't are called solitary bees. There are about 20,000 different types of bees. Wow!

One-third of the U.S. food production depends on them. They pollinate flowers that turn into fruit, vegetables, plants, and trees.

How? Bees carry pollen on their bodies and legs from one flower to another. Solitary bees are fantastic pollinators because they spill more pollen than they bring back to their hives. One solitary Red Mason bee spreads more pollen than 120 worker honeybees.

Why is spreading pollen important?

The pollen fertilizes plants, which allows them to grow fruits and vegetables. Can you imagine a world without apples, oranges, or carrots?

SOLITARY BEES

Solitary bees get their name because they don't hang out in big hives with lots of other bees. Each female is a Queen bee and worker bee rolled into one. First, she builds a tube nest. Then she sets a ball of pollen mixed with nectar at the end of the tube and lays an egg on it. Next, she builds a wall to separate this egg from the next one. She repeats the process until the tube is filled.

What's cool is that she chooses whether to lay male or female eggs.

Female eggs are always laid first and males second.

Why?

Because male bees hatch quicker than females.

A solitary bee lives for between one and three years and lays around twenty to thirty eggs in her short lifetime.

HONEYBEES

Honeybees live in colonies. Each hive has one queen bee, many female worker bees, and male drones. They all have jobs.

The queen bee lays the eggs—over 1,500 a day! The worker bees clean the hive, collect pollen and nectar, and care for the offspring. The drone's only job is to mate with the queen.

Only female bees can sting. The venom is stored in a sac attached to its stinger. Most bees can only sting once.

Another three interesting facts: They can see all colors except red. They can see far. And they can smell even farther.

HOW AFRICANIZED BEES ARE LIKE THEIR HONEYBEE COUSINS

Africanized bees look similar, but the honeybee is slightly larger. It takes a bee expert to see the difference.

They both produce honey.

They both respond to what they feel are threats in the same way: by stinging intruders.

Both types of stings deliver the same dose of venom.

Their colonies are made up of a queen bee, male drones, and female worker bees.

Their queen bees can lay over 1,500 eggs per day.

HOW AFRICANIZED BEES ARE *DIFFERENT* THAN THEIR HONEYBEE COUSINS

A European bee colony produces five times more honey than an Africanized bee colony.

Because Africanized bees are quicker to respond and sting without limits, they are more dangerous.

They attack in greater numbers and pursue their victims for greater distances. Plus, the killer bee colony can remain agitated longer.

Killer bees react to noises or vibrations even when there is no threat. There is no retreat. They will chase a person for up to a quarter of a mile.

Killer bees have a shorter development time frame and quickly grow into 40,000 bees.

There is a 75% chance of being in a deadly attack if you are in the path of a killer bee swarm.

HOW DID AFRICANIZED KILLER BEES END UP IN THE UNITED STATES?

Over seventy years ago, a scientist in Brazil was trying to produce a better honeybee. Unfortunately, an experimental queen bee escaped and migrated north. It took forty years for them to arrive in the United States. Jesus Lopez was the first American to be stung. He survived, but two years later, Lino Lopez died from a bee attack.

The killer bees like warmer climates and are primarily found in the southern States. (Texas, Arizona, California, Nevada, New Mexico, Oklahoma, Louisiana, Arkansas, and Florida)

TAKE HEART

Swarming bee attacks do happen, but you're more likely to be struck by lightning than to be killed in a bee attack.

SAFETY TIPS

If you live in an area where there are killer bees . . .BEE SMART!

- If you see a swarm, get inside your house or car. Close the doors and windows.
- Don't play dead.
- Don't scream or wave your arms.
- Don't swat at the bees.
- If you're outside, run as fast as you can in a straight line. Bees can chase you up to 200 hundred yards.
- Protect your face. Pull your shirt over your head to prevent stings to your eyes, nose, or mouth.
- Don't jump into a pool or a lake. The bees will wait for you to come up for air and attack.
- Be careful while using loud lawn equipment.
- Never attempt to remove a hive on your own. Leave it to the experts.

More Mario Bee Jokes

———

When do bees get married?
When they find their honey!

Why was the bee was fired from the barber shop?
Because he could only give buzz-cuts.

What's a happy bumblebee's blood type?
Bee positive!

What kind of bee is hard to understand?
A mumble-bee!

What did one bee say to the other when they landed on the same flower?
Buzz off!

What do you get when you cross a doorbell and a bee?
A hum-dinger.

What's a bee's favorite sport?
Rug-bee.

What is the last thing to go through a bee's mind when it hits a windshield?
I'll bee seeing you.

What do you call a bee that's been put under a spell?
Bee-witched!

KILLER BEE RESOURCES

Learn even more with these useful resources!

National Geographic video:
https://www.youtube.com/watch?v=d-7kKqgPEGs

**Arizona Department of Transportation
Safety Briefing:**
https://azdot.gov/business/programs-and-partnerships/adopt-
highway/safety-requirements/safety-briefing

BEE CULTURE
The Magazine of American Bee Keeping
https://www.beeculture

United States Department of Agriculture (USDA)
Invasive Species Information
Africanized Honeybee
https://www.invasivespeciesinfo.gov/terrestrial/invertebrates/
africanized-honeybee

The adventure doesn't have to end.
Leave a review to help others discover and join in on the excitement.

THE I ESCAPED SERIES

I Escaped North Korea!

I Escaped The California Camp Fire

I Escaped The World's Deadliest Shark Attack

I Escaped Amazon River Pirates

I Escaped The Donner Party

I Escaped The Salem Witch Trials

I Escaped Pirates In The Caribbean

I Escaped The Tower of London

I Escaped Egypt's Deadliest Train Disaster

I Escaped The Haunted Winchester House

I Escaped The Gold Rush Fever

I Escaped The Prison Island

I Escaped The Grizzly Maze

I Escaped The Killer Bees

I Escaped The Saltwater Crocodile

More great adventures coming soon!

———

JOIN THE I ESCAPED CLUB

Get a free pack of mazes and word finds to print and play!

https://www.subscribepage.com/escapedclub

Made in the USA
Monee, IL
03 October 2024

67181798R00179